Cardinal House

THE BLACKWELL BROTHERS
BOOK IV

K.L. TAYLOR-LANE

Written by - K.L. Taylor-Lane
Cover Design by - Leah Maree at Designs by L.M.
ISBN Paperback - 978-1-917276-01-6

Mark,
Because no heart could ever love me like yours.
Same coffin.
Same headstone.
Same consecrated earth.

Obsession.

As a Blackwell, it's my curse.

It lives in all five of my brothers. Two hearts thriving
with it, three of them rotting, but I didn't believe in it.
Didn't want to believe that it would latch itself onto
me, sink its claws bone deep and never let go.

Until I meet her.

Suddenly, my whole world shifts, my focus is her and
only her, and I won't stop until she's mine.

Then, all too quickly, she's gone.
Stolen away from me in the night, my heart is in pieces.

Rain. Blood. Coffin.

But I won't give up.

I'll fight to bring her back to me, uncover her past, and
hunt the people that hurt her. Can I defeat the
monsters that haunt her, or will I end up being the
worst monster of them all?

Playlist

Better Days - If Not for Me

wipe your tears - Halsey

Like A Villain - Bad Omens

Another Life - Motionless In White

Scream - Blind Channel

Pretty In The Dark - Ashley Sienna

Not Afraid Anymore - Halsey

Feel Me Now - If Not For Me

The Death of Peace of Mind - Bad Omens

Werewolf - Motionless In White

Time And Time Again - Papa Roach

The Diary of Jane - Breaking Benjamin

The Drain - Bad Omens

Learn To Crawl - Black Lab

Chemicals - Love And Death

Take It Out On Me - Thousand Foot Krutch

Note from the author

Please be aware this book contains **many** dark themes and subjects that may be uncomfortable/unsuitable for some readers. This book contains **very** heavy themes throughout so please heed the warning and go into this with your eyes wide open.

For more detailed information, please see content listing in back of book.

The characters in this story all deal with trauma and problems differently, the resolutions and methods they use are not always traditional and therefore may not be for everyone.

This book can be read as a standalone. However, it is recommended you read this series in numerical order for maximum enjoyment.

This book is written in British English. Therefore, some

spellings, words, grammar and punctuation may be used differently than what you are used to. If you find anything you think is a genuine error, please do not report, instead, please contact the author or one of her team to correct it. Thank you!

This book and its contents are entirely a work of fiction. Any resemblance or similarities to names, characters, organisations, places, events, incidents, or real people is entirely coincidental or used fictitiously.

*Cardinal House is a dark, gothic, MF, romance. Please read with caution, the characters in this book do not and will not conform to society's standards or normalities. This book does have a *happy ever after.**

*The Blackwell Brothers series is a series of interconnected standalones, meaning this book CAN be read as a separate entity, you do not have to read the first books in this series to enjoy or understand this story. However, for maximum reader enjoyment, it is recommended you read the series in the order shown.

Reading Order

Book 1 - Heron Mill (Hunter and Grace)

Book 2 - Heron Mill Tenebris (Hunter and Grace)

Book 3 - Rook Point (Thorne and Haisley)

Book 4 - Cardinal House (Wolf and Luna)

Book 5 - Magpie Manor

Book 6 - TBA

Wolf

CHAPTER I

Thunder rolls and claps overhead, no rain falling yet, but I know it's coming, can feel it hanging heavy and low in the black clouds. My feet are silent as we make our way across the open field of tarmac, my youngest brother, Raine, at my back.

The car park is empty, all except for one vehicle in the far back corner of the lot. A 1999, Lotus Esprit GT3 Turbo in faded lime green is angled across three spaces. Its back end spun out, the front crushed into a light pole with a steady cloud of smoke wafting from the mangled bonnet.

It wasn't the plan to follow a low level drug dealer tonight, but when the call came in on our way back from a body drop off. Our eldest brother, Thorne, telling us to track and chase this fool for our biggest employers, The Swallows, a crime family we often act as disposals for, we did as instructed.

After all, it is what we do as Blackwells, deal in death.

Only, we took chase for less than three minutes before he was careening into the empty car park and crashing into the railings. Still, I wasn't planning on doing anything else exciting tonight, so I suppose this is better than another evening stuck down in the morgue.

"You check the back," I instruct Raine as we come up on the smoking car, guns drawn, steps slow.

We don't know who or what else could be in the vehicle, what weapons he has, and despite my hunch that this is exactly what Thorne said, just a simple grab and bag, I don't wanna take any chances.

"Got it," Raine replies lowly, tone thick and tired, his body moving around me and stealthily loping towards the back end of the destroyed car.

Adjusting my grip on the gun, I bend down to peer into the cracked window. The guy's dark eyes are open, unseeing through the shattered windscreen. Blood covering his face from where he looks to have headbutted the steering wheel, body half slumped out of his seat, more red dribbling from his ear and down his neck.

Ah, fuck.

"Raine," I say loudly, trying to get my brother's consistently wandering attention, "Come 'ere."

Elbowing the remaining glass out, I reach in and feel for a pulse, but even as I do, I know I'm not going to find one. I've been disposing of corpses for more than twenty of my thirty-four years on this planet, I know when I'm looking at a dead thing.

My fingers slip in the warm blood, but I feel around anyway, just to confirm what I know, this'll be our second body drop off of the evening.

"He's dead," I tell Raine, drawing myself away from the window, turning to where I see my brother hovering beside the back bumper. "Call it in and we'll get this lot moved, might need Archer, too, for the tow."

Raine stares at me unblinking, his dark brown eyes, so much like our four other siblings', are wide. Deep violet circles beneath them look ghoulish under the flickering glow of the street lamp above. His choppy hair is a messy wave across his forehead, white licking burn scars threading down the side of his neck, disappearing beneath the round neckline of his t-shirt. He stands rigid, staring at me, and I sigh so heavily it feels as though my lungs deflate.

"For shit's sake, Rainey! You're fucking high?" I know he is now that I stare back, the way his pupils are blown wide, his jaw clenched tight but still fucking swinging, his shoulders shaking.

I sweep a hand over my head, my black hair tied up in a loop at the crown of my skull. I tuck my gun back into the holster, and pull out my phone, dialling Thorne. He answers before it even fully plays the first call tone in my ear.

"Wolf," he answers smoothly.

"Can you and Archer get over here? Got a disposal and a vehicle that needs crushing, Raine needs to go home," I tell him, staring at our brother.

"Got your location, on our way," he replies calmly, the soft taps of his dress shoes echoing in the background. "Is he high again?"

"Yes," I grit out, both angry and sad that this seems to be becoming a regular occurrence.

Thorne says something but I don't hear him as Raine cocks his head at me, his brow scrunched, eyes lifting from my booted feet up to my head, slow, until his gaze reconnects with mine. That's when I notice the gun still clenched in his hands, his finger on the trigger as he lifts it, aiming at me, arms trembling.

"Raine," that's what I say, my lips forming the words, I know I say them but I don't hear them, the phone still pressed close to my head. "Put the gun down, brother, you don't wanna be aiming that shit at me." My words are slow, calm, patient.

Thorne's voice is unusually sharp in my ear, his words a quick clip, "Archer is the closest, he is four minutes out."

"Raine," I repeat, "Rainey," my mouth feels impossibly dry. "Bro."

"You're a liar," he says coldly, his dark eyes nothing more than black holes in his face, his warm olive skin sallow under the shadow of the street light.

Blackwells don't tell lies.

That's our family's one rule.

Something we never do.

Lie.

"What have I lied about?" I'm cautious and slow, and Thorne is still talking but I hear none of it. "Tell me. Talk to me, Rainey."

"Don't," he spits, voice full of vitriol. "Do *not* call me that, only my brothers call me that." He shakes his head, "Only *she* called me that," he chokes out, bottom lip trembling. Arms fully extended, his gun on me, aimed at my chest with steadier hands now, "I'm not dealing with this anymore," he breathes out shakily,

bringing his hand up to his head, gun still aimed at me, he smacks the heel of his hand into his head. "You're not there, you're not there, you're not there. She's not fucking here!" he shouts.

"Raine."

I don't hear anything after I speak his name, just the scuffle of feet, my ears ringing even before I hear the boom. A gun firing. The phone in my fingers dropping to the ground. I watch in slow motion as it bounces on the tarmac, the screen shattering, little splinters of glass pinging across the ground.

My knees hit next, and it's the first time I think I blink. Slow and fast all at once. I can't get my arms out in front of me as I fall. The rough black surface scraping my cheek as air oomphs free from my chest, jaw bone crunching as my face connects with the ground. Grit and stones sharp against my flesh, my temple pounding as my skull ricochets off the tarmac.

Coldness washes through me, limbs like ice, my mouth is open and I taste dirt, copper thick in the back of my throat making me want to swallow, but it's like my tongue is frozen, swollen, touching the roof of my mouth.

Time seems to warp, the world bending and curling around me as I sink into the gravelly surface beneath me, swaddled by it as even that goes soft. I can't feel it anymore, nothing but the cold, which rips through me like ice, making me shake.

There's pinching in my eyelid, trembling warmth against my cheek. A face I recognise draws level with mine, big dark eyes, sparkling and wet. I feel my lips moving, but nothing comes out, no sounds to my ears but high pitched humming, loud and constant, as though I've been to a basement metal gig and stood beside the speaker all night.

The man's lips move too, fast and soundless, and my eyes close again, the warmth lost and I sink into the cold. Like shallow water welcoming me home, I let it take me under, an embrace from an old friend.

Death's fingers curling into my soul and severing it gently from my spine.

Luna

CHAPTER II

Night shifts are all the same in the trauma department.

Busy, loud, chaotic.

Tears and wails and grief are the soundtrack to my workdays. There is the thick scent of blood, like it's taken up permanent residence inside of my nostrils. Then there's the bleach, clinging to everything like death has disguised itself with the eye-watering scent, wrapping itself around this part of the hospital.

My white, rubber clogs are silent as I run down the wide corridor. Wheeling the resuscitation trolley back to emergency room two from five for the sixth time tonight. There've been two stabbings, both of which were fatal, and now I'm tearing back down the hall for the fourth gunshot wound, the three people before now in body bags beneath us in the morgue.

The success rate here is low.

Well, it is when I'm on shift.

That's why the others call me those nasty names.

They think I'm a bad omen.

The double doors fly wide as I smash the metal trolley through the entrance. One of three doctors stuffing gauze inside the open chest wound of a large man as another grabs the defibrillator.

Everyone moves in a blur around me as I take several steps back, out of the way to let them work. I'm not a real nurse, I'm just a night shift healthcare assistant. I check blood pressures, take bloods, ask patients how they are feeling, dress wounds and check stitches. I'm also the person who does the clean up.

Once this room is finished with, I'll be sprinkling a spill kit over the puddles of blood on the grey-speckled, white lino where it leaks from the body atop the gurney. I'll be disposing of the bloodied couch roll, the gauze, needles, and sterilising various medical instruments.

I stare unseeingly ahead, my back to the doors, my eyes on the scene.

Chaos.

Sweat beads on my nape beneath my thick black hair coiled into a large bun at the base of my neck, rolling droplet by droplet down the pale curve of my spine beneath the dense fabric of my sky blue scrubs.

There are a dozen bodies in this room, the air thick with stress, the temperature hot with pants of quick breaths, but adrenaline keeps each of them moving, breathing, working.

I imagine what their hearts look like banging around erratically inside their chest cavities. How hard they hammer to force blood through their veins. They're doctors, nurses, medical professionals that are used to this type of pressure, but I wish, not for the first time, that I could see beneath their skin.

Hands by my sides, I circle the pads of my index fingers over each of my thumbs, then run my thumbs along the lengths of my middle fingers.

Waiting.

For what's to come.

The inevitable.

Death.

The thudding of the body against the table is loud, the sound of another attempt at dragging a soul back into its shell using sudden shocks of electricity. I've witnessed this all tonight already, nothing really successful came of it then, I'm not particularly hopeful now.

"Beaumont!" My head snaps up at hearing my last name. Doctor Swiftson glares furiously at me from the corner of the room, the front of her green scrubs saturated with blood, "Get that family into the waiting room and out of my corridor, girl!"

Swallowing, I fist my hands, only just hearing the commotion at my back, now that my attention has been drawn to it. I turn, facing the windowed doors where a group of large men are all standing, peering in through the windows.

Pulling the door open just wide enough for me to squeeze through, I slip through the small gap I create and find myself almost backed back into it as I let it close, my hands flat against it.

Immediately, they all shout at once, demands, questions.

Is he okay?

Is he alive?

What's happening in there?

My eyes ping between each of them, three large men, tall, muscular, all with similar colouring, tanned, olive skin, dark hair, dark eyes. Each of them dressed differently, but all of them are coated in blood.

"Come with me to the family room," I tell them

quietly, my voice a low rasp that I rarely use unless I have to. "Then I can get a doctor to come and speak with you."

"No. We're not leaving our brother in there!" One of them barks, making me flinch back. "We're not going anywhere." He pins me with dark eyes sliced with shards of green, his hair a straight flop shoved messily away from his blood-smeared face. "Not until we know if he's gunna be alright."

The second man says something then, his features similar, a long white scar slicing through his right brow, his face screwed up into a snarl, something menacing, angry.

The third man stands between them, dressed so perfectly, a pressed suit, his hair slicked back and parted to one side, his eyes like endless black pits. There is dried blood along his jaw, his cheek, but he is otherwise perfect in his appearance. He silences the other two with nothing more than a look, and then those eyes come to me, and it feels as though the floor falls away beneath my feet.

Instinctively, I shrink back, knocking into the doors, the fabric of my scrubs getting pinched in the opening as they swing a little and close, snagging me backwards, making my feet stumble. But the suited man reaches out, his hand on my elbow, catching me before I can fall. He releases me just as quickly as he aided me, pushing his hands into the pockets of his black slacks as though touching me was a mistake.

"We are worried about our brother, I am sure you can understand that," he says politely, his voice deep, loud, assertive, proper, every word pronounced perfectly.

I glance over my shoulder, through the glass, the crash team works on the man on the bed, too many people crowding around him to see, but I suppose this is natural. What they feel. Fear, I suppose, at the unknown. Someone they love in the hands of strangers. Fate the only thing at play here.

I'm sure it wouldn't help them to hear what I have to say about that.

That a gunshot wound to the chest, the bullet still squirming its way around inside of the heart doesn't usually end well. I can only see one foot, a black boot, the laces hanging limply from the suede shoe, shaking like little worms with every jostling movement the medical staff surrounding him make.

A doctor moves out of the way, revealing another who has his hands, painted wrist deep with blood, hovering over the patient's chest, and one of the men around me makes a pained sound. Slowly, turning back to face them, I find the smartly dressed man's obsidian eyes still fixed on me.

"If you'll let me take you to a room just off of this corridor, I can go back in there and find out what's going on for you," I tell him gently, my heart lurching in my throat as the angry looking man with the scar through his eyebrow growls at me. "I don't want them to call security and kick you out."

The man directly before me eyes pinch, but he nods, albeit reluctantly, his hands coming free from his pockets, "We will not be placed out of ear shot," he tells me lowly, authoritatively, and I find myself nodding at the negotiation.

"Please, come with me." I push between them, trying not to brush them as I squeeze through.

I lead them to a staff lounge that doesn't see much use here in this department, always so chaotic, no one ever manages to snag a sip of water, much less a break. But it has couches and a water dispenser, a restroom at the far end. The three men file inside the brightly lit room, all of them in black clothing makes them look a little obscene in the sterilely decorated space. Once they're inside, they all turn to look at me, and it feels more than a little intimidating, like three predators and their potential prey. It makes me think of home with my uncle's guards, and I feel myself shrinking back.

"I'll come straight back as soon as I know some-thing," I tell them with a nod, my eyes on my feet as I start to back out of the room.

"Hey," the man who shouted at me calls, and I flick my gaze to his. "Don't let my big brother die, okay, sweetheart?" His voice cracks, making me swallow.

That's an impossible promise to make, and I feel the pressure start to weigh on my shoulders, instantly curling them inwards, an attempt at making myself smaller.

I don't really understand grief. I don't remember ever losing someone and feeling sad about it. It's always just been me and my uncle Nolan.

Names the others call me out on the ward rattle violently around inside of my head. Mocking and jeer-ing. How I always only seem to bring death. Every patient I'm in the room with dies. Because of me.

But I nod a lie to the man with the weak smirk before backing out of the door.

I hurry down the hallway, the white walls seemingly endless. This weird feeling of suddenly wanting this man to live feels as though someone is pressing down on my shoulders, pulling at my insides.

The doors swing open as I reach them, the room emptying fast, and the man on the trolley is being pushed out of the room. Oxygen mask over his face, wires and tubing over his arms, padding over his chest. I see glossy black hair, sallow skin, dark brows over closed eyes, but before I can get a proper look at him, he's rushed on by. Another team of doctors waiting for him at the opposite end of the hall.

This is good.

A good sign if they're not leaving him there. They're still rushing. Moving quickly. That means there's hope.

That means death has not yet come.

Nurse Barker steps out of the doors, the last one in the room, she looks at me, pulling the blue mask from her face revealing wrinkled lips and a dimpled chin. "They're going into surgery, tell the family, and then get this cleaned up."

CHAPTER III

B*lackwell.*
That's the name scrawled in dark green pen across the whiteboard pinned to the door as I stand before room twelve.

The three men from before are already inside, standing over their unconscious brother, even though I'm pretty certain they shouldn't be. But I saw the doctor speak with them only a short while ago, looking around before she ushered them inside, and there they've remained since.

Eight hours of surgery and one retrieved bullet later, the man lives.

For now.

I'm not sure why death follows me so closely, but it does, and everyone seems to know it.

As though they can sense the dark cloud haloing my head, the black cloak covering my shoulders, billowing out behind me as I traipse through the sterile white halls. Marking patients' ends as I pass with nothing more than my presence.

I'm not sure any of that is really true, but it feels that way.

It's why I hover outside this room now.

I'm supposed to be checking the patient's stats hourly now that the senior nurse has declared him stable, but I can't bring myself to cross the threshold, not after he was saved.

What if I ruin that?

I shouldn't even be here now, my shift ended an hour ago, but Swiftson told me I had to work an extra half shift, so I won't leave here now 'til at least midday.

Indecision makes my head hurt the longer I stare at the closed door. I take a step back, immediately knocking into someone, the breath punching out of me as I spin around, my pen clattering to the ground.

"Honestly!" Felicity shrieks. "What are you doing standing in the middle of the walkway?!" she spits at me, lips pulled into a sneer. "You're supposed to be checking on the criminal!" *Criminal?* "Do you ever do what you're told, you little freak?" She tucks a wisp of bleached-blonde hair behind her ear, smoothing her hands down on either side of her head as though bumping into me has ruffled her into a complete flustered mess. "Like, how is it we get paid the fucking same but only one of us is actually any good at the job?" she huffs through her nose, pinching her lips together tightly. "It's not fucking logical."

"I'm sorry," I say quietly, dropping my gaze, fingers blanching white the harder I grip the edges of my blue clipboard. "I didn't see you. It was an accident."

"Yeah, well, clearly you being born was a fucking accident." I glance up at that, the way she says it, so dismissive, so viscous.

Cutting.

Something heavy develops in my chest.

"I said I was sor-"

"Yeah, yeah, you're *sorry. Lunatic Luna's* always *so* fucking *sorry.* You always this sorry when your patients drop dead, too?" Felicity cocks her head, her light eyes wide, brows lifted high on her head, as though the mocking is a legitimate question.

Brow collapsing, my nose scrunches, an involuntary reaction to her words, but my eyelids feel hot and my chest feels tight and I just want her to stop paying me any attention at all.

"You're such a fucking weirdo," she scoffs when I don't answer. Dropping her hands to her thighs, she bends forward, putting her face right into mine, cocking her head, "Good luck in there, *Loony*," she whispers. "I hear *they're* all killers too." She lifts a hand to my face, her fingertip bopping the tip of my nose with every word as she sing-songs, "Just. Like. *You*."

With that, she straightens, strutting away, her long legs carrying her down the corridor. End of her blonde braid swishing across the tops of her shoulder blades like a swinging scythe.

Only when she's disappearing around the corner do I take in my first real breath since bumping into her. My lungs burn, and my heart thuds hard in my ears, but I need to do my job before she tattles on me again. I really need this job. It's the only thing I have that's mine.

Rolling my shoulders back, I dip down to retrieve my pen at the same time another hand, this one large and tanned with pale green veins ridged along the back of it, beats me to it.

In a crouch, I glance up, the formal suited brother holds out my pen, clicking the end of it to retract the nib as he offers it to me, "Your pen, Miss…?"

"Oh, um, well, Lu- Beaumont, but everyone calls me loon- Luna," I shake my head, pushing up to stand, the man's scent making my head spin, salt and leather, something sharp like a lightning storm. "I'm Luna," I whisper on an exhale, dropping my head, I reach out slowly, taking my lime green pen from his fingers as he too comes to stand, and shove it quickly into my breast pocket.

"Well, Luna, it is nice to officially meet you," the man doesn't smile, but his words sound kind and truthful.

On an exhale, I offer a tight smile, dropping my eyes back down to the ground.

"You need to come in?" he asks me, reaching past me to plant his hand flat against the door, pushing it inwards.

My eyes roll towards the small opening, the other two men still stand over their brother, side by side like sentry guards. I suck on the inside of my cheek, squashing it between my molars, contemplating entering the room.

The man holding the door pushes it wider, an invitation, as though he can sense my hesitation. But I take it for what it is, letting him prop open the door, I step inside, and as he follows me in, the doors swinging closed at our backs, it feels as though all the air in the room gets sucked right out.

All eyes fall to me, my steps feeling heavy as I move towards the bed. Head lowered, I reach the monitor, snagging the pen from my pocket, I scribble down the figures and diagnostics on my clipboard, checking the level left in the IV and making a note of it.

Nobody speaks as I work, but the weight of their collective gazes feels like boulders slowly building on my shoulders. Sweat beads along my spine, moisture gathering at the nape of my neck, my eyelids feel hot and my vision feels blurry, eyes bulging in their sockets. Studying the steady graph of the patient's heartbeat, I start to count every spike inside my head. Making a few final notes on my board, I click my pen, tucking it back inside my pocket and then turn to make my way back out of the door.

"Luna."

Hearing my name stops me still. The smartly dressed man with a voice just as smooth as his suit makes my spine rigid as I face the doors out into the hall. The clipboard feels heavy in my hands, short fingernails cutting crescents into the plastic coated board. I worry that he heard before, what Felicity said, what she called me. I worry he's about to say he doesn't want me inside this room anymore checking on his family member.

Instead, he calls out a politely spoken, "Thank you."

And it feels sincere.

June is supposed to be dry, but it's raining as I make my way home, taking the shortcuts through side roads and back alleys. Raindrops pelt down like bullets as they hit the top of my head, soaking into my black hair and running down my neck, my forehead, dripping into my lashes. It feels nice though, the coolness of it, because despite the rain it's still warm.

Cars drive by, their tyres speeding through puddles gathering along the side of the road, dirty water splashing up the sides of my legs as they pass, soaking into my beige linen trousers. The material gets heavier and heavier the wetter they get, the band around my waist sagging low on my hips the further I walk.

It's only when my toes cross the threshold of my garden path that the rain miraculously stops. I squint up at the sun breaking through the clearing wisps of cloud, the heat of the rays washing over me like a blanket of warmth. I spend just a moment enjoying it, the way the heat feels prickling across my pale skin, the little hairs on my arms drying and dancing in the light breeze. Eyes shut, I tilt my head back, bathe in the sunlight for the first time in years, and then I drop my gaze, straighten my neck on my shoulders and pull my shoulders back.

At the end of the straight brick pathway, dotted with weeds and yellow dandelions growing between the red blocks, is a large, two story, Victorian house. Two intricately carved white pillars on either side of the front door support a small, square balcony above enclosed by rusting, white, metal railings. Large Sash windows line both levels, three huge windows on either side of the balcony and front door below.

It looks like a fancy home that just needs a little love, but inside, it needs something else.

Steps slow, I swallow, making my way towards the front door, feeling my breaths coming a little too fast. Anxiety claws inside of my chest like a wild animal trying to break free, and for a fleeting moment, I allow it.

The panic.

Fear.

I'm twenty-nine years old, but when I step inside

this house, I'm still the same frightened six year old little girl that was sent here to live with an estranged uncle she'd never met.

It was terrifying that first year.

Now I'm almost numb.

"Luna," Uncle Nolan calls from the parlour as I try as quietly as possible to close the creaky front door, shutting out the sunlight for the darkness. "Come in here."

The first burn of tears heats the backs of my eyes, nostrils flaring as I breathe in deep, the musty air of the foyer infecting the back of my throat giving me the urge to cough. Dry and gritty, I swallow down the feeling, letting the shudder rip through my chest to settle the internal tremor.

"Luna!"

My feet move before I can think about it, a small smile curling my mouth in auto response to his summoning, it's not worth wearing anything less.

The parlour has extravagant high ceilings, carved coving connecting walls to ceiling, a smooth, decorative finish that's covered in cobwebs and dust, greying out the pearly white finish. There are huge portraits and art pieces in gold filigree frames lining the forest-green, damask wallpapered walls. And heavy, velvet drapes in raincloud silver, thick with dust, blocking out the world beyond the panes.

Uncle Nolan sits in a sage green leather armchair, smoking his usual Hamlet cigar, a putrid stench that's ingrained in every inch of this house. A newspaper open over his knee, one leg folded across the other, his foot dressed in expensive leather bounces casually as he reads over the black and white news spread.

Uncle Nolan is a large, trim man, his lean, muscular build dressed impeccably in a pale grey pinstripe suit. Jacket folded neatly over the arm of the opposite chair, his white shirt sleeves rolled up neatly to his elbows, waistcoat still buttoned, pocket watch still attached, but his tie is removed, the tail of it peeking out from his trouser pocket.

It isn't fair that he looks the way he does. The way he makes my skin crawl should, by right, make him ugly. A beast with a snarling, dripping maw, glowing red orbs and razor-sharp talons blading from his hands.

Instead, he has warm green eyes that he can make look soft and inviting, and a smile that could outshine even Her Majesty's crown jewels when he wants to be charming. His dark hair is just starting to grey at his temples, but in a way that makes him appear youthful for his age.

Those green eyes spear me on the spot as I stop

behind an empty armchair matching the one in which he sits. Fingers curling over the back of the worn leather, I wait patiently for him to speak. Ignoring the other men he has stationed around the room. Security guards. Or something. I'm unsure what it is my uncle does, but I know whatever it is, it's not something good. There are always armed men here, standing sentry around the house, every room, every hall. I have grown up here knowing not to pay them any attention.

Uncle Nolan doesn't like it.

Already knowing what he's upset with me about, I feel my breath funnel into my lungs as though it's filtering through sludge. Leaning forward, he ashes his cigar in the crystal-cut ashtray opposite him on the pouffe, leaving it to rest there. His gaze scans over the parts of me he can see above the chair when he sits back, my white blouse clinging to my upper body where it's saturated with water, my bundled hair dripping down my spine.

"You're wet," he states almost questioningly, despite the fact, I know, even with the curtains closed, that he knows it's been raining outside.

I say nothing in response, holding his eye. He purses his lips, his head canting slightly to one side, as he rolls his gaze over me a second time, dismissively.

"Where have you been?" he asks smoothly, that slippery smile starting to worm itself onto his face.

I know he knows that too.

Because my uncle always knows everything about me.

"At work."

A dark brow lifts easily on his forehead, and the look he gives me slides like melting ice down my spine, "Did I give you permission to be outside of this house during the day, Luna?" He twists the gold jewellery he always wears around on his right ring finger, a big circular signet ring with the letter B embellished in it.

The tremble is involuntary, I couldn't stop it if I tried, "No, sir," I respond quietly.

"No," he tuts, sighing with a slow shake of his head as though he hates to be having this conversation. His short hair is perfectly lacquered to sit to one side, unmoving when he smooths a hand over it, before running it down his chest, dropping his arm to rest his wrist on the leather arm of the chair, hand hanging over the edge. "And you didn't even think it pertinent to call."

"I'm sorry, sir."

"Mm, you don't look very sorry to me." I blink, my tummy flip-flopping as he wets his lips. "You didn't call me, so I have had no idea what you have been doing or where you have been for the last five hours. Not only did you not ask me permission to work an extra half shift. You did not call me. And apparently, you also think it appropriate to walk around outside in public," he sneers at my white blouse like it is a thing of disgust, "like *that*."

"I'm sor-"

"I thought you were lying dead in a ditch some-where, worried sick, and all you are is *sorry*?" his dark brows lift high on his head, expression open for my response, but I don't give one, this is how it always goes. "That's what I thought."

He tuts, uncrossing and recrossing his legs over the opposite knee. He turns his attention back to his paper, lifting it up so it's open before him to read once more. Long seconds of silence drag by before those menacing green eyes flick back up, finding mine once more. My bottom lip trembles, my insides sinking at the look of cold violence in his gaze.

"You're dismissed. Go upstairs and wait for me in the bedroom."

Wolf

CHAPTER IV

"Where's Raine?"

Those are the first words out of my mouth.

Cracked and dry. So. Fucking. Dry. It feels like the roof of my mouth is sandpaper when one of my brothers pushes a cardboard straw between my lips, the water at a disgusting lukewarm temperature, but god, does it taste fucking good.

"Not here," Thorne says plainly, honest and true, my older brother is never a man to mince his words.

"Get him here," I groan.

The pain in the centre of my chest feels like an

elephant sitting atop my sternum with a fire laced sword shoved between my ribs, every breath laboured and bone fucking dry. The cough that comes shoots out of my mouth and has me bowing in agony. Body curling into itself like one of those little grey woodlice my nephew Atlas always picks up and holds out to me before stuffing them into his pockets.

Eyes gritty beneath shut lids, I flop back on the bed, my entire body aching, and a roaring headache pounding in my temples.

Jesus.

"Wolf, you need to relax, your blood pressure is spiking and then you will have the nurse in here berating me for working you up," Thorne tells me, his tone brokering no argument. "Raine is fine, he feels bad, but he is fine."

Finally opening my eyes, I squint hard, my lashes crusted over, the wash of bright white light spearing my pupils like a blade, "Fuck me," I groan out, gritting my teeth in a molar-cracking clench, as I attempt to sit my arse up.

"Easy," Thorne hisses, his hands on my upper arm, upper back, "I'll move the bed, lie back down." Pressure from the flats of his hands against the fronts of my shoulders has my spine gently reconnecting with the weird half sponge, half air-filled mattress. "Right," he says, a white controller in his hand with an array of different coloured buttons. "This should do it."

With that, the back of the bed starts to push forward, and I'm sitting up, panting at the crunch in my abdomen, but I feel better than I did lying down, less like I nearly died and more like I'm about to.

"Fuck me, I feel like shit." Sweat beads across my brow, gathering at my temples, and I feel cold all over.

"You have been shot before," my brother states.

Thorne, ever the wordsmith.

"Yes, I have. Too many fucking times, but never point blank by my own brother. Jesus Christ, it's like there's a fire in my lungs," I complain, letting my head drop back with a thud. "Why aren't I on the good shit? How long have I been out?"

"Which question would you like answered first?" Thorne drawls.

He slides his hands into his slacks pockets, cocking his head just slightly to one side. His perfect wave of black hair is styled neatly with his usual side-parting, his dark eyes like a black night's sky intent on mine. He blinks once, slowly, and although his face is completely stoic, I can feel his teasing smile. He does that now. Smiles. Real ones. Since Haisley came into his life.

"You're such a fucking fuck." I exhale a huff of breath through my nose.

"I know." He licks his lips, straightening his head on his shoulders, "One, you *are* on the *good shit*. And two, three days."

"I'm tired as fuck," I moan, a jolt of pain spearing through my lower back, vibrating through the discs of my spine, the cords of my neck.

"Yes, well, you died a few times, I am sure that is quite exhausting."

"I don't even have the energy to give you a reaction to that, bro," I sigh heavily, breathing as deeply as I dare. "What's the damage? Healing time?"

"Few more days here for monitoring, fluids, antibiotics, but you are looking at a slow six to eight weeks recovery."

Slowly, I blink, staring down at my chest. A huge white gauze bandage covers the wound so I cannot see, but it feels as though a crater has been blown through the centre of my heart. The tape holding it down is stuck like a second skin and the thought of peeling it off when my body aches so much makes nausea roll in my belly.

I think of our youngest brother. The tape that held gauze to half of his upper body, his face, his neck, covering burns inflicted by our own mother. He was nine when she started changing her *cleansings*, spouting a bunch of culty bullshit, and changing up our *treatments*.

I wish I didn't love her.

"I want to see Raine," I swallow thickly, a lump in my throat, "I want to see our brother, Thorne." I look to him, my eyes, so much different in colour to his, are glassy, his face a blank picture of calm, but I know he's hiding something. "Where is he, Thorne, where the fuck is he?"

"He has not been heard from since it happened," he tells me reluctantly, and for a long second I just stare at him.

Thorne lied to me.

I get it.

I would have tried to lie to him too, were our roles reversed, however, as Blackwells, we do not tell lies.

I'm plucking off little round sticker discs and tugging on IV tubing before I can think much more. Raine is vulnerable. He's going through something right now and he's out there, alone, probably getting even more fucked up, and it's because of me.

"Wolf!" Thorne barks, my feet kicking at the sheets and cotton blankets tangled around my legs. "Wolf!"

Machines beep, an alarm sounds and pain shoots through every inch of my skull, but no one is with him. He probably thinks he fucking killed me.

"Wolf!" Thorne shouts this time, and the only reason I stop is because he shoves me back down, *hard*, and the pain that bolts and spears in the centre of my chest seems to grow and radiate in waves through my limbs. "Enough! Get in the bed, you fucking neanderthal."

He tuts as he lifts my leg back onto the mattress. Shaking his head as he starts to untangle the sheets hanging off the edge and bundled on the floor, nothing covering me but a pair of black boxer briefs. The same ones I supposedly died *a few times* in. It makes me suddenly want them off.

"Those are fresh, Archer and I dressed you ourselves this morning." That's how well we know each other, my five brothers and I, we don't really need to use words to communicate, we just know each other that well.

It's why I know we need to find Raine.

"Thorne I-"

The doors crash open, and a harrowed looking old bat bursts in with a frown and a glare. Most people would probably cower away from her, she looks like a mean fucking bitch. Grey hair pulled back into a bun so tight, it's as though she's trying to smooth out the wrinkles in her aged face. The short woman struts aggressively across the room, every footstep closer makes her seem more and more angry.

"What do you think you're doing, boy?" she sneers, directing her question at me. "You think we saved you just so you could throw a temper-tantrum like a spoiled little brat?" She bangs her fingers onto the clacking keyboard, shutting up the beeping sounds and alarm.

The dimple in her chin deepens as she turns to glare at me, her lips pursing tightly, the creases around her mouth etching into her skin like cracks. She doesn't say anything more, scowling down as she resticks a bunch of coloured discs with wires to my chest and sides, puts my IV back in. I stare at her name tag, *Senior Nurse Betty Barker*. Should be *Senior Nurse Batshit Bitch*.

Thorne says nothing as he finishes unwinding my sheets, laying them back over my legs. His hands slide back into his slacks pockets, watching her finish, my heart rate spiking wildly on the monitor screen when the nurse finishes getting me hooked back up.

"Relax. Or have a heart attack. You might not be so lucky the next time," Nurse Barker spits, throwing Thorne a narrow eyed glare, before turning and storming out of the room, the doors banging shut behind her, but I can still hear her voice bellowing orders halfway down the corridor.

"Fucking hell," I groan, panting for breath.

"I told you I did not want the nurse coming back in here," my brother says with distaste.

"She's a fucking nightmare," I grunt, shutting my eyes and laying my head back. "Raine shoulda shot her instead."

There's quiet for a few minutes as I pant to catch my breath, only the sound of Thorne folding himself into the large chair at my side, quiet as ever. So I don't miss it when someone enters the room, the doors opening once more.

Breathing slowed, I open my eyes, hoping by some miracle it's Raine, but instead, someone else steps through that makes my heart start hammering all over again.

The woman's hair shines like black oil beneath the rays of the sun, parted straight down the centre, tied back at the nape of her long neck. Her uniform is sky blue, which, against the white iciness of her skin, makes her glacier-blue eyes pop like neon lights in a dark room. She's tall, maybe five-ten to my six-six, her shoulders slim, arms soft, skin clean of ink or freckles or scars.

Her eyes blink, just once, as she takes me in. Her gaze roves up from the bandage over my chest to my face, the stubble over my jaw that is usually shaped and short and neat, feels too long now that someone has paid it attention, even if it was just a cursory glance.

My skin feels hot, the longer she holds my gaze, I feel the air in my lungs stilling, warming, like there are kindling embers inside of them. Those blue eyes are almost clear, the pupils so black, it's like the lake at Heron Mill frozen over in winter, the dead night's sky free of stars above.

She lowers her head, severing our connection and I take my first breath since she appeared in the doorway. She starts to move closer, only twelve feet between us, but it feels as though she's daggered my heart, the way it thuds hard and fast in my chest, the rapid beeping of the machine beside my head. I'm not sure I could be embarrassed by it if I tried.

It feels as though I've been ensnared in a trap designed to kill. Barbed wire and crushed glass and razor blade sharp spears, all of it capturing me, piercing my skin, sinking deep into my organs and wrapping me up in blood and obsession.

I hate it.

The way my insides react to her.

It's involuntary.

Her eyes are different, but other than that…

She looks like my mother.

I feel sick.

Gritting my teeth, she comes closer, stopping beside the monitor. I track her movements, the way her small hands hover over the keyboard, long fingers elegantly tapping the keys, the clacking loud. The beeping stops, her hands drop from the keys and those bright eyes come to mine again, they remind me a little of my sister's. Grace has two different coloured eyes, but one of them is an icy-blue, it's more surface level water than this girl's though. These blue orbs want to drown me.

Her gaze flicks to my chest, and automatically, mine follows. The gauze is stained red, a steady seeping bloom in the centre of the covering. That's when I feel the pain again, but it feels dull now, in comparison to how my heart ached and pounded when she appeared in the doorway.

"Hello, Luna," Thorne greets quietly, my head snapping in his direction at the ease in which he speaks this stranger's name.

"Hello, Mr Blackwell," the girl replies softly, her voice rough, a little gravelly, as though these are the first words she might have spoken today.

Luna.

Sweat gathers along my hairline, beads of moisture gathering across my forehead, but the rest of me is cold. An infection of ice shoots through my veins, forcing goosebumps to raze across my flesh, and my heart hammers harder again. The wound feels as though it reopens, grows, turning into a black hole of my own despair.

I don't want this woman in here.

I don't want my brother greeting her like they are already familiars.

It's been three days.

I need to go home.

"Wolf," Thorne says, and the buzzing in my ears seems to wither away and die.

On the opposite side of the bed to her, I look to him, his immaculately suited body folded effortlessly into the hospital chair, fingers resting delicately atop his knee. You wouldn't look at this well dressed, straight-postured man and see a killer.

"This is Luna," I stare at my brother so long I feel my eyeballs drying out, but I can't conjure any thoughts to make my mouth form a reply. "She has been taking care of you throughout the nights." Thorne is not one to smile, though he does it more now, but his lips curl at one corner as he flicks his gaze back to the woman.

Luna.

The name feels too comfortable inside my head. Like I could say it too easily.

Too much warmth associated with it.

Too much comfort.

Luna.

Thorne stares at me, and I can feel my lips part, the air funnelling in through my teeth, and the first words out of my mouth are like poison, "I want a different nurse."

"Wolf," he frowns at me, those black brows dropping low over his even blacker eyes. "Do not be rude." Looking over me, back to her, he says, "Please ignore my brother, Luna, he is a barbarian when he first wakes up."

My molars ache where I clench my teeth so hard, staring at him, but the harder I clench my jaw, the worse the ache in the rest of my body feels, so I loosen it up, pull air in through my nose, try to breathe normally.

"Nurse Barker asked me to change your dressing," the girl, the woman, *Luna,* whispers, her voice cracking, it makes my fucking guts twist. "I can see if I can ask her to do it, it's not a problem."

I feel the cool air move into the space beside me, her soft footsteps tracking her away, I don't look, but I drop my head back against the bed, stare up at the ceiling before shutting my eyes.

"It's fine," I grit out. "Just get on with it."

Wolf

CHAPTER V

This is torture.

Her long fingers carefully peel off the tape holding the large bandage to my chest. This is day three of consciousness and I am starting to lose my fucking mind.

The gentle touch of her gloved hand against the hardness of my pec sends goosebumps across my flesh, my nipples pebble into tiny hard points and the tendons in my neck are so taut it feels as though my head's going to shoot off of my shoulders.

"Sorry," she whispers for the millionth time.

My eyes are shut tight so I don't have to look at her. So I don't have to see that long inky hair. She wore it down in a braid yesterday, the end swishing against her lower spine. I want to rip it out of her scalp by the roots.

I say nothing in response.

The stickiness of the tape tugs at the little hairs covering my skin, almost ticking my flesh. It bothers me more than it should, the way she is so quiet and so calm and so careful with me. She reminds me a little of Haisley, all of that time I spent with my brother's love, how careful she was with me, I with her. It was natural, the roles we fell into, I was there to protect her whilst my brother got his shit together enough to go back to her. But she is gentle, all of the women in my family are, Grace is, the way she is with creatures and nature and her sons. You wouldn't think she were capable of the bloody mutilation messes I've cleaned up for her.

My mother was never gentle, not by the end. She was cruel and manipulative and violent, and we let her do whatever she wanted to us.

For love.

A hiss escapes me when soft fingers tear off the tape in one quick rip. My eyes flying open and immediately falling onto her.

Her.

Luna.

Ice-chip eyes and alabaster skin. Everything about her is icy and pale, all except for that hair.

Luna is staring at me, her expression blank, as it always is, but it's as though, despite her blank look, I can feel her anger towards me.

Perhaps anger is too strong of a word, dislike maybe, or irritation.

Maybe she can't fucking stand me, the way I wish I couldn't stand her.

"*Ouch*," I exaggerate, showing too many teeth with my snarl, but she doesn't react, she hardly even blinks, those heavy fans of onyx lashes a mere half flutter over her bright eyes.

This time, she doesn't say sorry. This time, her chest stills, the tips of her fingers like an electric zap where they rest over my heart. Spikey stitches jutting out of the centre of my chest, she brushes over them with a ghost-like touch, but her eyes never leave mine.

It's as though time slows, not to a complete stop, but enough that every breath feels like I'm inhaling grave dirt, the consecrated earth burning its way down my oesophagus. It tastes like death on the back of my tongue, my future, my brief past, where my heart let me down four times before they could stabilise me enough to dig around inside of my chest cavity for the 9mm piece of metal.

That's why I can't stand to look at her.

Can't stand *not* to look at her.

Because when I look upon this delicate face, pale pink lips almost the same shade as her skin, her top lip so much plumper than the bottom, it makes her look like she's wearing a constant pout, her lips pulled into something that almost resembles a moue. Her nose long and straight, pronounced, but still soft on her face between the high arches of her cheekbones. There is not a blemish on her skin. Not a freckle, not a mole, a scar, a birthmark, she is heavenly, untouched, and my insides twist with the way I would like to mess it all up.

See redness bloom in the shape of my fingertips around the pale length of her neck. A bruise dug deep into her clavicle, each little crescent shape mark a bright pale blue from my teeth. I want to see my hand-prints on her arse, beard burn from *my* face in the creamy junction of her thighs. Mostly, I want to feel her long fingers tear the band from my loop of hair, thread into the chin-length, black strands, her palm cradling the crown of my head before she twists the inky strands and rips my head back.

"I am always very careful with you."

That's what she says, it's spoken with her usual dulcet tone, quiet and soft, but a little rough, gravelly, like she doesn't often speak. Doesn't use her voice. And it's all I want her to do. With me. Speak. No matter what it is she says, I want to hear it.

"I know," I sigh, scrubbing a hand down my face. "You are." Her eyes flick between mine, her face soft and blank, I want to see emotion on it, a smile, a frown, anything. "Thank you," I tell her, and she looks away, continues checking my wound.

It feels sinful, these quiet moments in the night, stolen together, the room is always dimly lit, the hall beyond bright light like the sun, but I can't relax all day, waiting for her shift to start. So when dinner is served and cleaned up, and the lights in my room are dimmed, I know it won't be long.

I find all sorts of excuses to get her in here, more often than just her blood pressure checks and wellness questions. None of the other nurses want to deal with me anyway.

Because of who I am.

What I am.

My last name.

Luna, though, is completely oblivious. Or so it seems. She is never cautious around me in a frightened way, she never looks at me too long, but when she does it's without any sort of judgement.

It feels good.

Too good.

I'll be discharged soon and I'll never see her again.

Saying nothing in response, she carries on assessing my chest, I let my eyes close once more, and her fingers leave my skin. The sound of her opening up a fresh dressing is loud in the room, and when her touch comes back to me, I flinch. It is like electric shocks bolting through my veins, bringing me to life with the mere touch of her. I wonder, not for the first time, why I'm such an arsehole to her.

It's like we're in the playground and I'm pulling on her pigtails and shoving her into the dirt. Because I *like* her.

What's worse is that so do my brothers.

My dad.

They're all on first name basis with her like they're longtime friends, and me, I can't even form her name on my tongue before I'm being a rude fuck.

My stomach clenches with thoughts of Raine. He's the only one who hasn't been by, hasn't text, hasn't called. No one knows where he is and no one can get hold of him. He has a lot of issues, he uses a lot of substances to cope with things that haunt him, and sometimes he'll disappear for days, he always comes back, but he's never disappeared after shooting his brother before either, that's what has me worrying.

But that's no reason to treat this woman, who is never anything but gentle with me, like shit.

I'm thirty-four years old, I need to get a fucking grip.

I open my eyes, lips parting to finally, *finally* speak her name, and the door's are swinging closed at her back as she leaves me alone once more.

I don't press the call button again for the rest of her shift, but I do manage to hobble out into the hall after watching her step inside one of the storage rooms.

"Wolf!" Luna whispers with alarm as I stumble into the tiny room, clinging onto a shelf for balance.

Shelves and shelves of dressings and bandages in different coloured trays line the walls, filling the room.

"What are you doing out of bed?" her bright eyes flick frantically over my shoulder, through the open door towards the hall at my back, so I slap out my hand and manage to dislodge it from the doorstop.

It shuts slowly, one of those soft-closing safety features, and then I'm slumping back against it, my breathing ragged in my chest, dizziness tightening my lungs, but I keep myself up, clad only in a loose pair of black boxer shorts, I stay standing.

"I was a dick," I say sternly, frowning at myself, "and I needed to apologise."

With a thud, my head drops back against the solid wood, no sound filtering in from outside the door, and I stare down at her, her big eyes wide on mine. She looks nervous but she doesn't flinch back, she doesn't try to step away, and she could, I'm useless in this state, and she's got plenty of space if she wanted to avoid me.

"I don't want to scare you," I whisper the words, closing my eyes for a second as black spots burst in my vision.

"You don't," she breathes, a shuddery exhale. "You shouldn't be out of bed, Mr Blackwell."

"Wolf," I rasp.

"Wolf," she repeats quietly, and it's like a tether tugs at my balls, heat sinking into my stomach.

"I love hearing you say my name," I confess, and it feels so unlike me, but it doesn't feel wrong in this moment, it feels important that she knows.

"We need to get you back to bed," she says, her voice still a whisper, cracking with urgency to get me to comply.

"I needed to get you alone, just for a moment," I push off of the door, fisting the metal pole of a shelving unit dividing the room.

Luna backs up, bumping into it, her head tipped

back, her pretty eyes on mine, "Wolf," she warns again, and it makes my dick throb in response.

I dip my face down into hers, clinging onto the shelving unit to hold me up, our lips almost brushing. She sucks in a sharp breath, my own rushing over her mouth as I exhale heavily. Her hands come to my chest, fingertips delicate over the rough gauze taped over my stitches.

"Wolf."

"*Fuck*, I love that," I murmur against her lips, my cock sitting heavy in my boxers. "Let me take you to dinner," I tilt my head, slanting my mouth over hers, my whiskey-caramel eyes flicking between her icy-blues. "I've been a grumpy shit with you," I lick my lips as I say it, catching her cupid's bow, her expression softening. "Let me show you I'm not really like that. Say yes, Luna."

"I can't," it's barely a whisper, but to me it rings loud and clear as if she'd shouted it at me.

"Okay," I lick my lips again, brushing them across hers, making her gasp in surprise, before I pull back.

Fuck, I want to kiss you.

Luna frowns, just enough to carve a little crevice between her inky brows, it makes me want to smile.

"I respect women enough to understand no means no," I tell her honestly, reaching up with my free hand to run my thumb along her jaw, smoothing the rough pad of it just beneath her ear. "Even if your rejection hurts worse than this bullet hole in my heart." I cough a laugh, spluttering with a deep, chesty groan.

"We need to get you back to bed, Wolf," Luna's eyes flare as she says it, her fingers firmer against my chest, they singe everywhere they touch, fingerprints burning into my flesh.

"Would you like to go to dinner with me, Luna?" I drop my head forward, staring down between us, my eyes shuttering closed once more.

"I can't," she whispers, her short nails curling into the bandage, "but it's not-" she cuts herself off as I look up into her eyes, our mouths hovering too close.

"It's not what?"

She swallows, glancing away, and I'm catching her chin, drawing her gaze back. The room is hot, and we're breathing each other's air, the way we are so close. I could devour her where we stand, but I don't lean into her further, not in the way I crave. Instead, I just hold her chin, gently enough she could escape if she wanted to, but she doesn't try.

"It's not because I don't want to." My eyes flicker between hers, icy-blue and bright, even in the shadowed space of this cupboard, trying to read her.

"What does that mean, Luna?"

"It means, I can't," she shakes her head, drawing in a deep breath. "You need to get back into bed before you get me in trouble."

Without waiting for me to say anything in response, she's hooking her shoulder beneath my arm and guiding me back to my room.

CHAPTER VI

The corner of my mouth stings as I dab it with a cotton bud slick with antiseptic cream. It's my night off work which automatically makes it the worst night of the week. The bathroom is in darkness around me, only a single tealight candle flickering on the edge of the sink. The orange glow lights up the underside of my chin, hollowing out my cheeks with shadows like a carving, ghoulish and grim.

Blood tinges my taste buds, the sting in my lip the cause of that, and I try not to think about the other pain. The way there's a type of pressure pushing down inside my pelvis, my lower spine, a sharp ache in my backside that I know will not allow me to sit comfortably for a few more days. There's numbing cream I can use down there, but the thought of touching it when it hurts so much makes my temples pound with an oncoming headache. And I'm sure he isn't finished with me yet. It's why he sent me to clean myself up. There was blood, and my uncle doesn't like mess.

Placing the cotton bud down on the basin, the space between the hot and cold taps, I stare at it, wondering how long I've been, how much longer I can get away with being in here.

Tears build, my face angled down, my gaze locked on the darkened plughole in the sink. I wish I were small enough to fit between the gaps, let the water from the taps wash me away. I don't know where the pipes would take me, but it would be better than here.

It would be better than here.

"Luna," Uncle Nolan bellows loudly from the other end of the hall, and just the sound of his voice has my stomach bottoming out.

Sickness rushes up my throat, burning on its ascent, I spin, dropping to my knees, and expelling everything inside of me into the toilet. Sweat beads across my forehead, my hands ice-cold and clammy, palms damp with dread. My arms are curled over the toilet bowl, hands hanging in, I reach up to flush the chain, my fingers numb as they find the handle and pull. When the water finishes spitting, I drop my forehead to my forearm and let my eyes fall closed.

I'm panting for breath, panic a hot dagger in my back, I won't have long. I need to get it together. I need to remember how to breathe. How to walk without pain penetrating through my coccyx, how to clear my face of expression or emotion. I need to remember how not to cry.

Bile comes up next, my upper spine cramping with pins and needles as I gag and heave some more, spitting into the clean water of the toilet. My knees ache, the bones crunching as I reach up to flush again, turning myself around so I can lean against the wall.

A knock rattles the bathroom door, followed by a short, "Miss Beaumont," from one of my uncle's guards.

"I won't be a moment," I manage to get out, my voice cracking, a withered broken thing inside of me, somewhere, deep down, that same six year old girl is crying.

It feels like I'm dying when I attempt to stand. Fingers clinging onto the edge of the basin to haul myself up. Trembling knees and shaky breaths get me up just enough to twist the cold tap, cupping a palm beneath it, I gather some water and swish it around my mouth, spitting into the sink.

I catch my reflection in the mirror, my blue eyes haunted, they look so clear they feel like I'm looking at someone else. The violet rings beneath my bloodshot eyes need covering, I can't be anything but perfect before I go back in there.

It's the first time I let myself think about the patient at work.

Blackwell.

Wolf Blackwell.

I'm not sure why thoughts of him come to me now. I have thought of his warmth many nights when I've been lonely and scared. And I don't even know why. He never says more than three words to me and they're always usually grunted and cold. A bit mean.

Him asking me to dinner was because he had a high temperature and is on a ridiculously high dose of intravenous pain medication.

And yet, I wish I could go with him.

Anywhere.

Away from here.

I think of the cupboard, his hot naked skin heating me through my scrubs, his breath on my face, our lips almost brushing.

I thought he was going to kiss me.

I think I would have let him.

Be my first.

He has these pretty eyes like dark honey, yellow-caramel, which remind me of an actual wolf's. With his tanned, olive complexion and his dark brows. Black hair, strong features and thick black stubble, he's like a man-wolf, one of those men that can shift under the light of the moon.

I think about him doing just that, fur sprouting, a snout elongating his face, dissolving his strong features into a dripping maw. I think of him bounding through my front door, racing his way up the stairs, and ripping all of my Uncle's men to shreds. He tears out my uncle's throat, before he comes for me.

He's slow and careful when he approaches, his thick, black fur drenched in crimson. But he dips his head, pushing his wet nose into the palm of my hand and nuzzles me. Curls his huge wolf body around me, and neither one of us cares about the blood as we settle together in a dark corner. Then he stays.

With a quivering hand, I reach up, pulling open the mirrored cabinet to retrieve some concealer. I dab it on quickly, patting it in with my fingertips before wiping my hands on the dark hand towel. I try not to think about anything else as I twist the door knob, letting myself back out into the hall.

The wall sconces are lit few and far between, just enough to make it to the end of the corridor without tripping over my own feet. I count ten men between the bathroom and Uncle Nolan's rooms, and knowing that he could call on any one of them to hold me down, and they would, without question, makes me want to vomit all over again. So I push the thoughts aside, my bare footsteps light against the worn runner carpet, my silken nightdress fluttering around my thighs.

The door opens from the other side as I approach the bedroom, revealing the fire roaring brightly behind the grate, someone must have added new wood. When I step inside, the guard stays where he is, on the inside of the bedroom door, and I sense another on the other side of me as I pause just inside the room.

Uncle Nolan sits before the fire, bare except for a pair of dark coloured boxers covering him. He looks handsome and strong, at ease in the way he elegantly lounges in the leather armchair. All open and carefree. Sated. Like he just had the best sex of his life.

It makes me sick.

"Luna," he purrs, the sound raking up my spine like a rusty pitchfork. "I thought you had gotten lost," he tilts his head. "And so early on in our evening too." He clucks his tongue, a soft shake to his head, he smiles, this loose, warm grin, that makes my insides knot as though they are snared in razor wire.

"I'm sorry, Uncle," I whisper, my entire body trembling so hard that little loose hairs drift around my face, catching in my lashes.

"No need to be sorry, sweet girl," he smiles, something carnal. "Come here."

He opens his arms in demand as opposed to invitation, and my feet start reluctantly dragging me forward. He pulls me carefully down into his lap, manoeuvring my legs over his thighs, tucking me into his chest, my face into the side of his neck. His scent is stomach-churning, because he smells like *us*, our scents combined together with sweat and blood, too much skin and too many unwanted touches. Tears burn the backs of my eyes, my eyelids hot and clammy as Uncle Nolan slides his hand down my spine, his fingertips grazing over the top of my painful bottom, only the silk of my nightgown between us.

He rests his chin atop my head, his other hand coming around my waist, holding me to him, his hand light on my hip. He doesn't need to hold me tightly, he knows I won't try to get away. I haven't tried to escape him since I was a very small child.

"I do not mean to hurt you," he starts, as he always does, with the niceness and the fake apologies after he has been particularly aggressive with me, impatient. "Sometimes, sweet girl," he hums, the vibration like a sonic wave penetrating my skull, "I get so carried away with you, your beauty makes me forget myself. You understand what you do to me, don't you, Luna." It's not a question but I am expected to answer anyway.

"Yes." I swallow, the feeling like razor blades attacking my throat. "I'm sorry, Uncle Nolan."

"Mmm, yes, yes you are," he hums again and my breaths are these short, laboured, painful things. "You know that we are going to have to do more tonight."

My eyes squeeze closed, fingers curling tight in my lap, "Yes, Uncle Nolan."

"I don't like hurting you, Luna," he tells me again, his words too soft and kind to be real. "It's why I've left you untouched here," he says, just barely grazing his fingertips over my mound, reminding me of my virginity, like a scythe swinging just atop my head. "Pure. I'm not trying to ruin you completely, I love you, sweet girl."

Completely.

Sickness churns inside of me, every part of my body feeling like it isn't mine.

I'm not sure it really is anyway.

Ever has been.

Ever since I arrived here, my body has been just for him.

To use.

So when he's using his grip on my waist to lift my hips, his fingers of the other hand sweeping beneath the silk fabric, tugging it up around my waist. He settles my naked bottom back down onto his thigh, and slides a thick, dry finger slowly down my crack.

I flinch, even though I try so hard not to, and his descent stops, his fingertip curling in between my cheeks, but it doesn't go anywhere, he's not moved low enough yet.

"Do I sense reluctance?" he breathes the question, his hand sliding from my waist to cup the underside of my chin, his thumb and fingers clasping my jaw in a painful grip, jerking my head up. "Do we need assistance now?"

I think of the men by the door, more out in the hall, the way they've seen everything and do nothing about what happens to me here. I get it. It isn't their problem. They won't get involved. They need their pay checks.

But that's the problem with the world, we watch these terrible things happen all around us everyday and never interfere because we don't want the bad thing happening to transfer onto us.

Fear is a wonderful ruler.

"No, sir," I whisper through pinched lips where he cranes my head so far back it squashes my face. "I'll behave."

His grip loosens, his hold relaxing somewhat on my face, allowing my chin to drop down a little. His green eyes soften, as though my words touch his heart. But they don't. That organ of his is charred to ash, incinerated. There is nothing left inside this evil man but rot.

He hums again, releasing my jaw completely to cup my cheek, smoothing his thumb beneath my eye. I stiffen at the touch, his gaze dropping to where the digit sweeps and I pray the dancing shadows in the room are enough to hide my likely poor concealer job. As it is, he must see nothing that displeases him because he smiles at me, and on anyone else, it would be attractive.

Holding my gaze, his hand still cupping my cheek, the finger of his other hand restarts its descent. A sharp breath daggers my lungs, the scent of his usual brand of cigars getting trapped in my nose as the tip of his finger circles my swollen back hole, his hand rough between my cheeks. He watches my face so intently, I daren't breathe too hard in case the tears start to fall. It takes everything I have left not to wince when he pushes his finger inside, immediately forcing it deep, shoving through the tight, painful ring of abused muscle.

The groan that rumbles in his chest, the grit of his teeth as he fucks his finger into me, adding a second far too quickly to stretch me out once more, is animal. He is feral as he grunts, his other hand dropping to my hip to thrust the dry, rough digits into me so hard my teeth rattle. I stare at his eyebrows unseeingly, so he thinks I'm giving him my full attention.

A scream gets trapped in my throat when he tears his fingers out of me brutally, leaving me empty and sore, but at the relief, I sag into his chest, my fingers curling tight beneath my chin, because I want to be held. I want to be comforted. I want someone to look after me because they love me, not because they hurt me.

But he's all I have.

Uncle Nolan coughs, a strange, empty throat clearing, that has his chest shaking as he swallows, "I thought I told you to clean up," he says coldly.

My eyes snap open, the smattering of coarse chest hair suddenly feels rough against my cheek, and my heart drums so hard in my chest, I feel like I'm going to faint.

Licking my dry lips, I whisper, "I did, sir." And it's the truth.

Panic is like a living, breathing thing inside of me, I don't even know what he's referring to right now, and the unknown is far worse. He grabs my upper arm, yanking me to my feet as he pushes to stand, and I cry out, unable to keep the sound from escaping. Uncle Nolan shakes me, his grip on my bicep punishing, but it's his other hand that has my attention.

Dark red blood covers his index and middle finger, the deep, almost black coloured liquid slides down the back of his hand, curling around the dip between his forefinger and thumb. My eyes are wide as I feel wet warmth dribble down the backs of my thighs, but I don't look, too afraid, too nervous to realise this could be real damage.

And I won't get help for it.

I could be left here to die.

I almost want it.

That doesn't look anything like it has before.

Uncle Nolan shakes me again, before releasing me abruptly with a hard shove. My arms flail, feet scrabbling, and I hit the floor hard, my back crashing into the grate covering the fire. Instantly, the heat singes me, the metal burning through my silk nightdress. I throw myself forward on instinct, trying to get away from the fire, but my arm shakes so hard when I land on my palm that my elbow gives out and I go crashing to the floor.

My chin hits the hardwood, clacking my teeth

together, pooling blood on my tongue. Stars shoot across my vision, and I don't try to get up again. Body tired and aching, goosebumps prick my skin, a cold wash comes over me like a blanket made of ice drifting down to cover me, chilling me to the bone like death.

Through blurry vision, I see yellow-caramel eyes and it's the last thing I see before everything goes black.

Wolf

CHAPTER VII

Two nights go by without Luna being on shift. Instead, I get this bouncy, flouncy, blonde bitch with a name like Trinity, or Flossy, or something. She has scowling, pale blue eyes, a snarl to her thin upper lip and a cockiness to her attitude that makes me want to knock her out just so I don't have to look at it anymore.

Usually, she only comes in to check my monitor, muttering about me being a 'criminal' under her breath, then jots shit down on her clipboard, and fucks off again.

Not tonight.

Night three with no sign of Luna and I'm starting to forget all about searching for my little brother. Who, honestly, like my dad said, is probably holed up in The Crypt, a cult-run, underground bar, drowning his sorrows in absinthe and uppers. Rather than dwelling too much on that, I'm thinking about hauling my arse out of this bed and searching the streets for Luna instead.

I feel restless and irritable, and the room is so stuffy with a window that doesn't fucking open -what's even the point of it?- I sort of want to throw myself out of it.

"-just because *she* doesn't show up for her shifts for two days, because *she's ill, I* have to be the one to cover her. And honestly, I have better shit to do on my nights off tha-"

"Who are you talking about? Luna?" I grunt the question, interrupting her, which from the narrow eyed glare she throws my way, she doesn't much like.

"Why? You miss the little weirdo or something?" she sneers at me, dropping her eyes down my mostly nude body with interest.

I've got the sheets covering my lower half, but my chest is bare because the heat inside this hospital, I'm almost certain, is what kills its patients.

I lift a brow, glaring right back at her, I'm not going to snap back and tell her that Luna isn't weird, because, well, she is, but, I think I fucking like that about her.

"Don't start that bitchy bollocks with me, just answer the question," it's said in a drawl, lazy, languid, like I couldn't really give a fuck either way.

It's kind of what I tell myself, too.

That I don't care.

Though, I don't find myself to be very convincing.

The blonde rolls her light eyes, popping her hip, "Yes, I'm referring to *Luna*." I hate the way she says her fucking name, like she's beneath her, less than, it makes me want to rip her tongue out. "The little liar's called in sick, wait, no, scratch that, her *guardian's* 'personal assistant' called in sick for her the last two days," she scoffs, rolling her eyes again. "Which, you know, is just sooo, like, a cop-out. It screams privilege, right?"

I blink at that, bewildered, quite frankly, at the jealousy pouring off of this girl that claims to dislike her because she's *weird*.

"Luna still has a guardian…" it's less a question, and more of an out loud thought, but Florence keeps talking as though I'm actually conversing with her.

"Yeah," she scoffs again, as though it should be obvious. At my frown, she rolls her eyes again. "She's like, not all there, is she, you know, mentally…" she screws her face up as she says it, like I'm stupid, and it's obvious. "I mean, clearly. How many other twenty-nine year olds do you know that still get 'looked after'?"

She looks at me, waiting for an answer, and honestly, I don't even know what to say to any of that. It doesn't really give me anything. If Archer were here, he'd gossip along with her and get every last piece of information he could squeeze out of this girl. And she'd do it willingly, give up her darkest secrets, spill her guts, because Archer is nothing if not seductively charming.

"Right," I finally say, and half of her face does this weird sort of scrunch thing, like she's both cringing, and thinking I'm a complete moron, either that or she's having a stroke.

"Yeah, so, anyway, guess you'll be getting her back tomorrow, that's what Josephine said after she took the call, and I'm getting four longgg days off." Fiona says, well, she actually says a lot more after that, bitching about every other staff member she has the clear displeasure of working -loose term- alongside in this department.

But all I can focus on is the fact Luna will be back tomorrow. That's how my next twenty-four hours drag by, waiting.

"Arrow's spoken to him," Archer drawls, kicked back in the hospital chair beside my bed, throwing a gobful of M&Ms into his mouth, they clack against his teeth before he crunches them with his mouth open. "He's trippin' balls, man, trippin', balls." Something dark falls over his face as he laughs, his eyes shadowed, the usual flares of green in them hidden by storm clouds.

"Why, what'd he say?" I ask, swallowing my own handful of colourful chocolate sweets.

Archer's gaze rolls back to mine, before flicking onto Dad's who's sitting the other side of me, opposite my brother. He's in a tailored, navy suit, sans tie and jacket which is folded over the back of the small plastic chair he brought in from the hall to sit on, because like I said, it's a thousand degrees in this fucking room. It's why I'm still shirtless, nothing covering me but a fresh pair of black boxer shorts. I was covered by the thin, white, cotton bed sheets, but I'm atop them now.

"The usual," our dad sighs, blinking up from his phone, the device clutched between both hands so he can type furiously. The man texts faster than any teenager, I'm sure. "Bleeding walls, moving floors, ghosts."

Dad shrugs, like it doesn't really mean anything, but the pinch of his brow, his dark brown eyes tight, I know he's worried. He just won't say anything while I'm here. With a bullet hole through my chest that itches like I've got fleas forming an army inside my sternum.

"Anyway," Dad says, pressing the lock button on the side of his phone and tucking it back inside his slacks pocket. "Your sister sends her love, as do the boys, she wishes she could come, but, well..." Dad shrugs again, but this time it's a looser gesture, warmer, familiar.

Grace grew up in a sanatorium, she doesn't cope well in hospital settings. That's why, with her and Hunter's fourth baby on the way, they have a doctor visit the house for ultrasounds and check-ups.

My younger brother Hunter delivered their three boys at home in their bathroom after spending months being trained to do so, the rest of us waiting just down the hall. He wasn't even nervous, he just knew he had to do it, *for her.* But this time, with a baby girl on the way, something that's not been birthed in the Blackwell family in over seven generations, he's scared utterly shitless.

"Where's Thorne tonight?" I ask, holding my cupped palm out towards Archer for another handful of sweets, Thorne's been here every night, even if he doesn't show until three-am, we work unusual hours.

"With Haisley," Dad grins, it's wide and real and a little bit wolfish. "Both of them have been staying at the mill to help in Rosie's absence." Rosie is Heron Mill's housekeeper slash nanny, and she loves her work, but she's going in for a second hip replacement and having a well deserved ten weeks off. And with Grace being seven months gone now, she doesn't have the energy to chase around three boys under six. "And I think all of the chaos has gotten to Thorne, so he's taken her out to dinner." His eyes sparkle as he says it, and although, due to a messy family drama, Haisley already bears our last name, they're not married...

"He's going to propose tonight, huh?" I smile as I say it, it makes my heart thud a little harder, it feels good, the thought of him getting down on one knee, tears in her eyes, hands covering her mouth in surprise.

They're perfect together.

"How the fuck d'you get that from that?!" Archer laughs, smiling widely now too.

It makes the room feel warm, not that it's fucking cold in here, definitely not that, but it feels like happiness.

Love.

Then the doors open, and at the entrance is the

woman I've been desperate to see. I feel all three of us, my dad, my brother and me, collectively stop breathing as our gazes swing to her.

That long, shiny, sheet of raven-black hair is braided forward over one shoulder, her icy-blue eyes are bright and wide. She's fucking beautiful.

But something's off with her.

And like wolves scenting blood, all three of us sense it.

She holds herself strangely, one of her shoulders dropped slightly lower than the other. She appears stiff, like a wooden doll with barely posable joints.

"Is it okay to come in, Mr Blackwell?" she asks quietly, one hand splayed over the door, pushing it inwards, the other by her side, long fingers curled around her blue clipboard.

She's not even looking at any of us as she speaks. Her eyes are on the space just over my head. She could just as easily be speaking to me, as she could Archer or Dad.

And it's the latter that speaks, "Of course, you can, Luna," he smiles warmly as he says it, shooting me a quick look. "Archer and I were just leaving," Dad says, pushing to stand, he smooths his big hands down his thighs, collecting his jacket and tie. "We'll be back tomorrow, son," he tells me, gripping my shoulder firmly as Archer unfolds himself from his chair on my other side.

I watch them both walk towards Luna, her tall, slim frame seeming to shrink back as they approach, and they catch it too. The way they slow their steps towards her, giving her a wide berth. With warm smiles, they both say goodbye to her as they pass, and then we're alone.

She almost limps towards me, but I likely wouldn't notice if I weren't looking for it. She's slow in her approach, like she's in pain, coming up beside me to scribble down things from the monitor screen on my left, giving me a much wider berth than normal.

"Luna," I say softly, as softly as my deep voice will allow, I'm gruff with the way I speak, but I try to soften it for her. "Look at me." Her eyes dart just slightly towards me, that pale-blue flicking to me from the corner of her eye before refocusing on the screen in front of her. "Please." It's a mistake when I reach for her hand, I know it is as soon as I lift my fingers from the bed, but even as I tell myself to drop my arm, I don't.

She flinches before I even make contact, a wince in her face like the sharp movement pains her, and it feels like a dagger through my chest. Give me a bullet over this any day.

I drop my hand back to the bed instantly, even though my fingertips tingle with the want to reach for her again, to make contact this time with that milky soft skin. But I don't. Instead, forcing myself up a little straighter in the bed, I turn fully towards her, my hips twisting so my entire upper body is angled towards her. My chest pinches, the skin feeling tight, but the pain is more like severe bruising now than fiery agony.

"Luna," she doesn't look at me, but I can tell I have her attention, her eyes are still on the screen but they're glazed, because she's listening to me, and I don't want to scare her off. "I'm sorry, about the other day, when I was rude to you, and what happened afterward. I just wanted to apologise. Again." Her bottom lip pulls tight, like she's clamping down on it with her teeth, her fingers pausing over the keyboard she was typing on only moments ago. "I'm really sorry about it." The last part comes out in a whisper, gruff and low, but she still doesn't look at me and I realise I'm holding my breath, waiting for her to. "I'm really grateful you're the one taking care of me."

She blinks. Hard. A flurrying flutter of her lashes over watery eyes, then she turns to me, and we're so close, the way I'm pushed up towards her, my height helping me get closer even though I'm sitting down. Our lips could brush, if I just lean forward a little, and it's all I can think about, but I stop myself from closing the scant distance. Staying right where I am, our lips hovering only millimetres apart, her breath feathers over my mouth, her scent dizzying me, sweet peas and fresh cotton, soft and subtle.

"Luna," her eyes drop from mine, her gaze falling to my mouth. "When I get out of here," her eyes come back to mine, wide and waiting, sparkling like stars in the night's sky. "Come to dinner with me." I don't ask it as a question this time, I know it's bad, but I don't want her to have the option of saying no. *Again*. "To thank you," I find myself tacking on the end, as if it'll help sway her.

She stares at me so blankly, I'd think she hadn't heard me at all, but the rush of her breath fanning across my skin is all I need to know.

She heard, and she feels *something* about it.

Right now, that's all I'm after, a reaction.

"Say yes," I hush, my lips almost skimming hers with my words, but I am so very careful not to let them touch. "Say you'll let me apologise with a fancy dinner and wine and too much dessert."

Everything is a whisper, it's like we're trapped in a bubble of tension, and I wonder if this is all just me. But then, with a shuddering inhale, I feel her fingers brush my collarbone as she reaches up resting her hand as light as a feather against the front of my shoulder.

"Your eyes are like a real wolf's," she whispers, that plump pout of hers actually brushing mine, my lips tingle like they've been shocked with electricity. "I think about them sometimes." My heart hammers harder and harder, blood rushing around like it's a race inside my body. "They're really pretty."

Trying not to think too hard about the fact she thinks about me too, I say again, "Come to dinner with me." Wetting my lips with the tip of my tongue, catching hers as I do, she doesn't flinch back. "Come to dinner with me," I repeat, her fingertips pressing firmer against my clavicle.

She exhales, gently pushing herself away from me. She steps back, just out of reach, because that's what I want to do. Reach for her. Earn her trust. Get her to tell me what's wrong. But she looks at me with big eyes, the blue crystal clear, and offers me a sad smile, a gentle shake to her head.

"I'm sorry, Wolf, I can't."

And then she turns away from me, crossing the room, nothing but the swoosh of the swinging doors left in her wake.

She's all I think about as I try to stay awake for when she has to come in again to check on me, but it's another nurse instead, and I realise with a new bloom of pain in my chest that she swapped with someone to avoid seeing me again.

I try hard not to think too much about what's clearly wrong with her tonight. The way she moved, the sad look in her eye. Whatever it is, it's well hidden.

Well practised.

And that just makes me all the more concerned.

CHAPTER VIII

N o one's ever asked me to dinner before, and Wolf's asked me on two occasions now, it's all I can think about on my walk home.

It feels odd that someone would want to take me anywhere.

Especially someone like *him*, when I'm someone like *me*.

It's too confusing. The feeling that swelled inside me was new, and it felt... good; that makes it dangerous, and I can't afford to get myself into any more trouble. It doesn't matter that no one can see me when I'm at the hospital. My uncle's guards do not follow me there, it's my only moments of freedom, of being unwatched, but I refuse to let myself latch onto the feeling Wolf Blackwell invokes in me. It won't do me any good to be thinking about him.

The sun's coming up earlier and earlier now, what with summer well and truly here. It's nice, for me, because it's the only time of the year I get to see the sun and not be scolded for it.

Still, I don't dawdle, because despite the pain etched into my bones, I won't get given any grace when it comes to the amount of time it takes me to get home. If I'm too slow I'll lose my walking privileges.

The early morning sun is hot against my black hair, warming me all the way down to my toes where it burns into the top of my head. I breathe in deep, even though there's not many pleasant scents to smell, but it's just nice to breathe air that's not contaminated with cigars.

I've never dreaded going home before. Not really. But this week, I find myself more and more reluctant to make it there. I wonder if death has been shadowing me for so long because it's been waiting for it to be my turn. Perhaps, by Wolf Blackwell surviving, because I left the room, I owe the grim reaper someone else in return.

Me.

He asked me to dinner.

My heart thumps, I think of his eyes again, and I can see them perfectly inside my mind, it's as though they're seared into the inside of my skull and I haven't even had that long to study them. I guess because of their unusual colour, they're just easy to remember.

Maybe I just really like them, so it's easy to be consumed, even if it is only inside my head.

I often imagine another pair of eyes, nothing else of a face, just the eyes. These ones are blue though, exactly like mine, and they're always warm, creased around the outer corners, like they're happy when they see me. I wonder sometimes if they're my own, and I'm just wishing mine were that joyful.

The big house comes into view and dread burrows its way back inside my marrow like an infection I catch whenever I step within the property boundary.

It's not until later that afternoon, when I finally start feeling myself relax, that I realise I shouldn't. I'm just nodding off in the chair in front of the fireplace, unlit and full of ash, my legs pulled up in a curl beneath me, that the door opens.

I sit up with a start, eyes wide, heart pounding, a tightness in my throat that feels like a boa constrictor is coiled around my neck.

"You were late home," Uncle Nolan says.

He's standing a few feet from me, the open door at his back, two guards stepping through to join the two that were already stationed in here when I made it home. I can feel the look on my face, more than my usual careful, blank mask, confusion twisting my features. I want to argue, for the first time in my life, I want to disagree, stand my ground, I definitely wasn't late home. I know I wasn't.

"I was informed you arrived home this morning at precisely five-thirty-three."

Three minutes.

Uncle Nolan's entire body trembles with his rage, but his voice betrays nothing, he doesn't shout, or raise his voice, or scream. He never does, never has, I wonder if I'd prefer it if he did.

"Well?" He taps his foot against the wooden floor, his arms by his sides, hands in fists. "Where were you?"

My mouth works, but no sound comes out. The book in my lap feels heavy, my feet feeling numb beneath me, and tears fill my eyes. I know my uncle loves me, that's why he gets so upset. He's protective of me, but I don't feel safe with him. And for the first time in my life, after the other night, I feel real, unbidden fear.

"I wasn't late home, sir," I whisper, staring up at him, my heart in my throat, because I never talk back.

"Excuse me?" His voice gets deep, slow, rough, it feels like a rumble, and my skin goes ice cold. "What did you just say?" he whispers, and it's a poisonous hiss.

Air shudders into my lungs, and I swallow hard, wetting my lips, "I wasn't late home, sir," I repeat, even quieter than before.

"Is that so?" he lifts a dark brow, and I hate it, the look he gives, cold anger, but I suddenly won't back down.

"Yes, sir," I hold his eye, until his gaze rakes down my body, the tension dropping out of his shoulders, his fists unfurling, before his eyes come back to mine.

Sickness washes around inside my belly, but I hold my stare, I don't let the wetness gathering along my lower lash line fall. I hold myself together, waiting. And, honestly, I don't know what's going to happen here. I have *never* talked back before. Ever.

"Paul!" Uncle Nolan suddenly yells, making me flinch.

He doesn't take his eyes from mine as the man comes into the room, and I don't dare look either.

Uncle Nolan licks his lips, still looking at me when he speaks, "What time did Luna get home today?"

"Five-thirty, sir," Paul says automatically, and I feel my shoulders hitch up around my ears.

"Precisely?" Uncle Nolan clarifies, still staring at me.

"On the dot, sir."

My uncle stares at me for long silent moments. The tension in my spine makes the skin pull tight around the small burns down my shoulder blade, they're in a sort of cross-hatch pattern from where I fell against the fire grate, they sting, but they don't look too bad.

There's relief now, somewhat, like a warmth heating the iciness in my veins, that I was right, about the time I arrived home.

Somebody lied to him, to get me in trouble?

"Are you lying to me, Paul?"

My head snaps up at that, and my eyes dart to the man at my uncle's back.

That's my mistake.

It doesn't matter that I don't look long enough to catch a glimpse of him to even be able to tell you his hair colour, just that tiny flicker of my eyes sends my uncle into a fit of rage.

With a speed almost inhuman, he turns sharply, grabbing the man and throwing him to the floor. The guard smacks his face into the hardwood, and blood blooms on his lip. My uncle turns the man over, and hits him in the face. His hands curled into fists, knuckles blanching, he punches the guard, the big gold ring he wears splitting the skin on the man's cheek.

There is so much blood, it's hard to see his face, the sound of flesh smacking flesh, bone and cartilage crunching, as Uncle Nolan beats the man's face, rolling around inside of my head like a violent echo.

Ice rushes through my veins, my heart beating so hard it threatens to crack through my chest cavity, but I don't move. I do nothing as my uncle kills a man with his bare hands. He's straddling the unconscious man now, the rest of the security team sentry around the room, and I don't dare look at them, but nobody seems to have any sort of reaction to the violence taking place.

The murder.

I don't realise tears are falling until my uncle crouches down before me in the same position I was in when he first came home. Frozen in the leather. Uncle Nolan reaches up, cupping my cheek with a hot, slick palm, smearing my skin with blood. I'm not sure I can tear my eyes away from the body on the floor. The man's head, *Paul's* head, nothing more than a concave, bloody mess.

I'm trembling when my uncle directs my chin with the firmness of his thumb, dragging my attention onto him from the corpse on our bedroom floor. His face is flecked with blood, splatters across his forehead, his cheek, chin, little droplets of it dripping off of his jaw.

The whimper that escapes me can't be stopped, I can't choke the sound down, as I heave in a sob. My uncle just keeps holding my face in his big hand, crouched before me, his green eyes soft considering what's just happened. It's as though he isn't affected by it at all.

"Do you see what happens, sweet girl," he says quietly, his cigar-tinged breath blowing over my mouth, "when you disobey me?"

Tears run down my cheeks, my eyes are burning, eyelids hot enough to burn, I feel my heart cramping, and I don't know what to think. I'm not sure I even have the ability to. My eyes roll back to the body, and a sob chokes me, seeing this man lying dead where I lay only a few nights ago bleeding in a different way.

Will this be me one day?

Slowly, I drag my gaze back to Uncle Nolan's green eyes, "I'm sorry, sir," I whisper.

"Mm, yes, I should think you are."

He releases my face, pushing to stand, drowning me in his shadow. The way he peers down at me, towering above me, is terrifying. Reaching into the breast pocket of his shirt beneath his waistcoat, he flourishes a white handkerchief before cleaning his face off with it. Meticulously wiping off his fingers one by one, he finishes cleaning his hands and then re-pockets the blood-stained square of fabric out of view.

"Get up, Luna," he orders, taking a single step back, and with jerky movements, I do. "Turn around."

Something inside of me shatters and crashes and I don't try to stop the feeling of hopelessness as it over-whelms me. The cries ring hard and loud, like a wailing that only seems to appear inside my head. Outwardly, despite my body trembling, I don't make a sound.

His fingers move to his fly, the zipper loud as he pulls it down.

Silent tears slip down my cheeks, running along my jaw, as I turn around. My hands trembling, he grips my arms from behind, just tight enough to hurt, but loose enough to ensure he doesn't leave a mark, he moves me around to the back of the chair. Sliding his palms down my arms, stopping when he reaches my hands, he moves them to curl over the back of the leather chair.

Back pressed to my front, he flips the skirt of my silk nightgown up, bunching the delicate fabric in his fist, he holds it up around my waist. His breath sluices down my neck, but all I can do is tremble, staring down with tear drenched eyes at the smashed skull, the oozing blood and pulp like substance seeping from it.

I hardly feel it as he forces himself into me, the tight

ring of muscle in my backside clenching tight as he shoves himself deep. Grunting into my flesh, his breath hot and quick against the side of my neck, he bottoms out.

Tears drip from my face, nails clawing into the leather under my hands, I hold on tight and try to relax. To let this happen without a struggle, without being held down. I try to drift off somewhere else when the pain ricochets up my spine, settling in the base of my skull, my hips colliding brutally with the armchair.

I close my eyes, thinking about what it would have been like if I had said yes, if I were to attend dinner with Wolf. What would he wear, where would he take me, would he cook? I have never been anywhere, but I think I would like to go everywhere if he were the one to hold my hand and lead me.

Wolf makes me feel safe when I'm with him, even though he's sometimes grumpy. He's handsome with that thick black hair pulled back from his face, those honey coloured eyes dressed in heavy fans of lashes. He has a squared chin, a wide set jaw, the back corners angular curves covered in a thick black stubble. There are piercings in his upper ears, black hoops in both shells of cartilage, multiple and unsymmetrical on each side.

His body is clearly treated like a temple. Ridges of

muscles wrapped up in tanned, olive skin. He has large thighs and dark hair along his legs, but it's not thick, and I bet it feels soft to the touch like the very sparse hairs dotted across his chest.

I picture his mouth, pout plump, his lips the same thickness both top and bottom. The slight upturned tip of his nose that makes the feature almost soft on his masculine face. And the way his brows are so thick they should probably look comical, but they're gently sloping arches over his eyes that tie everything in together instead.

I think of his lips brushing mine, his breath on my skin and I can almost imagine more.

With him.

So as my uncle exhales hard against my neck, his face nuzzling into the side of my throat, I picture Wolf instead, but like a slap to the face, the image inside my head doesn't stick.

Because Wolf, Wolf would never hurt me.

Wolf

CHAPTER IX

The hospital agrees to a nighttime discharge because that's the hours my family keeps.

And we paid them off.

It definitely did not have anything to do with me wanting to see Luna.

Our eldest brother, Thorne, not quite a year older than me, is the first one through the door, followed quickly by Archer and Hunter, entering the room in an arrowhead formation.

Thorne is elegant when he enters, dressed in his usual black-on-black suit, shoes shined and polished, hair immaculately swept into place.

Hunter stalks in like a predator. A scowl on his face, a tear in the hem of his t-shirt, dark hair shoved messily back. Hands curled into fists, he glances around the room like he's looking to pick a fight with a piece of medical equipment.

Archer saunters in last, wearing his usual smirk, hair a mess, slices of it hanging in his eyes, until he tosses it back like he's in a shampoo advert, grinning wide when he catches my eye.

"He lives!" Archer cackles, his smile all straight, white teeth.

Doesn't matter that I saw him last night, where I was, and still remain to be, far from my deathbed.

"That's not funny, I actually almost died, dick'ead," I frown, scowling at him as he lifts my duffle bag from the floor, and tosses it over his shoulder.

My legs are hanging over the side of the bed, joggers on, sans underwear, I was so out of breath after showering for a whole four minutes and towelling off, before trying to reach my feet to hook my bottoms on, I couldn't be fucking bothered.

I breathe out hard, everything feels fucking exhausting, all this moving around is not fun. I suddenly wonder if going home alone to Cardinal House is even a smart idea. That huge plot, all those buildings.

Jesus Christ, I'll have a lot of work to do.

I insisted I'll be fine, but... *will I?*

"You need help?" Hunter grunts the question, staring at me through the straight, black hair that's fallen over his eye.

"Fuck off," I huff stubbornly, I know I was shot, but I don't want to need help.

But the door opens at his back, a wheelchair pushing around my brother, his dark eyes on it as the woman steering it just narrowly misses running over his toes.

Luna wheels the chair right up to me alongside the bed, her long fingers curling around the handles. She looks up at me, my chest heaving as I continue to catch my breath, still bare without a shirt, and she lifts her brows.

The action makes me want to laugh.

She doesn't pull them high, not in the way Haisley would, fast, and lifted on her forehead, arched with wide eyes and pursed lips. She'd demand I get in the chair without any words passing between us at all.

But this, the way Luna is so fucking delicate and blank, but I feel like I can see whatever it is she isn't showing to the rest of the room, it makes my breath hard to catch for an entirely different reason.

"You need to use this," she says softly, her voice still that rough little crack.

It's all I hear in my dreams now.

"And if I don't?" I challenge, lifting a brow, my heart bangs around inside my healing chest cavity and I'm sure it can't be good for my health, but I don't care.

At least I'm not hooked up to any more monitors that bleep when it happens, it was starting to get embarrassing, the dramatic beeping when my heart rate rose high, it only happened every time she entered the room.

She frowns slightly, only just barely enough to create a tiny little crease between her black brows, "You'll end up back here," she tells me like I was asking her a serious question, and not just playing around.

"Oh, sweetheart," Archer purrs, draped like a human sloth in the chair behind me as I peer over my shoulder to scowl at him, my duffle bag on the floor discarded by his feet again. "Don't you know..." he cocks his head, his sentence only half finished, it's not a question.

Luna blinks, almost adorably confused, she's so fucking smart, but she just doesn't seem to get social cues, banter, jokes, it's all sort of lost on her.

"Know what?" she asks, genuinely unsure of what Archer could possibly mean.

I stare at my brother harder, his playful grin widening, his eyes still on her, "This is exactly where he wants to be."

I sigh heavily, scrubbing my hands down my face, before lifting my gaze onto hers, my hands thudding into my lap.

"Why would you want to stay in the hospital?" she whispers, stepping around the wheelchair so she's in front of me, and she genuinely doesn't know why.

Despite Archer winding her up, he's not wrong, I'd stay here forever if it meant I'd get to spend every night with her.

Without thinking, I reach over to cup her face, and she doesn't flinch this time, she doesn't step back, she lets me touch her, and my heart sings.

"Because you're here," I whisper back.

And it doesn't matter that my brothers are here. It doesn't matter that we've only just met and don't really know each other. It doesn't matter that she doesn't fully trust me yet, not enough to tell me her heartache, her secrets, her joy.

None of it fucking matters because I just know I want her.

I can feel it.

The pull in my core, a tether to my soul, something invisible and overwhelming joining me to her.

Can you feel it too? Tug back, baby girl, tug back and let me see you.

Those crystal blue eyes peer up into my own, her cheek cool in my warm palm. I hold her gaze, licking my lips, and I watch as her eyes drop to my mouth, flicking right back up to mine.

"Let me take you to dinner," I breathe the words almost over her lips once more, because I tugged on that tether that's somehow knitted us together with a sparkling silver thread, and she came. "Let me take you anywhere," I stare into her eyes, "everywhere." Our lips brush with every word now as she leans into me, letting me rest my other hand on her waist, both of hers coming to rest against my chest.

Luna's bottom lip trembles, I can't see it because we're so close, but I feel it quivering over mine, and I want to draw back, a frown on my face, but when her shuttered lids lift, her eyes glassy with tears, something clenches inside of me and I don't push. I don't push her, even though I want to demand something from her.

Someone's hurt her, I know it, so many little things have been coming together inside of my brain, and I've been driving myself insane trying to understand without asking her.

But I'm leaving here now and I don't want to go with her thinking I didn't care enough to ask.

"Who's hurting you, Luna," I whisper over her mouth, tightening my grip on her waist, just enough for her to feel my fingers flex against her ribs.

Her lips part, her eyes fluttering closed, a breath heavy from her nose. I want to kiss her. Take her away from here. From these people who treat her like shit and whisper about her behind her back.

I want to wrap her up in my arms.

Protect her from the world and everyone in it.

Even me.

Her eyes open, flicking between mine, she closes her mouth, silence loud in the moment, all I can hear is the rapid thundering of my heart.

She steps back, dropping her head and wringing her hands.

"Luna."

"You need to use the chair, or I'll get in trouble," she swallows, bringing her eyes up onto mine from beneath her lashes and all of the air leaves my lungs. "You can get out of it once you pass the entrance doors to the hospital. I'll be in the hall with your medicines."

With that, Luna backs away from me, avoiding Hunter as she leaves the room, my eyes following her as she goes.

I breathe in deep, closing my eyes, huffing sharply with a shake of my head, I ball my fists, but there's nothing I can do.

Well, there is, I could kidnap her from here and lock her up with me. It wouldn't be the first time one of the Blackwell men has done just that, it's also highly unlikely to be the last. Blackwells do not think clearly when it comes to their obsessions.

I thought I was immune.

I've got two brothers who have found love with their obsessions, and another three brothers heart-broken by theirs. Neither group of them ever really sold me on the idea.

Fuck, this is rough.

Thorne steps between my knees, a white t-shirt gathered up in his hands, he holds it out to me, and I thread my head and arms through so he can pull it down my back.

"Thank you," I sigh, scrubbing a fist to my eye, I can feel a stress headache coming on already, and I feel fucking exhausted.

"She reminds me of Gracie," Hunter says with a little less hostility in his voice than usual, he always gets like that when he talks about his wife. When I turn to look at him, his eyes already on mine, the same shade as Dad's and the rest of our brothers, only my own are different, like Mum's, he shrugs, "You'll have to make her an offer she can't say no to."

Nobody else says anything as between Thorne and Archer, they get me in the wheelchair, and Hunter manoeuvres me out into the hall. Luna's there, waiting at the end beside the lift, a green paper bag in her hand and a small stack of papers.

Her blue eyes track me as I'm wheeled towards her, Archer ahead of us, Thorne behind. She passes the paper bag to Archer as he thumbs the call button for the lift and then drops her gaze to me.

I don't say anything to her as the lift doors slide open, Archer and Thorne both step inside, and Hunter turns us around, wheeling me backwards into the lift so I'm facing outwards.

Luna reaches out, holding out the papers in her hand, but I'm not looking at those, I'm only looking at her.

"Wolf," she says, and I hate how much I love the way she says my name, all low and rough and almost scolding, it makes me want to laugh. "You need to take these."

The announcement to signal the elevator doors are about to close calls out, *'Lift going down.'* So I reach out as though to take the papers and snatch her wrist instead, yanking her into the lift just as the doors close at her back. She stumbles, dropping into my lap as I pull her into me, capturing her around the waist with my arm.

Little loose hairs drift across her face as she exhales sharply, the papers from her hand slowly drifting towards the floor.

"Wolf," she says breathlessly, and my entire body hums with satisfaction.

Her glacial blue eyes are locked on mine, and I can feel her heart beating like a drumming in her chest.

"I'll be back here everyday until you tell me yes," I say softly, speaking into her ear. "Everyday."

She stares at me with longing, want and fear. And that bottom lip trembles again, the way it quivers, it's like my undoing. I'm starting to wonder if the fear is all because of me, am I being too pushy, am I frightening her, intimidating, is all of this too much.

"Please," she whispers, one of her hands coming up to touch the hollow of my throat, her body turning towards me so our noses almost brush. "Don't."

"Why not?"

"Because I'm not…" Luna looks down, sadness in the pout of her lips.

"Because you're not what?" I sigh, then breathe her in, her scent sweet and clean.

She looks up at me, her eyes filled with tears, real pain in the slope of her brow, she whispers, *"Free."*

I'm scowling, I don't mean to, but I can't stop myself, "Luna-"

The lift doors open, dinging as they do, interrupting us. Her head automatically turns towards the hall, and she throws herself out of my lap, stumbling to right herself as a large man dressed in all black is standing there, I assume waiting to use the lift.

"Miss Beaumont," the man says, "you're required to return home immediately."

Her entire body trembles, Archer immediately pushes between her and the man, Thorne is next to separate them, and Hunter pushes me out next, the lift doors clattering closed at our backs.

"What's this about?" I grunt, pushing to my feet, pain pulses inside my chest, and my legs feel like they're about to buckle, but I get my arse out of the chair and push Luna behind me.

The big guy blinks at me, his dark eyes roving to the girl at my back, he can't see her, but he stares at the centre of my body like he can.

"It's okay," Luna whispers behind me, stepping around to stand in front of me. "I'll just go and get my-"

"No, I'm afraid you're required to leave now, Miss

Beaumont," I glare at the big guy as he ignores the four of us blocking her, his eyes lazy in a way that has alarm bells going off inside my head.

I turn to face Luna, clasping her upper arms and spinning around with her, so I'm all she can see.

"Do you know this guy?" I ask her, her eyes on the floor. "Luna, look at me," her blue gaze lifts, glassy with tears. "You don't have to leave with him," I tell her, meaning it, I'm already planning out our life together inside my head. "I can protect you." She looks up at me, this fractured, sad smile curling her lips, I decide in this moment, I hate it, it's all wrong. "I can keep you safe."

"I know you would," she smiles again and it feels even worse, even sadder. "I know you want to," she breathes, her entire body still trembling, she lifts her hands to my wrists, circling them with her long, cool fingers. "But you can't." She squeezes them just once before dropping her hands, slipping free from my own. "It was really good to meet you, Wolf," she whispers, dropping her gaze, she starts to move away.

My hand snaps out, grabbing her upper arm in a tight grip, that on skin as pale as hers, will probably leave a mark. I hate how appealing the idea is.

"Don't walk away from me, Luna," I whisper, breathing hard, staring at the side of her dropped head, eyes downcast. "Don't walk away from me. I'll find you."

She swallows so hard I can almost hear the gulp, and then she turns to me, hidden by the wall of my brothers, she whispers, "You won't," with that same broken smile, but it feels more like she says, *I hope so.* "Please, let go of me."

I release her arm like she burnt me, and I don't turn around because if I do, I won't let her go. And it feels important to me that I should. I can't have a fight in the hospital, I can't have a fight full stop, I'm in no fit shape to even put on my own socks for fuck's sake. But Thorne is, he stops her without touch, simply turning to face her as she moves away from me stilling before him.

"If you ever need an unusual favour," he says calmly, "for taking care of my brother, I owe you a debt," his voice is low, hushed. "You just call this number and let it ring."

I turn my head, watching as he slips a plain black card into her hand, the only thing on it is a number in gold foil. I have only ever seen Thorne give out a single other one of those cards, the man does not owe anyone a debt.

"Miss Beaumont," the man says, summoning her again.

A growl rumbles in my chest. I want to stop her. Kill this man. Kidnap this woman. Tuck her up inside of me and keep her. I would do anything. I already know it. If she told me to put a gun to my own head and pull the trigger, I wouldn't even blink. But I'm letting her leave anyway.

"Goodbye, Wolf," Luna whispers and that's what it feels like.

When I turn and watch her back as she makes her way towards the exit, the man taking her not close enough to touch her, it doesn't make me feel any better. Her shoulders are pulled back, spine straight, footsteps mechanical.

It looks like a death march.

Wolf

CHAPTER X

The following night we're expecting rain, but the air is warm, and I sit out on the back steps of the kitchen at Heron Mill regardless. I couldn't go home. Not yet. It just felt too strange to be by myself tonight. And it seems as though everyone of my brothers are staying here right now anyway. Well, everyone except Raine. Who, apparently, is safe. I'm not sure anyone would tell me the real truth right now, but they respect me enough that if something really bad had happened to him, they'd tell me.

Plus, I think I'd feel it.

I think I'd know.

The six of us are tied together in ways no one would ever quite be able to understand. The love we have for each other, our family, far surpasses that of anything else I've ever felt.

The door is open at my back, letting in some of the warm summer breeze and probably an endless amount of moths as they follow the glow of the hall light beyond the dark kitchen. I peer out into the dense trees, seeing nothing, but hearing so much. The swooshing of the leaves in the breeze, the call of owls, the snuffles of hedgehogs.

"I can't sleep either." My stepsister turned sister-in-law's voice sounds at my back, her footsteps silent as she makes her way closer.

Tyson and Duke, Grace and Hunter's two Dobermans, bound down the steps beside me, rushing out into the dark trees. The light press of Grace's fingertips against my shoulder comes next as her swollen, bare feet appear beside me on the step.

She's slow to step down, my hand lifted in offering to guide her safely down. Once her bum meets the concrete beside me she breathes out a big sigh.

"The boys were easier than this," she says quietly, staring up at me with mismatched eyes, a gentle smile. She drops her gaze, palming her big, round belly lightly, brushing her fingers over her nightdress covered bump, "I'm so uncomfortable." She blows a long strand of blonde hair from her face, her eyes coming back to mine. "What's keeping you up, Wolf?"

I huff a breath, shaking my head, "I'm restless."

A small smile tips her lips, "So's this baby." Grace stares out at the forest beyond, one hand on her bump, the other still in mine. "Are you worried about Raine?" she asks softly, concern in her voice, she tightens her fingers over mine.

I sigh, looking down at her, her face pinched with worry, "Not really. I think he'll be just fine." Deep down, I believe it too. "You don't need to worry about him, Grace, he's a big boy, he'll come back." She tilts her face up, her eyes meeting mine, one a warm hazel, the other an icy-blue, it makes me think of Luna. "I wouldn't lie to you," I tell her with a smile.

"Blackwells don't tell lies," she recites easily, something that's been etched into each of our brains since Mum left, before that too, but Dad really drilled it into us after she was gone, now Grace is passing it down to her boys.

"Blackwells don't tell lies," I agree, squeezing her hand softly.

"Are you staying here a while?" she asks after a few minutes of listening to the quiet.

"I don't know."

"Tell me what's really on your mind," she whispers it into the darkness, and I look down at her dainty hand in mine, the wedding bands bright even in the dark on her ring finger. "I may not tell lies, but I can keep a secret." She chuckles a little at that, and I swear, even now, almost seven years after she first appeared in our lives, it's still a shock to see her so emotive.

"You know about my nurse?" I ask her, peering down at the side of her face as she bumps her shoulder softly into mine.

"Of course, I know about *your* nurse," she smiles wider, pulling in her bottom lip as she lifts her gaze back to mine.

"Hunter tells you everything, huh?" I grin at her.

"Sometimes," she smiles back and it feels good, having her with us. I can't remember not having a sister, and I'm glad that I can't because this feels too good to miss out on. "What's she like?"

It throws me. The question. Because truly, what is she like?

"Her name's Luna."

Grace hums happily, "Like the moon."

I drop my gaze, staring at the thin material of my light grey joggers, my knees almost pushing through the worn, aged fabric, "Her skin is like the moon." Grace's smile falls, but not unpleasantly. "Her hair is as black as the night sky, darker even than that maybe, like her skin reflects the sun and her hair consumes its light." I breathe in a shuddery breath, staring down at Grace's hand in mine. "Her eyes are bright blue, clear though, like a glacier." I think of the way Luna says my name and my heart starts to drum to a beat only it can hear. "She's sad."

'Your eyes are like a real wolf's.'

"You could make her happy," Grace whispers, her head cocked to one side, a strand of thigh-length hair falling forward of her shoulder. "You're a bit grumpy sometimes, but you have the purest smile of anyone I know." My heart clenches, an ache in my chest that has nothing to do with the healing gunshot wound. "I think you should go get her."

I stare out at the trees, Tyson and Duke racing back towards us through the brambles, a large stick swaying between both of their mouths. They sit at the foot of the steps, staring up at Grace with dripping maws. I nudge her shoulder with my own, in exactly the same way she did to me, and it brings her smile back.

"Silly boys," she tuts, shaking her head loosely as she stares down at them. "I think it's time to get this baby to bed." She sighs heavily, a small grunt escaping her as she shifts her swollen feet, stretching out her toes.

"Hunter," she calls quietly over her shoulder, "help me up, please."

We smile at each other as he appears from the shadows. Both of us knew he was there. He's never far away from the woman that he loves, but luckily for us, he doesn't snatch her away like he used to.

I want that.

With Luna.

"Thanks, sis," I turn my head, resting my chin over my shoulder.

"You're welcome." She smiles softly down at me, Hunter's hands beneath her arms pulling her to her full height, leading her into the house. "Goodnight, Wolf."

The dogs trot up the steps behind them, brushing past me as they go, "G'night, Grace."

The clock in the kitchen ticks loudly, as though it's the mill's way of calling me back inside. So I pull myself up on the iron handrail, and lock the door behind me, only to find Archer sitting at the table.

"How long have you been there?" I ask, grabbing a glass from an overhead cabinet and taking it to the sink.

"Long enough."

Filling the glass with water, I pop a painkiller from my pocket and swallow it down, "What you thinking about, Arch?"

My younger brother by only a year looks up at me

as I rest my arse against the edge of the sink, his hands steepled together atop the red and white chequered table cloth. It's a wipe clean one, made of that thick, shiny plastic stuff, lucky really, because my nephews, Atlas, River, and Roscoe, like to colour in the white squares with paints.

Archer swallows, holding my gaze, face blank, like he's seen a ghost, he whispers, "*Her.*" My blood runs cold, goosebumps racing across my flesh like little erupting volcanoes. "How her hair shone in the summer and her eyes swallowed me whole." his words reminiscent of what I just said about Luna in my conversation with Grace.

Every part of me feels like ice, they never talk about *her,* Archer, Arrow, and Raine.

"He thinks he's seen her." Archer breathes the words like they hurt him to say.

"Who?"

"Raine called." Dread cramps my stomach as I think of that phone call. "He was out of it, babbling a bunch of bullshit." Archer looks up at me, his hands thudding against the table. "He's *there* you know."

Magpie Manor.

We don't speak of it after what happened there.

"Dancing around with shadows and ghouls," Archer laughs but it isn't humorous. "He's managed to get Arrow to follow him there now." He shakes his head, "Chasing a ghost girl," he snorts, huffing a dark laugh. "He wanted me to go with him." He looks at me then, sharply, like he's pleading silently, but I don't know what I can give.

"It's alright, man, you don't have to go back there again, Arr-"

"It's not fair!" he explodes, throwing himself to standing, the chair clatters to the floor, palms of his hands landing flat on the table. His chest heaves, black hair falling into his eyes. "It's not fair that she was taken from us," *us.* "And now Raine thinks because he's the fucking baby, he can get fucked up and drag us all down into the pits with him! Well, he can't! It's not fucking fair that he's doing this to us!" Archer's chest heaves, a sob lunging up his throat. His voice cracks and bleeds, and I'm dropping the water glass into the sink, crossing the room and taking my brother into my arms. "It isn't fucking fair, I loved her too and I don't get to bring her back." Archer sobs, his entire body trembling, heaving as he breaks down in my arms. "It isn't fair."

"You're right," I say, kissing the top of his head fiercely, "it isn't fair." I swallow, thinking of his girl, thinking of my Luna. "It isn't fucking fair what happened to you, and it isn't fucking fair that Raine's bringing this all back up now. But if I know you, Arch," I tell him, holding him tight to me as he cries in my arms, his face in my chest, my heart breaking inside my chest. "It's that this didn't break you before, and it's not going to break you now." I swallow past the lump in my throat, "You're one of the strongest men I know, and we'll get you through this, okay?"

Archer's body trembles as I keep holding him tight. He draws in air, settling his breathing, his hands fisted against my bare back, knuckles pressing into my spine.

"We'll get you through this, okay, Arch?" I mumble against the top of his head, swaying him slowly in my arms.

"No! No," he shoves off of me. "We're not letting the same thing happen to you." He sniffs hard, wiping his arm across his nose, he pushes his hair back, sniffing again. "We're going to get Luna, don't fuck up by walking away, Wolf. It feels like the *right* thing to do because you're a good man. But you're also a fucking Blackwell, and we don't give up. Don't lose your girl before you've even got her." He's panting, his chest heaving, shoulders rising and falling, rising and falling. "Don't end up like me," he whispers, his cheeks shiny with smeared tears, eyes red and bloodshot. "Let's go and get Thorne."

Wolf

CHAPTER XI

Archer howls out of the rolled down window like an animal. Despite the rain lashing down, drenching his face, he doesn't seem to care.

"Yes!" he shouts, dropping back down into the front passenger seat with a thud.

He howls again, using his hands over his mouth to project the sound, and then he leans across the centre console, shaking his soaked hair over Thorne. Our eldest brother tuts, using the control on his driver's side door to roll Archer's window up.

"I love boys' night!" he whoops, his legs spread

wide, head lolled back on the headrest of his leather seat, water running down the sharp bone structure of his face. "Why don't we do this more often?"

"You mean sneak into girls' bedrooms in the middle of the night and snatch them from their beds to sate your brother's wolfish appetite?" Hunter drawls from beside me in the backseat of Thorne's car, his face pulled into his usual stern scowl.

"Yeah, that!" Archer chuckles, this loud, raucous sound that is the polar opposite from his sobs less than an hour ago.

"*Gee*, I wonder," Hunter huffs, crossing his arms over his broad chest. "I don't want to be here," he grunts with a sigh. His dark eyes coming to mine, "I'll do this for you, but you know, I'd obviously rather be in-"

"Your wife," Archer interrupts. "We all know that, but, Hunt, man, I don't know if you know how this shit works, but it doesn't matter how many more times you nut in her, she's already knocked up, all the spunk in the world isn't gunna make it twins," Archer slaps his thigh, mouth open wide, head thrown back, laughing like a hyena.

"Archer," Thorne warns lowly, trying to stop the impending collision.

But Hunter's face draws into something dark, his

eyes narrowing on the back of Archer's head, who's now humming a tune under his breath and tapping his fingers on his thigh.

"Watch what you say about my fucking wife," Hunter warns lowly, his brow pulled low, eyes shadowed. "I know you've got shit going on, but that's your sister. Show some fucking respect," he hisses the last word before leaning forward and punching Archer in the bicep.

Archer, seemingly unaware how close our brother is to ripping his throat out, peers out the window, rolling his shoulder, like he hardly even felt it, "Sorry."

Hunter exhales, a short, sharp breath, but he lets it go.

For now.

"She is on the move," Thorne says calmly, each of us leaning forward in our seats to stare at the screen in the centre of the dash, the little blue dot, representing the business card with the tracking chip he gave Luna, moving fast.

"Where the fuck would she be racing to at four in the morning, isn't it her night off?" Archer mumbles, less like an actual question and more like he's speaking all of our thoughts out loud.

I've had a bad feeling since Archer decided to drag Thorne and Hunter out of bed and get us all in the car.

It feels wrong, somehow, what we're doing, but I don't think that's the source of my dread. It's as though, as soon as Archer told me to get my girl, everything moved at a million miles an hour and it suddenly became urgent.

The thuds of my heart banging around inside my chest are loud in my ears as Thorne takes an unexpected left turn. The blue dot is moving so fast, racing its way across the map, Thorne accelerates harder, effortlessly following the marker.

"Something doesn't feel right," I say out loud, but nobody comments.

My insides churn, my gut twisting into knots as we keep driving.

"Maybe she dumped the card," Thorne offers up, "we know the location of the card, not the girl."

"Yeah, plus, she wasn't at a house anyway, was she? Where did you say it was originally, Thorne? A pub?" Archer asks, peering up, his black hair falling into his eyes.

"Yes," Thorne replies, cold and quiet, his tone has goosebumps raze across my flesh.

"So, maybe the card fell out of her pocket or her hand when she was get-"

"Getting dragged out of a car." I don't know why I say that, but it feels like truth. "Thorne," I say my brother's name like he's my lifeline, and in this moment, that's how it feels, my anchor. "Drive faster."

Every fucking twist and turn makes sickness swirl inside my gut. I've never felt both so hot and so cold all at the same time before. There's a pressure inside my skull so intense it feels like the bone is going to crack.

The streets get darker, street lamps busted, bulbs blown. The buildings grow bleaker, boarded up windows and steel barricades replacing doors. It's silent inside the car, bar the hammering rain assaulting the roof and our collective breathing, mine much harsher than everyone else's.

The blue dot stops on the map, and we get closer and closer, the blue marker still unmoving and I don't know whether I'm close to screaming or vomiting.

Thorne stops near the edge of the docks, the blue dot blinking in the same spot for the last few minutes, and despite the pull in my wounded chest, I'm tearing my way out of the vehicle without thinking of any consequences. My brother barks my name at my back, the sound of the other car doors opening and closing loud in the echo of the rain. Thunder claps directly overhead making me flinch, my shoulders hunching up around my ears as lightning lights up the river ahead.

I swipe an arm across my face to clear the rainwater from my eyes, and find her slumped in the shallow water.

My heart drops into my stomach, tears filling my eyes and pain bolts up my thigh bones as I rush towards her, my knees crashing to the wet ground. There's so much blood and flesh and tangled black hair. I'm not even sure what it is I'm looking at. She looks mangled, the way her body is positioned. Long limbs twisted together, blue scrubs torn and stained with large dark patches, thick, raven coloured hair strewn across her pretty face, plastered wetly to her icy skin.

A sob catches in my throat, hitching my chest, and I don't breathe as I crawl forwards in the shallow water, weakly dragging myself closer. My backside hits the gravelly riverbed, water seeping into my clothes. I'm pulling her up into my lap, smoothing down her hair, kissing the crown of her head as I cradle her in my arms.

The storm rages overhead, but I barely feel it, the cold air whipping around us, the pelting rain punishing my skin, the thunder cracking and lightning flashing.

The weight of her feels different than it did just last night, when I dragged her into my lap at the hospital, whispering words over her lips. She was light and stiff, but she wanted to give in, the way she rocked slightly into me, as though it wasn't intentional, didn't realise she was doing it. She felt the pull between us too, the tether.

She feels a lot heavier now, like the entire world is weighting this dead girl's body.

I can't strangle the sounds that fall from my throat, rocking back and forth with her in my arms as I cry. Sobs ripping their way out of my bleeding heart, choking their way up my throat. Luna's body is floppy, her head heavy on her shoulders, and as if to punish myself, I bring my fingers to her throat, holding my breath, closing my eyes, I still the jerky rocking movements and feel for a pulse.

Long seconds pass and there's nothing. I keep my fingers pressed to her neck, denting her beautiful pale skin with the pressure, but I don't feel anything. Panicking, I lift her up higher, shushing her pointlessly as if to calm her as I rest my ear over her heart. I clench my eyes shut tight, holding my breath once more, desperately praying to anything that will listen to let her come back to me.

Give her back to me.

The cry that spills from my lips is that of a wounded animal when I still get nothing. I'm curling her up into my arms, bundling her limp body into my chest, and crying into her neck.

I'm not sure how long I sit in the water, rocking

back and forth with Luna's body, but my brothers stand guard around us on the shore. Even though it's raining, even though the longer we stay here the more at risk we are of being spotted. But none of them rush me. Not until the sun is just lifting behind the dense black clouds still spilling mourning tears, and Archer drops into a crouch before me, his booted feet in the river too.

I'm quiet, still clutching her to me, trying to warm her freezing body up, but my own teeth are chattering now, my skin like ice, rain and river water soaking me through to the bone.

"We've gotta move, Wolf," Archer rasps, his voice thick but gentle. "Let's get you both into the car, yeah?" I'm nodding as he and Hunter help me up by gripping my elbows, our footsteps splashing, nobody tries to take Luna from me as Thorne leads us all back to the car.

Hunter threads the seatbelt around us both, being careful to move the strap so it doesn't press against her as he reaches across and buckles us in. Thorne drives once everyone is seated, and I am silent. Barely hearing the murmurs from my brothers' hushed conversation, I blink, staring unseeingly at the back of the headrest in front of me. I can't bring myself to look at her again.

"Take me home," I manage to get out, my voice strained. "I want to do this myself."

Nobody argues with me as Thorne flicks on his

indicator, the ticking of it like a hammer to the head. I squeeze my eyes shut tight and listen to the static humming in my ears. My hands hold onto her so tight I'm sure it'd bruise, and I loosen my grip for just a second before I realise it just doesn't fucking matter anymore.

Grief strangles the heavily thudding organ inside my chest cavity like barbed wire pulled taut. And in this moment, I'm praying for the healing bullet wound to open back up. Let my blood ooze and spill, and my soul leave my body to find hers.

It isn't fair I only just found her and now she's gone.

It hits me like an artic lorry smashing into me at high speed, I'm the one that got her killed. If I hadn't pulled her into my lap in that lift at the hospital, if that man hadn't seen us when the doors opened.

I should have followed her. She was scared, we could all see it, but I let her go.

'Because I'm not free.'

Archer's words roll around inside my head next, *'Don't fuck up by walking away, Wolf. It feels like the right thing to do because you're a good man. But you're also a fucking Blackwell.'*

But I already did walk away.

I am a Blackwell.

And I'm not a good man.

I think of dinner earlier tonight, nearly the whole family together, all of us around the table, eating steak and ale pie whilst this girl, this perfect, perfect girl was beaten to death.

There's pain in my temples, a pulsing ache in my forehead.

This is all my fault.

The drive onto the property as we reach Cardinal House is long.

Thorne navigates the wet gravel perfectly, the grind of the tyres is a welcome sound as we get closer to my home. I stare out at the graveyard on our left as we pass it, the dirt road overgrown with grass and weeds. New potholes forming because of the cracked, dry earth suddenly being flooded with rain. More things for me to fix. I suddenly don't see the point.

Eventually, the car pulls up to a stop outside my front door, and I stare at it for a long time before deciding where we need to be.

"Take us 'round the back," the words scratch on their way up my throat, my stomach convulsing as my vocal cords protest.

"Wolf," Hunter says from beside me, his big body angled towards his door, giving me and Luna as much space as possible.

After a quiet moment without response, Thorne lifts the handbrake and takes us around the two connected buildings to the back door we use for disposal transfers.

They leave because I ask them to, once they help me out of the car, I watch my brothers drive away before heading inside.

The building is cold and dark as I carry Luna through passages and hallways, taking us down a few steps into the morgue.

Reluctantly, my arms protesting our separation, I lay her limp form down on the ancient, white tiled slab, positioning her so she's lying flat on her back. Pushing my own hair out of my eyes, my hair tie having come loose somewhere, I take a deep breath, flick on the bright overhead lights, and finally take a proper look at her.

Her lips are violet, her skin pale, blue veins stark like lightning forks beneath her skin. Her blue eyes are closed, there's a slice in her throat, just above her pulse point. A gash in her temple, stretching back into her hairline and bruises blooming across her delicate face. I study the side of her head, my thumb sweeping beneath the wound that looks like a bullet scrape. I track it into her thick hair, parting the inky strands to follow it all the way to the back of her skull. This would have bled a lot, but there's no way this could have been the cause of death.

I'm suddenly wondering if she drowned, and I could have given her CPR had I not been in such a fucking state. But I picture her lying in that water, and bile rushes up the back of my throat. I spin around, heaving into the deep steel sink, my chest aching, throat burning as I empty my stomach into it.

What if I made her leave the hospital with me?

What if I'd snatched her up and chained her to me, forced her to come with me and my brothers?

Why did I try so fucking hard to be a good man, to want her to come to me?

She's dead because of me.

Good men, heroes, they never fucking win.

The bad guy, the villains, the ones who stalk through shadows and bathe in blood, those are the men who win.

Pain swells in my chest, pounding in my temples, and tears drip down my face, but I don't think of her as mine in this moment. I can't, or I won't be able to get this done.

Mechanically, I grab the scissors, cutting through her stained, wet clothes. I ignore the mottled black, purple and green bruises as I carefully lift her limbs, threading the clothing out from underneath her and dropping it into the black bag hanging open at the end of the table. Thorne's card wet and crumpled, the corner just poking out of the breast pocket of her top.

The river water and rain has mostly cleaned away any blood, but I'm struggling to find an injury that could be the cause of death. Nothing is adding up, unless it's internal damage, haemorrhaging, and from the bruising, it's likely.

Carefully, I lift her upper half forward into a sitting position, using my forearm to band across her bare breasts, I scan her back, nothing but more bruising, one in the shape of a fucking boot. My teeth grind and I gently lay her back down, turning her onto her side, I step around the table to get a better look, my hand gently clasped over her shoulder.

The bruising that I find on the backs of her thighs, her buttocks, fingerprints and blunt blooms of purple has bile painting the back of my tongue. But I can't not look, I can't not know, whatever it is she had to go through, endure until death... Me only seeing the evidence shouldn't be hard. She had to go through it, the least I can do is look, to know for sure. It'll drive me insane, all the what ifs, the not knowing.

With trembling hands, I reach out, smoothing my rough hands over her soft skin, skating my palms over her soothingly, like I'm saying sorry for what I'm about to do, and I wish the bruising was enough for me, but I have to know. I part the flesh of her bruised cheeks gently and find the evidence I expected. And it doesn't make me feel better knowing for sure that she was sodomised, probably until it killed her, or she was so near death anyway, maybe she begged for it.

Suddenly, I can't feel the disconnection anymore.

This isn't just another body in my mortuary.

I can't just do this like she's nothing to me.

Like she hasn't infected my blood, wrapped herself around my heart and strangled me with that soft, clean scent of hers. The slow blinks, blank expressions, that tiny hidden smile she gave me, reluctantly, but she did it, and it was for me. It felt fucking amazing.

My soul fucking bleeds black for what it can't have.

It isn't fucking fair.

The sobs rip out of me like an exorcism. The pain in my heart is enough to kill me, and I wish it would. In this moment, as I slip to the floor, my fingers clinging onto the edge of the table. I know. I know that I'll never be able to get the image of her cold, lifeless body out of my head for the rest of my life.

Luna

CHAPTER XII

The pain pulsing in my eye sockets is like nothing I've ever felt before, heavy and dull and sharp all at once. There's a pressure in the front of my skull, and a burning along the left side of my head. My fingers twitch, my arms running with pins and needles, and my legs feel like jelly.

I take a deep breath in and the air is hot, humid, like glue in my lungs when I inhale, but my body is trembling with cold even beneath the blanket covering my bare skin. And if I could feel my flesh properly, everything feeling asleep, numb, I'm sure I'd have goosebumps springing up along my flesh.

Swallowing hurts my dry throat, my tongue thick and heavy in my mouth. I part my lips, sucking in more sticky air, my throat feeling like razor blades have slashed through my vocal cords. I twitch my fingertips, wanting to rub my fists over my eyes, my lashes glued together with sleep. I lie still for a moment, squeezing my shut eyes, attempting to open them whilst my hands come back to life.

It takes me too long to get my brain to tell my fingers to reach up to the side of my head, to feel the searing, dull ache. To rub across my eyes, wipe the sticky corners of my mouth. But as I bring my arm up, the blanket slipping off and slinking to one side, my knuckles tap on something above me.

Terror races through my blood as I lift my hand again, only a few inches above my body, my knuckles collide once more with something hard, covered with silky fabric. I drag my fingers along the material, loose where it hangs from whatever it's attached to. Straining hard to open my eyes, panic gnawing inside my chest, clawing at my bones.

Everything is dark, my eyes open in slits, but I can't see my hand over my face. My elbows tight to my body, only inches between them and the sides of whatever is over the top of me. My breathing is harsh, and my voice cracks when I open my aching jaw, crying out at the pulsing pain in my temples, but words don't come as I realise I'm in a box.

How did I get here?

Without thought, the humid air funnelling wildly in and out of my lungs, I cry out with unrestrained panic. My fists banging on the top of the box. My movements are limited and my elbows bang against the sides as I pound on the box, wood, I think.

I can hear nothing but my quick, rasped breaths, my eyes wide and bulging despite the pitch darkness. My heart hammers so hard inside my chest, I can hear the rushing of blood in my ears, the sound of it pulsing through my veins.

In this moment, nothing hurts, my panic elevating high above everything else. My head doesn't hurt anymore, there's no feeling in my limbs, but I curl my hands into fists and punch as hard as I can into the wooden top above me. I grab the silky fabric between my fingers, my nails snagging in it as I fist it tight, trying to split through it. It shreds eventually, my jaw clenched, teeth gritted, my chest tight with a held breath as I tear it apart, my muscles screaming in protest.

Panic ebbs and bleeds as I start to picture what my box looks like. Shiny wood, a curved top, brass handles, two on each side.

Please, please, please, don't let this be what I think it is.

I kick my feet, punching everywhere I can reach, panting hard and sucking in too much air.

I still. Terror like fire in my veins, but I'm getting dizzy and the air is too thick with my panting breaths, I just need to stop for a moment. I let my sore eyes close, slow my panicked breathing into something slower.

Carefully, like a caress, I slip my hands into the torn fabric, running my fingers along the wood. Bending my knees as much as I can out to the sides, a bit like frog's legs, I slither down the length of the box on my back, tearing more material with the flex of my elbows as I continue feeling along the wood.

A sharp breath pains my lungs when I feel it, the wood is punctured, caved in from the outside, long, sharp pieces like daggers piercing through the silk. A hole. A rush of air leaves my lungs, and I shimmy my way back up so I'm lying straight and flat once more, and then I crunch my aching body upwards as far as I can, bending my knees out to the sides, pulling my feet together between them, and then on a deep inhale, holding my breath, I kick up.

The cry shreds my throat as it tears its way up from my chest, the large wooden shards piercing my feet, but I don't stop, kicking and kicking and kicking. The entire box rocks side to side, but the wood is giving way, the sound of it splitting, my pounding kicks. Then my toes slip through, and there's air on my skin, cold, and icy. No dirt. It feels like the single greatest moment of my life.

I shimmy back down the length of the box, reaching for the hole, my shoulders protesting at the stretch, and then with all of my strength, I punch through. Gripping the pieces of wood, I tug and tear and bend and flex. Yanking and pushing and shoving the broken pieces with all of my strength. The box rocks side to side like I'm in a canoe on a rough sea, the top splintering more and more.

Wet warmth dribbles down the backs of my hands, my palms, curling around the insides of my wrists, but I don't stop, this new surge of energy fuelling me on. I fight my way through the barrier trapping me inside the box and then I can finally kick my legs out, using my forearms and elbows to keep my weight, I push and wriggle my way out of the jagged hole I enlarged. Wood scraping and cutting my naked skin as I thrust my hips up, using my palms to help push me free. My legs flop down, nothing but cool air beneath my stretching toes, but I don't let it deter me, I don't worry about what's around my flailing legs, I just want to get out of the box.

The wood scrapes my breasts, chafing my nipples,

splinters embedding themselves into my skin. I thread an arm up, squeezing my elbow close to my body and shoving my hand out of the hole, my fingers slapping clumsily over polished wood to help me hook my way out.

Shoulders shimmying through next, one and then the other, and then my spine is bowing, my head slung back, neck arched, my body slithers its way to the floor.

With a thud, I land in a heap, my forehead scratching along the split wood, vinyl flooring like ice beneath me.

It takes a moment to adjust, my chest heaving, mouth open, gasping in the cool, fresh air. Eyes blinking in the darkness of the room, lighter than the pitch blackness of the inside of my box, but dark all the same. I peer around the space, cataloguing the things I can make out as the pain returns to my body.

It wasn't gone before, but it was numbed, for my fight to freedom. That's what it feels like as I squint hard, eyeing the strange room. It's mostly bare, what looks like steel countertops running along both sides of the space, a tiled table in the centre, and then, at my back, off centre, but still nothing around it, a stand holding my box.

Coffin.

My breath shudders in and out with a trembling

exhale, my knees protesting as the caps grind into the hard floor, fingers slapping and curling clumsily over the edge of the countertop to pull myself up.

Dizziness rattles around my skull, my legs like jelly as I grip tight to the side, my head hanging forward between my shoulders. Pain pulses through every inch of me, my insides feeling like they don't belong, my skin feeling wrong somehow. There's agony in my knuckles, my fingers numb, wrists and forearms shaking with the effort of holding myself up.

Other than the fact this room looks like a morgue, I don't know where I am, or how I got here. I'm vulnerable, bleeding, naked, and I really want a glass of water. Without much more thought than escaping this room, hands slapping down against the metal worktops, I make my way towards the door, three steps up to reach it. I grapple for the handle, my movements sloppy and uncoordinated, but it opens easily, unlocked.

My head feels fuzzy, floaty and light, but the pain in it is heavy, pounding in time with the hammering pulse in the side of my neck. The corridor beyond the door is dark, and I can't make much out with the strain in my eyes, but the walls are light coloured, the wallpaper one of those textured ones with foamy swirls.

My hands propel me along the wall, my body slumping heavy into it, shoulder dragging as I claw my way forwards. Exhaustion rolls through me like a spell of death, and I don't know why I was in the box.

Coffin.

Blinking hard, my eyelids heavy, I come to a wide opening, stopping to catch my breath, I peer down the corridor, a vast open archway at the very end of the hall with a soft flickering glow cast across the carpet.

My feet welcome the softer surface as I stumble towards the next wall, my toes curled, bleeding. I can feel splinters in the bottoms of my feet, blood running down my hands, and my head spins again, a tightening in my belly. It feels like my organs rearrange themselves inside my gut as my head spins, my stomach dropping.

Suddenly, the hallway seems so long, the soft orange flicker of light stretching further and further away from me. I swipe a hand over my face, dislodging tangles of black hair away from my cheek, shoving it from my lashes. The thick, straight lengths hang down to my lower spine, brushing over my hip bones where long strands slip forward, curtaining my face as my head hangs low.

Still clawing at the wall to keep myself up, I stare at my bloody feet the whole way towards the light. Sagging with relief when my toes touch the circular glow cast out over the carpet, the flickering orange spilling across the wide archway.

Through the overwhelming dizziness, I lift my head just enough to roll my eyes up to the top of their lids, staring ahead with pain in my temples as I strain my eyes.

The room is large, rows of chairs separated by a long aisle I find myself standing at the end of. Ahead of me, at the front of the room is a table, dressed with a white table cloth, a large gold cross standing in the centre of it. There are candles on either side of me, the source of the light, white pillar candles nestled beside flower arrangements that have wilted and died, petals limp and rotting, their leaves curled and dry.

My nose twitches against the smell, and I slowly move forwards, my feet shuffling almost silently across the carpet. I cling to the backs of the seats as I make my way down the aisle. Ankles rolling and elbows bowing with my weight as I finally make my way to the front seats.

Breath ragged, my chest aching and pulling, the dizziness like a black veil starting to drop over my vision like the final curtain call, I choke back a sob. Fear lacing through my veins again like liquid poison as my head rocks.

There's a man that I couldn't see before, sitting in the centre of the front right row of chairs. His knees spread wide, his broad back bare, warm, sun-kissed, olive skin dark in the shadows. Silently, I move closer, my mouth working to speak, to call out, to ask for help, but nothing comes. My head spins, white sparks exploding across my vision.

I focus on the man, his eyes closed, chin-length, black hair draping across his face where he hangs it forward. His muscles bunch in his arm as he suddenly throws his head back, eyes creased tight as he lifts a bottle of amber-coloured liquid to his mouth. Lips suctioning over the top, bubbles drawing upwards in the liquid, Adam's apple bobbing in his stubble speckled throat, he gulps the liquid down. His cheeks hollowing with each pull of the alcohol, before he stops, the bottle clenched precariously between his thick fingers. He's gasping for breath, spluttering with a dry cough, and that's when he opens his eyes.

Vision aimed at the ceiling, he leans his large body back in the chair, the wood creaking as he rests back. The button of his black jeans popped open, zipper lowered, the bottoms hanging low on his carved hips. He blinks hard, letting the bottle between his fingers thud softly to the carpet. With a swipe of his hand over his mouth, he rubs the back of his wrist across his eyes, sniffing hard as he holds his forearm there.

Licking my dry lips, I breathe hard, my vision blurring in and out of focus. Pain pulsing through my pelvis, my lower spine stabbing, I wince, a tiny, animal-like, whimper escaping my teeth like a hiss.

The man whips his head in my direction, throwing himself out of the chair, his bare foot kicks the bottle, knocking it over, the liquid splashing out onto the carpet. His mouth hangs open, his jaw and cheeks covered in a light layer of black stubble, his eyes glowing like kindling embers in the shadows.

He steps towards me, and I don't flinch, I don't try to dodge him when he dives forward, catching me in the hooks of his large arms as my knees finally give out. The man crashes to the floor with me, cradling me in his arms. And a sob escapes me at the same time it does him.

His warmth sinks into me, my eyes too heavy to keep open, I'm limp in the cradle of his body, and despite not knowing him, the stranger holds me tight and all I feel with the foreign feeling touch is safe.

Wolf

CHAPTER XIII

Disbelief wars with logic inside my head.

She was dead. When I pulled her from that water, she was dead, her chest wasn't moving. I couldn't get a pulse. I can't understand it.

"Maybe her vitals were just so weak you couldn't get a read on them," Archer suggests with an awed whisper, threading a needle into Luna's inner arm. "You were sobbing, it was raining, thunder. You couldn't think straight. There was a lot going on."

His hands are so much steadier than mine right now. I wanted to do this myself, but I can't stop shaking. He was outside in a car. Despite my earlier instruction of leaving me alone, my brothers thought it best one of them stay close by. It only took him three minutes to run inside when I called.

"The water pressure probably helped slow the bleeding," he says absently, a crease between his brows as he too finds this whole thing hard to believe.

"I thought I was seeing a ghost," I whisper numbly, trying not to disturb the girl I almost suffocated inside a coffin I couldn't bring myself to cremate.

It felt too final, too soon to say goodbye when I'd only just found her.

I cleaned her up, laid her inside the casket, covered her with a blanket.

I close the lid.

Hiding her face. All that perfect, ice-white skin bloomed with marks and bruises swaddled in a blanket of mine. The polished wooden top gleams under the harsh white light, my hands sliding over it, running across the wood.

It's the final nail in the cavity of my chest where my heart has withered and died. I lock it away, ready to bury it with her.

I want to climb inside this box. Curl my body into hers, join us both together in the fire that's to come next. I thought about putting her in the ground, but laying her in the earth, the weight of it atop her. Letting her rot, worms and insects eating their way through her like a delicacy. I can't do it.

A cry bursts from my trembling lips and my curled fists come down over the end of the coffin. I don't feel anything as I bleed, my bones aching, grinding, the skin of my knuckles splitting, spilling, oozing.

It feels as though my heart is weeping as blood dribbles from my abused fists. Crying out for what it didn't even have.

Thorne has always been my anchor, I his, but then he met Haisley, and she became that for him. It left me floating, far out at sea, no anchor, no tether, no line to draw me back in.

Nothing until her.

Instantaneous.

That's how it felt when I stopped being angry at the world and let myself see her for the first time.

How delicate and gentle and quiet she was.

Was.

Sickness churns in my stomach, but there's nothing left inside of me but acid now. Bile choking its way up the back of my throat as my fists continue to smash through wood.

I stumble back, my arse hitting the floor, chest heaving and heaving as I look up at the mess I've made.

It's supposed to be perfect.

She is so perfect.

This needed to be done right.

I should have been the last thing she saw. I would have held her and comforted her and let her know it was okay to go. To pass on, even without me. I would have made her feel safe.

'Because I'm not free.'

My heart bleeds black and my soul cries blood, but there's nothing I can do.

As a Blackwell, we deal in death. Create it, clean up after it, bury it eight feet deep.

But we don't feel it.

We hardly blink, collecting body parts and bones, soaking up blood, and discarding human tissue like it's everyday trash.

But this…

Staring at the broken coffin of a beautiful girl I could see myself one day marrying, it doesn't feel like only her death. It feels like my own.

Tears slide down my cheeks, my jaw clenched tight, heat swells across my eyelids and I can't bear to sit and stare at this fucking box any longer.

There's nothing left for either of us here.

Not tonight.

Rain.

Blood.

Coffin.

Images of her standing there, trembling, candlelight casting her in an eerie glow. Blood and scrapes and slices all over her naked body. Her knuckles broken, fingernails snapped too low, blood curling around her wrists, forearms, dripping from her fingertips.

She could have suffocated.

"What happened to her hands?" Archer asks softly, as we both study the blood racing down the length of clear tubing now connecting my arm to hers.

Luna.

Her blue veins bright beneath the ashy white of her pale skin, her eyes closed, gunshot wound to the side of her head clean and red. My t-shirt is on her upper half, my boxers on her hips, a blanket covering all of her. I watch my blood rushing down the tube, feeding her with it, and my heart clenches and swells at the possessiveness I feel, a piece of me inside of her.

She infected my veins and now I'm infecting hers.

To heal.

"She beat her way out of her coffin."

I'm disconnected as I say it. The words foreign sounding to my own ears as I stare down at her, all delicate and soft and *alive*. I swallow hard.

"Wait, what?" Archer chokes as he fumbles with the plastic wrappings from the tubing and needles.

Slowly, his dark eyes spliced with green lift to mine, his chin over his shoulder, he licks his lips, staring at me silently. We're in the visitor's room, an echoey space that feels like a fish tank, one wall of it made of glass with heavy open drapes framing it. The space once used for loved ones to come to view their deceased, but Cardinal House isn't open for business anymore. Only disposals happen here now, and those bodies are never fit for viewing. But this space has the most room for medical equipment, it felt better than putting her in my bedroom. I want her to want to be there.

"I put her in a coffin because I wanted it to be..." I huff out a breath, shaking my head, *nice* isn't the right word. "I couldn't just throw her in the furnace, Arch."

He frowns, nodding his head, "I wouldn't have been able to do it either." His words are whispers scraping up his throat, his gaze unfocused as he stares down at the floor. "You got her back though." He blinks up at me, scrunching the papers and wrappers into a ball in his fist, "She's here now." His Adam's apple bobs hard in his throat with his swallow, before he sniffs hard and pushes to stand. "Sit on that stool," he instructs, checking the tape on the needle in my arm as I do as instructed. "Keep yourself elevated higher than her."

"Arch," I say lowly, my deep voice rough, "if I could bring your girl back to you, you know I would, don't you? All I want is for you to be happy." Tears prick my eyes as he absentmindedly rubs over his wrists, faded scars from many bindings marking his skin. "I love you."

He looks up at me then, eyes shining, jaw clenched, "You think there's any way she's still out there some-where?" he whispers the question, holding my gaze, fucking hope shining in his eyes.

I roll through every possibility inside my head, it's been over twenty years since she went missing. The likelihood of her being somewhere alive and well is slim, but I suppose not completely unheard of.

"Maybe," I shiver as I say it, licking my lips. "But I don't think it's good to go chasing ghosts."

He cocks his head, top section of hair longer than the shorn sides on either side of his skull, black hair hanging across one eye, he flicks his gaze from me to Luna.

"Hang onto this one, brother," he says, throwing the rubbish in his hands into the waste paper bin, before his eyes come back to mine. "Don't let her out of your sight ever again."

CHAPTER XIV

Everything feels warm.

My toes curl and stretch as the arches of my feet pull, an ache running up my calves like a cramp that's still fading. I flex my head back, the curve in my spine feeling stiff and sore, but I'm so comfortable, I don't want to wake up yet.

The pillow beneath my head is so puffy it's almost wrapping up around my ears. There's soft cotton touching my skin, the light pressure of a weighted quilt over the top of my body, it feels like I'm sleeping in a cloud.

That's why my eyes suddenly snap open, my heart

thundering in my chest, lungs heaving with panicked breaths.

"Shhh, it's okay, you're safe," a deep, gruff voice says from beside me, making me flinch, a hiss escaping my teeth as something snags sharply in my arm.

Blinking hard, I look up with heavy eyes, and suck in a hard breath.

The handsome man from when I woke up before sits beside me.

I was in a coffin.

I fought and crawled my way out of it…

Is any of this real?

His eyes are like whiskey, rich honey yellow, warm but hard. His black brows are pulled in a tight dip, his forehead creased, and his attention is all on me.

"You're safe now," the man whispers, "I'm going to keep you safe."

"Where am I?" my voice a cracked whisper, I swallow hard, licking my dry lips.

The man turns, sitting on a stool higher than the bed I lie in, reaching for something on his other side, before turning back to me, a cup in his hand, a white paper straw. He leans closer, guiding the cup to my mouth, the straw to my lips.

"Drink," he encourages, those unusual coloured eyes holding mine.

I take the straw into my mouth, gently sucking up cool water. It feels incredible sliding down my parched throat, the inside of my mouth coming alive again as I swallow it down.

"Not too much," he says, then, "we're at my house," he tells me, taking the cup away and placing it back down. "How are you feeling?"

I stare up at him, my eyes dropping from his stare to the black stubble covering his jaw, following the stark cords in his neck to the round neckline of his black t-shirt grazing the hollow of his throat. My fingertips twitch, wanting to touch him there, like it's familiar, as though I've done it a hundred times before.

"Luna," the man says, my eyes snapping back to his, my lips parting.

Luna... that's me.

He speaks my name knowingly, like we're familiars, friends, lovers?

Tears fill my eyes, my breath burning as I hold it tight. Staring up at him, he reaches forward, tucking a strand of hair behind my ear. Instinctively, I lean into his touch, his skin so, so warm, his palm and fingers calloused, but the way he lets me nuzzle into his hand, sweeps his thumb beneath my eye, cups my cheek, makes my body relax, my breath exhale in a rush. But the tears fall all the same, he makes me feel safe, and I don't know who he is.

"Luna," he whispers, and I know that's my name, *I know that's my name*, but I don't know his, and- "Do you remember what happened, baby?"

Baby.

"No," I shake my head, lifting my hand to press over his, bandages and tape and gauze wrapped around my stiff fist. "I don't remember." tears roll down my cheeks, wetting his hand, but he doesn't lean back, he doesn't pull away. "I don't remember who you are," *but I don't want you to stop touching me.*

He sucks in a breath, pain and something else darkening his features, but he doesn't move his hand away, and he doesn't try to, my hand still over the top of his.

"It's okay," he hushes, the pressure of his hand on my cheek the only thing I can feel. "You don't have to remember anything right now, all you gotta do is feel better." He offers me this tiny, sad smile and I swallow hard, my throat thick, my face wet. "Don't get upset," he whispers, sweeping his thumb across my cheek, "I'll look after you."

My eyes slam shut tight, tears squeezing free, a sob rattling my chest, my body jumping with a core deep cry, but the man doesn't release me, he doesn't move away, I don't scare him off.

"It's okay," he repeats, over and over, spreading tears across my cheek with the smoothing of his thumb. "You can cry," his deep voice is a gruff whisper, rough but soothing, and as my entire body trembles with my sobs, he just sits and lets me ride it out.

Sniffing unevenly, my breaths too stuttery, I blink my eyes open, and find his already on me, soft and open, "I don't know anything, my head's all," I purse my lips, pulling in a deep, hard breath, "fuzzy." The cries soften, and he's still shushing me, patient.

"I'm Wolf," he says calmly, "Wolf Blackwell," his hand like fiery warmth against my cheek.

"And how do I know you?" I manage to get out, hiccupping on the words, my eyes wide and wet on his.

He frowns a little, his face pulling tight briefly before smoothing out again. I can smell him now, his skin so close to my nose, the strong scent of disinfectant, but something else too, *him*, lilies and teakwood. It doesn't feel familiar but it feels *safe*.

"I was shot," he says blandly, like it doesn't really mean anything, but a small gasp escapes my lips all the same, my fingers tightening over his on my cheek as my heart clenches with worry. "I'm okay, now," he reassures me, this pained smile curling one corner of his lips. "You took care of me, in the hospital."

He stares at me a moment, letting it sink in, and, "I work there."

He smiles then, nodding, "You do."

Exhaling slowly, I feel my chest loosen slightly, "But why am I here with you?"

Wolf's eyes narrow, one of them twitching at the outer corner, "Because somebody hurt you, and I found you, brought you here to take care of you."

Everything inside of me feels like it's being rejected out of my skin, because, "You thought I was dead."

"I couldn't get a pulse, or a heartbeat, or a- *fuck*. Anything! I should never have put you in that coffi-"

"I'm okay," I tell him quickly, doing what he just did for me, reassuring.

The split tips of my fingers slide beneath his, wedging between the underside of his hand and my cheek.

"I could have killed you," he whispers. "Look what happened to you because of me," he sighs, dropping his gaze and I find myself desperately wanting to claw it back.

"But you didn't." I lick my lips, cracked and dry, glancing down at my other arm, a clear tube connecting my inner elbow to his, it makes my heart swell and flutter. "You wouldn't have meant to hurt me," I breathe the words, his eyes slowly lifting back to mine, uncertainty in his gaze, his chin still dipped. "I- I know that." I frown as I say it, unsure *how*, exactly, I know that, only that I do. But a sudden wash of panic overwhelms me, my body going cold, despite my skin feeling hot, "What happened to me, Wolf?" he shudders at the question, but he doesn't shy away from it.

"Honestly, I don't know. All I know is how I found you, and-"

"How did you find me?" The words are barely a whisper, but Wolf is leaning down so close now, I can feel his breath on my skin and it sends signals to my brain that are confusing for someone who just clawed their way out of their own coffin.

Would he have buried me?

"Dead," he cringes a little, but his eyes shine, yellow-caramel, glass orbs, mesmerising. "In the river, beaten, shot, and-" He pulls himself up short, stopping the next words, his breath leaving him in a rush, but I grip his fingers, squeezing, telling him with my eyes to say it. "Sodomised."

It's as though the word triggers the pained nerve endings in my entire body, because suddenly everything seems to come back online, like I've just been shocked with a million volts of electricity, and it *hurts*.

"I'm going to protect you, keep you safe."

"Who would do... *that* to me, why would they kill

me? Am I…" I lick my lips, pain vaulting through every inch of my skin. "Am I a bad person?" My gaze lifts, eyes flicking between his, as his face hardens into stone.

"No. You're not a bad person, you're just someone that other people thought they could hurt. You did nothing wrong."

"How can you know that? What if I'm in a gang or something?"

What if I hurt people and deserved to die?

What if I'm a murderer?

He laughs, but it's not humorous.

"You're not anything you're thinking, Luna." Wolf's hand flips in mine, his fingers lacing though my own, the scarred backs of his knuckles grazing my cheek. "You're not bad, you're not in a gang. You haven't committed any crimes."

"But how can you know?" Tears well up again, and my face hurts too much to keep crying, the side of my head burning with every wince and pull of my features, the skin too tight.

"I just know." He shrugs loosely, running our joined hands over the arch of my cheek.

"How was I in a coffin?" I ask, scrunching my nose.

"Oh. Well, I- this is a funeral home," Wolf tells me. "I… *look after* people once they've passed away."

It feels as though that statement has a lot more

meaning to it than that, but I don't press, this is all too much to take in anyway, so I just nod, like that's enough.

"Why can't I remember anything?" it's vulnerable and the sound makes me feel sick inside, but I just... *trust* this man, even if I don't know why.

Wolf swallows, his dark, stubble studded, throat rolls with the motion, his plump lips curl together between his teeth, the dark rose-pink colour blanching briefly as they pop free. "Sometimes, after something traumatic happens, or we get a head injury, we forget things for a while, sometimes everything, sometimes a little." He smooths his hand down to my jaw, his fingers fanning out over my face, thumb to the tip of my chin, my own hand falling away, dropping to my side. "It'll come back, whatever you don't remember, it'll come back, just don't try to force it, okay?"

With a deep frown, I hold his gaze, my insides feeling like they don't belong, my skin itching and tight, like it doesn't quite fit.

"Let me take care of you," Wolf whispers.

Dipping his face back into mine, I think of our arms joined by a tube ferrying blood, presumably from his veins into mine, and I glance down at it, staring at the clear plastic filled with rich crimson.

"Why do you want to?" it's the breathiest whisper I

can manage, my voice crackling, but I don't look at him, I breathe him in instead, this scent that I feel like I know, but not well, as I stare at the tube. "Why would you look after me? Why did you look for me? How did you find me?"

Sharply, I look up at him, my head pounding in time with the frantic banging of my heart. His eyes are on mine, and the emotions in them change quicker than the wind, so many things flash across his face before his features smooth out.

"I looked for you because I had a bad feeling. I found you because my brother gave you a card that had a tracking chip in it. And I want to take care of you because before all of this…" Wolf glances away, blowing out a breath that rushes over my face. "I wanted us to be more."

I blink, my eyes feeling droopy, everything feeling light and heavy all at once, "More?" I whisper.

He dips his face closer, our noses brushing, a strand of straight, black hair dropping from behind his hair, tickling across my cheek.

"I wanted you to be mine."

Luna

CHAPTER XV

I nner arms sore, my muscles ache all over, my head pounds, and my eyes burn, but I pry them open despite the sting because of the man in the chair beside me.

Wolf Blackwell.

His chin-length hair is down, the coal coloured strands tucked behind his pierced ears. His head is turned against the side of the high back chair, his temple resting against the worn leather. Something about the chair makes me uncomfortable, the longer I look at it the worse my head pounds, but the man sleeping in it is far too pretty in slumber not to stare at.

Rose-pink lips sit in a plump pout making him look boyish, his jaw is sharp, harsh angles with a square chin, high cheekbones and neat, black stubble styled tidily on his cheeks. His eyes are closed, heavy fans of dark lashes that curl high atop his cheekbones, but beneath those lids sit these warm, fiery, honey, whiskey coloured orbs that I want to stare into for days.

It's dark in here, but being so close to him, the shadows only seem to carve and enhance his features like he's a piece of art in a museum and I'm just a lucky girl with a nice view.

I think this is the first time I've really woken up since the other day, when we talked.

'I wanted you to be mine.'

Something flutters around in my belly at the thought, a warmth spreading through my chest, but then I glance at the chair again and it's like ice water dousing me.

As much as I don't want to, I'm going to have to wake Wolf up. My bladder is full, my legs have pins and needles, and my lower back is twinging from lying in bed so long. I feel thirsty and uncomfortable, and I want to bathe. I want to wear fresh clothes, and for my skin to smell like soap, and the pressure in my pelvis is starting to hurt.

Wolf's hand is in one of mine, grip tight even in

sleep, my fingers are bandaged, taped up and swaddled in gauze. The last couple of days have been a blur. The only parts I can remember when I woke are Wolf's warmth, his fresh breath fanning my face, his gentle touch with rough hands. A divine contrast, this man is built like a beast, huge muscles, broad shoulders, tall and towering, but he's soft and caring, *with me.*

"Wolf," I say quietly, my voice cracking, but he doesn't stir.

Shadows fill the space around us, this strange cube like room. There's no light in here, no window for the outside world, but one wall is glass, and I move my eyes there now, peering through the darkness.

My skin ripples with goosebumps, my eyes wide, trying to see in the pitch dark. The space feels open with the glass partition, a large empty room on the other side.

It feels as though demons and ghouls are creeping through the obsidian, my eyes seeing blurs of shadows moving amongst the darkness, but I know there's nobody there.

My breathing is ragged, my lungs burning as I strain my eyes, trying to see. I turn my attention back to Wolf, his soft snores like a hibernating bear, a smooth, deep rumble that shakes me to my core with comfort. There's a creak then, and my heart lurches into my throat, perspiration sticking my hair to the back of my neck, my forehead beading with sweat.

I fly up in the bed, every muscle protesting, but my eyes flick to that horrible leather armchair again and I feel unsafe, something inside of me repels against the idea that that chair is just a chair. It feels impossibly more, even though I don't understand why.

Suddenly, all I can see is bone and blood and deep red seeping across dark wooden floors. I see flickering candlelight at the edges of my vision and my own reflection staring back at me, a split lip. Then there are blue eyes, familiar, but they are not my own, and my insides curl and rebel and force acid up the back of my throat.

I'm flopping to the floor, on the other side of Wolf, my knees and hands crashing into the hard ground. Keeping my eyes down, I crawl forwards, not looking up as a cool breeze feathers over my heated skin. I don't want to see, so I don't look. If I don't look, I can't see, and I can't be scared.

The top of my head bumps into the corner junction of a wall, pain splitting down the side of my face as black spots blur across my vision. I reach out for the wall, curling myself up into its corner and try to stop seeing those eyes.

There's a glint in my vision, large, strong hands that

are like Wolf's but not. Gold, something big and gaudy and too flashy on a fist made of violence. I'm shoving down the shorts I wear, knowing I mustn't have them on, supposed to be bare. I kick them away quickly, trying not to be caught. There's a terrible rasping sound growing, louder and louder, closer and closer, and the images in my head are coming to life around me like an old film cast over the walls.

The floor is falling away around me, my head curled into my drawn up knees, hands fisting tightly over my ears. Wet warmth meets my bare feet, soaking my bare skin, and my tummy twists with shame, but I can't look up and I can't open my eyes, and even still, the images come. The blue eyes, like mine, but not my own, the large hands and the flash of gold. The blood, the bone, the sound.

It echoes in my ears, thumping, groaning, silence. Eerie and calm, soundless, blocking out the noises of the world above. Pain explodes in my head and my eardrums feel like they're about to burst. And then the water comes over me in a wave, silent and wet, then there's a voice, a scent. Harsh hands on bruised flesh, heat flush with my back. A rocking motion that has pain shooting through my coccyx, up the spasming bones in my spine. Sticky, thick, slick slipping down my legs, a scent, strong and smoky and sweet, it makes me gag, my stomach revolting when it's all I can smell.

A whimper passes my lips, and I know I shouldn't make noise; I am to be silent, *sweet girl.* Silence. I clamp my hands over my ears harder, my painful knuckles going numb as I smash them against my ears.

Big hands come to my shoulders and I flinch so hard I crack my forehead against my knees and stars shoot through my head again like the milky way is spitting them out and unable to stop.

"Luna."

One word and I'm scrambling, dropping my hands and shoving down onto my knees, wetness beneath them as I drag myself through the puddle. I'm launching myself forward until I collide with a broad chest that smells like lilies and teakwood and I suck it down like it's the only oxygen I can stand.

"Luna," Wolf mumbles, his lips to the crown of my head, pressing kisses, over and over against my hair.

Big and warm and safe.

My entire body trembles in his hold, and although he drops back to his bottom with a thud that rattles my teeth, and his chest huffs out a short, surprised *ooft*, I've never felt safer or more secure, in my life.

And I don't know how I know that, only that I do.

Tears streak my cheeks, wetting Wolf's throat, where I bury my face in the hollow. Hot, little puffs of breath turning into water vapour against his skin, a cry cracking out of my dry throat as he holds me close. Squeezing me so hard it feels like he could snap my spine, but I want him to hold me impossibly tighter, closer. Break open his chest cavity and wrap me up inside of him.

"It's okay, baby girl, I've got you," he hums against the top of my head, his breath hot over my scalp. "You're safe."

But I don't feel safe, not inside my own mind, "There are monsters," I whisper, my hands curled into fists, squeezed beneath my chin.

"The only monster here is me, Luna," Wolf hushes, little, sweaty strands of hair blowing across my face. "And I'm *yours*." His arms squeeze me tight, while his hands smooth up my spine.

"It hurts," I whimper, squeezing my eyes shut tight as a dull ache seems to thud in my bottom.

"I know it does," Wolf kisses my hair again and I press myself tighter into him, no part of me touching the floor, every inch of me is cradled in his lap. "But I'm going to make sure you never hurt ever again."

The bathroom light is off, the door ajar for some light to creep in from the hall. My head is splitting, an ache in my eyes as Wolf tilts my head back, tipping another bowl of water over my hair.

He sits at the side of the clawfoot tub, pressed up on his knees, a pair of fresh jogging bottoms on his legs because his other ones were wet.

Because of me.

Shame heats my cheeks and I drop my head forward just as he douses me once more with the bowl of water, and I splutter as it runs into my nostrils. Wolf's hand swipes over my face, his calloused skin comforting as he rubs water from my eyes. He runs a soapy cloth over my skin, washing every part of my battered body, his touch gentle and soft with my bruises and cuts.

Even though it's four-am, Wolf cradled me, rocking me, soothing me in a puddle of pee, before hearing my request for a bath and obliging without protest. He didn't say anything about it, even though it's embarrassing and makes my cheeks heat, he still doesn't mention it. As though it never even happened.

I haven't told him about the chair. Or the eyes. I didn't tell him anything because he hasn't asked. I don't think I could tell him anyway. None of it makes sense. To be frightened of a chair.

"What's that pout for," he chuckles lightly, more water from the bowl rushing down my back.

"Headache," I lie, but also, it's not a lie, I really do have a headache, but that's not why I'm pouting.

"Blackwells don't tell lies," he says quietly, as though to himself, but it feels nice, to hear it, to feel the real truth there.

He hums, his hands finding my bruised shoulders and massaging slowly, the pressure light, warm and heavy, welcome.

"I'm not a Blackwell," I reply quietly, his hands stilling for just a moment before continuing their ministrations.

"You're a Beaumont," he says, and the whole sentence sounds wrong, like he's not really directing that at me at all, even though that *is* my name.

Beaumont.

Something I did remember, my name.

"Ready?" he asks a few minutes later, the warm water cooling quickly inside this cold house.

"Yes," I blink up at him as he stands.

Reaching back down to run the flat of his hand

over the top of my head, being careful to miss the long bullet scrape in my scalp. He smooths the water out as he presses down, wringing out the long tresses by curling the strands around his fist and squeezing the water free.

Wolf pulls the plug, draining the bath, and then scoops low to grab me up, my hands already reaching for him as he bends forward. He sits himself down on the closed toilet seat, cradling me in a towel and carefully pats me dry.

The towel is huge, big enough to fit both of us, but it's just for me, warm and fluffy and large enough to swaddle me up in. He lifts up another, this one slightly smaller and lays it over my head, lifting my hair from my back and wrapping it up.

And then he just holds me.

His chin to the top of my head, arms secure around my waist, my back, and my eyes close as I breathe him in, lilies and teakwood, strong and floral, warm.

"What did you dream about, Little Moon?" he asks me quietly.

Wolf has a naturally deep voice, it's a bit gruff, gravelly, loud, but he quells all of that when he speaks to me.

"Monsters," I whisper back, my lips brushing his

chest, the barest smattering of dark hairs over his tight, tanned skin.

"What sort of monsters, baby girl?" he asks me in a hush, both of us still and comfortable, relaxed where we're curled up together in the steamy bathroom.

Two words, and I don't have to think about them at all before they fall off of my tongue, "Human ones."

Wolf

CHAPTER XVI

It's not watching as such, the way my eyes track her every movement, twitch, yawn, blink, breath, it's more a needy, psychotic study.

Luna slept for days, only waking up to reach for me. Whimpers and pained cries disturbed her sleep, but she only woke through the silent moments, when the nightmares must have been at their worst. Her heart pounding, her eyes snapping open wide, and her hands clammy and clawing for me, the bed often wet.

It's fucked up because I'm fucking living for these moments.

She needs me.

I'm sick.

Though, because of her terrible sleep patterns, I've had the bare fucking minimum myself. It's why I sit out here now, on the front porch of the mortuary. Luna out cold inside, the door open at my back, the summer air catching on the breeze and rushing through the dark halls. I bring the blunt to my lips, inhaling slow and deep, my lungs filling with the expansion of my chest.

There's nothing around here for miles. I bought up one-hundred-fifty hectares surrounding this place. I snapped it up for a good price too. The last owner died, his son wanted nothing to do with the property, I bought it, then started buying up all the land surrounding it.

Perfect for disposing of body parts.

It's what we do, after all.

Specialise in.

The Blackwells.

Disposals.

It's what my girl does too, *'cleans up messes.'*

Match made in hell.

I reach down to adjust my cock. It's constantly fucking throbbing now. Not an issue I've had in the past, but even in the hospital, a fresh bullet hole through my fucking heart and I was poppin' a fucking boner every time I thought of her.

I might be taking care of Luna. I might be nursing her back to health. I might be preparing to take out every last motherfucking cunt that ever looked at her wrong, let alone touched her.

Killed her.

But I still want her. In all the baser, carnal, sinfully depraved ways any Blackwell man wants the object of his obsession. I look at her lying there in that makeshift bed, my place at her side, an armchair pulled in from one of the many unused rooms for me to sleep in. I could put her in my bed, but I want her in there when I don't have to restrain myself.

I'm not sure I could, even with her injured, even with her frightened and cowering at every unusual creak in the old stone building. So we'll stay in the visitation room until it's time.

She doesn't like to be left alone. Even when she uses the bathroom, I wait outside, the door ajar, while she takes care of her business. But every few moments, she calls my name making sure I'm still right there, and blood shoots to my cock like a bolt of lightning.

Sticky-sweet smoke drifts from my nostrils, my exhale slow and drawn out because, *fuck*, it feels good to be sitting out here in the middle of the night without it fucking raining. July is right around the corner but summer is officially here.

The moon is big and round, shining high in the sky, a blanket of stars twinkling in the black. The smoke from my spliff climbs towards it, a thick white cloud obscuring my view for a moment. I think of my sister, Grace, probably outside too right now, at the mill, she always is on a night like tonight. Drawing my phone from my pocket, something she now has and uses, albeit occasionally, she often forgets she's even got one and leaves it somewhere for the battery to die. But I send her a message all the same.

WOLF

You up?

GRACE

Yes.

Are you looking at the sky too?

She sends a picture of the moon, it's blurred, the camera not held steady, a white blur across black, the tip of her finger over the bottom of the lens. But I smile at it, leaning back in the rocking chair, the wood creaking with every tilt backwards.

WOLF

Sure am, lots of stars tonight.

GRACE

So many.

How is she?

Sighing, I breathe deep, drop my head back against the high back of the chair, and continue to rock. Thinking about what to say. How to say it. Good. Not good. Totally dependent on me and I love it?

WOLF

Getting better. Goodnight, sis.

GRACE

Goodnight, Wolf.

Thumb over the lock button, I press it, letting the bright screen dim to black and repocket it in my loose joggers. Smoke floods my lungs, filling my chest, making it tight. I'm not a regular smoker, only having the occasional spliff to relax at night, but when I feel this good, this calm, my muscles loose and body boneless, it makes me wonder why it's not a more regular thing, although lately it has been. It's the only thing that sent me off to sleep over the last week.

"Wolf?" Luna's dry voice calls out nervously, anxiety laced, her tone high.

Flinching, I snap upright in the chair, head whipping over my shoulder, eyes wide, peering into the darkness.

"I'm here," I call back, readying to stand, but she appears then, in the mouth of the hall, her hand against the wall to keep her steady.

Her approach is slow, footsteps careful, her feet are still tender, but the bandages are off now, the splinters and shards of wood I removed weren't too deep.

The decking is cool beneath my bare feet as I stand, moving towards her, intending to get her back into bed. She's not been moving around without me at all since we arrived here ten days ago, but I think that's more to do with wanting to need me as opposed to a physical thing.

"Hold on, I'm coming," I tell her, stabbing out the joint, flicking the roach into the ashtray resting atop the railing of the porch.

"Can I come out there?" she asks, stilling her steps.

The house is in darkness, but the moon's rays flare across the entrance hall, shadowing her movements just enough for me to make her out.

"With you, Wolf?"

That's what gets me every time, her saying my fucking name, it's like a shot of adrenaline stabbed directly into my heart.

"'Course you can," I move towards her, her steps restarting, hand guiding her along the wall.

As soon as I reach her, nothing but the pitch darkness of my shadow falling over her, she lifts her gaze, and that icy, winter-blue stare daggers me through the chest.

Her hands find my biceps, long fingers smoothing up my arms, curling over my bare shoulders, she buries her face against my chest, nuzzling over my heart.

"I woke up and couldn't find you." Her breath feathers over my skin, goosebumps rippling across my flesh, my nipples pebbling. "I thought you left."

She trembles against me, nothing but one of my t-shirt's covering her body. It drapes over her like a tent, slipping off one shoulder, exposing the milky skin wrapped over the slope of her neck.

"I told you," I exhale slowly, dragging in a deep lungful of her as I dip my nose to the crown of her head, my hands sliding up her back, "I'm never going to leave you, Luna."

She exhales at that, her entire trembling body slumping against me, allowing me to draw her in closer, mould her body into the curl of mine as I arch over her, scooping her up into my arms bridal style.

Her legs hang limply over the crook of my elbow, crossing at the ankles, heels of her feet bumping against my outer thigh as I turn with her in my arms back to the open door. My feet move us towards the porch, the moonlight casting us in its glow, and I carry her back to where I was sitting, setting her in the wide rocking chair, placing myself on the floor at her feet.

"Were you smoking?" Luna asks me quietly, her voice never much more than a whisper.

A shiver works through her that I feel run down my spinal cord and into my coccyx where her shins press against my spine.

"I was," I tilt my head back, letting it rest against the cap of her knee.

"It doesn't smell…" she lifts her eyes from mine, staring off into the distance with a small frown.

"It doesn't smell what, Luna?" I respond just as quietly.

I've been doing this all week, encouraging her, in these small moments where she offers me up something unfinished, like she's remembering something but isn't sure, to give me her full thought. And she struggles with it, as though that's not something she's ever been able to do before.

I had Thorne send me over everything he could find on her. Parents, home life, schooling, friends. Alarm bells screamed inside my head when I received the final report. It was only a page and a half long, and the home address was wrong. Raine is the better tech guy, but he's still at Magpie Manor with Arrow doing only the devil knows what, so perhaps he will be able to find out more once he comes home. Until then, I only know what I did already, her name's Luna Beaumont and she works at the hospital.

"Putrid," she finishes wrinkling her nose.

A laugh barks out of me at that, my head knocking back into her bony knees, "And what *does* it smell like?" I ask curiously, watching the scrunch of her face melt away as her eyes once again find mine.

"Nice."

"Nice?" I smile up at her. "You think weed smells nice?" I raise a brow, my smile curling my mouth.

She looks at me in that way that only Luna can, her expression blank, her eyes wide, but it tells me so many things, "Yes, better than cigars."

Cigars.

"You smoke many of those in your time, baby girl?" I keep smiling wide, watching as she shudders at the endearment, but it feels false quickly, watching her eyes drop from mine, to her hands in her lap, like that statement means more to her than either her or I know.

"No," she says blandly. Slowly, her eyes draw back to mine, lifted beneath heavy black lashes, she tucks a strand of inky hair behind her ear, "I don't think so. I don't think I know how."

I lick my lips, reaching into my pocket, I pull the tin of ready-rolled joints out, flipping the lid and removing one. I look back up at her, gesturing with my head for her to come closer. She puts her bare feet onto the floor, my t-shirt slipping off of her slim shoulder further as she rests her hand against the back of my neck, climbing around to move in front of me.

Luna stands over me, the moon at her back, washing her alabaster skin in a silver-grey. It makes her appear ghoulish, a spectre, the moon a halo around her head. She stares down at me, the long expanse of her legs seemingly stretching on for days. The bruises are still deep. Dark purple and splotchy green, red-strawberry spots bleeding beneath the skin, but since the mockery of a second blood transfusion, my blood type fortunately O-Negative, she's been doing okay. Better.

"Come here, Luna," she looks down at my lap, eyes dragging up my bare chest, finally settling on my own. "Climb into my lap."

She doesn't hesitate, but her movements are slow, her body still achy, her hands, in particular, still tender. Fingers taped on each hand, bound together, immobilised to heal a broken knuckle on each fist.

Guiding her down, my calloused hands rough

against the silky expanse of her thighs, she settles over my lap. Tightening herself close, threading her arms beneath my own, curling them around my ribs, fingers knotting in the centre of my spine.

She breathes me in deeply, her breasts brushing my chest through the thin cotton, and that's when I feel it. Trying hard not to freeze as she squirms even closer, settling, but I know she feels when I lock up. The hot, hot heat of her cunt singes against my lower abs, *bare* against my skin.

"Luna."

"I'm sorry," she whispers, attempting to pull back from me, withdrawing into herself, shrinking and withering and *dying*.

"Do you not-" I lick my lips, trying not to be nervous around her about these little things she does unconsciously, so far, I haven't liked any of them because of the meaning behind them. "Do you not feel comfortable wearing knickers?"

"Um, I- I'll go and-"

"No," I stop her, curling my arm around her back, drawing her in flusher, like a punishment to myself.

The feel of her hot flesh against the ladder of my abs is criminal, but the way she's not looking at me now, stiff in my lap, feels worse than my own self control issues.

"Luna," I lick my lips, "look at me." Craning my head back to look at her. "You don't have to wear underwear if you don't want to." Her crystal clear eyes flick between mine, shining with unshed tears. "But you *are* allowed to, if you want to. There's no rules in this house to say otherwise. When it's only me and you, you do whatever makes you comfortable," I tilt my head to the side. "There's no shame in this house, Luna," I say softly, catching her dropped gaze, "okay?" I whisper, my free hand lifting to tip her face, my thumb to her chin.

"Okay, Wolf," she whispers, my mouth slanted over hers, her breathy words feathering across my tongue.

"Do you want to tell me why you keep taking them off?"

She hesitates to put them on as well, it's like a warring indecision in her after she gets out of a bath, an array of fresh clothes left out for her to choose from.

"You don't have to tell me," I smooth my hand over her head, keeping her face before mine, so I can see her.

She sucks on her lower lip, her eyes on the base of my throat, she swallows and heaves in a deep breath, "I keep thinking I'm not supposed to have them on."

"Do you know why you think that?" I sweep my

thumb down the side of her throat, eliciting a shiver in her.

"Just a feeling I get, like I'm not right," she whispers.

"Not right?"

"Like I'm going to get punished for wearing them."

"Thank you for telling me," I kiss her forehead, my mind spinning, but the instinct to rage, to hit something, to scream, to pummel someone to death is overwhelming.

Smoothing my hand up her back, her long hair draping around us like a curtain, I offer her a smile, curling my fingers into the hair at the nape of her neck and tugging gently.

"Now," I say, shifting so I'm more comfortable on the hard wooden decking, ignoring the feel of her pussy grinding against my stomach. "You wanna try this with me?" I ask her, holding up the unlit joint between us.

Her eyes track it, taking it in, and then she wets her lips, looking back to me, she nods, "Yes. What will it feel like?"

"Well, this bud in here doesn't contain any THC, that's the shit that gets you high, 'kay?" I explain.

"Okay."

"This stuff'll just make you relax, you'll get a lil sleepy and soft, it won't make you dizzy or sick."

"Okay." Luna swallows, staring at the rolled joint between us, her knees around my waist squeezing against my ribs.

"I won't ever let anything bad happen to you," I whisper, tugging lightly on her hair, my thumb grazing her nape where my hand's tangled in the underneath of her inky strands.

"I trust you." She licks her lips, the words coming out automatically, zero hesitation as she eyes the joint.

The erratic pounding in my chest rattles my sternum, heart threatening to burst its way through as my heart-beat echoes dramatically in my eardrums. A cold chill slithers its way down my spine, the hot press of Luna's cunt flush with my belly, the rest of her supple, soft skin moulded to my body. Draped over me like I'm a designer chair and she's the model atop it for an expensive shoot.

I slip the joint between my lips, reaching up behind her to grasp the lighter from the railings, I spark it up, my lungs filling with sweet smoke as the embers burn bright. She keeps her eyes on my mouth, watching the part of my lips, the thick white smoke creeping out slowly between my teeth. It makes them feel numb, sensitive, then I part my lips fully, open my jaw and blow out the rest of the smoke into the warm breeze.

"You want to try? Or you want to shotgun it?"

She scrunches her brow, the pert tip of her straight nose crinkling, "Shotgun?" she questions, but I don't explain, my cock like steel in my pants, selfishly, I just want her lips on mine.

I've regretted not stealing a kiss from her, all those times in the hospital I coulda done it, I think she woulda let me.

But I was waiting for her to come to me.

I move my hand in her hair, gripping the back of her neck tightly, tilting it back, instead, "Open your mouth, Little Moon."

She gasps lightly, which is perfect as I inhale from the joint, and close my mouth over hers. Allowing the sticky-sweet skunk to pass between us. Her eyes are wide on mine, her lids drooping as some of the smoke filters slowly into her lungs, the rest of it I release into the darkness, my lips parting reluctantly from hers.

Eyes shining, she coughs a little, right in my face, making me curl my bottom lip in, mashing it between my teeth to suppress my grin.

"How's that feel, baby?" I ask her roughly, my voice gruff, hand clasped over the nape of her neck massaging the tight muscles there.

Her body melts into mine, her hips shifting and grinding her pussy against me. We both freeze then, as

I take another toke of the weed, my hand stilling on the back of her neck, thumb digging into muscle.

"I'm sorry," she whispers, glancing down between us, but she doesn't move, as my gaze, too, drops between us.

Even in the dark, I see it, the colour in her cheeks, beneath the blanket of stars, the moonlight falling across us, her shadow the only thing between us, but the ladder of my abs are now shiny and slick with her arousal. And I know she can feel my cock digging against her arse cheek, but she makes no move away from it, and I'm still holding the marijuana smoke in my lungs as she finally lifts her eyes to mine, her teeth gnawing on her lip.

Her small hands drop from the back of my neck to the space between us, slipping down my bare chest leaving goosebumps in her wake. Her long fingers fiddle with the hem of the black t-shirt of mine she wears, some of her fingers taped up because of her broken knuckles. Something I still have guilt about, but in this moment, when she drops her head to mine, our combined breaths coming hard and fast between us, both of them tinged with smoke, I move first.

LUNA

CHAPTER XVII

The weed is forgotten as he flicks it from his fingers, his arms threading up my back, hands curling over my shoulders, his mouth surging against mine.

Wolf's lips are soft yet hard, plump and desperate and pressured. He hauls me up against him, higher in his lap, my pussy rubbing up against his hot, hard belly, the rippling muscles catching my clit. My hands fist in his hair, tearing out the elastic that holds it tight in a loop at the back of his skull. He moans into my mouth, biting my bottom lip as my fingers card through his hair, gripping at the roots and yanking his head back.

He growls into the kiss, the sound vibrating my tongue, running down the length of my vocal cords, and expanding in my chest like fingers of heat stretching and curling and claiming my heart. His big hands are firm on my shoulders, heavy, his fingers curled over my trapezius muscles, kneading and digging to pull me in closer.

Wolf Blackwell kisses like death.

As though the grim reaper is hovering at his back, peering over his shoulder just waiting for the right moment to strike and he doesn't want to miss his chance.

It's stolen.

This moment.

From the next life, he drags it into this one by the throat, kicking and screaming, and then he tears it to pieces so the moment can't be taken from him.

Wolf Blackwell kisses like death, but I've never felt so alive.

His kiss is a claiming. Like he needs the taste of me permanently seared into his tongue. The feel of my lips moving hungrily against his to survive. His breath is a hot wash of desperate desire as he tears his mouth from mine, flicking his tongue across my top lip before sinking his teeth into the bottom. He stretches the skin out, his teeth nibbling before he lets it go, the wet flesh slapping against my bottom row of teeth and then he's diving in again.

I'm not sure what I'm doing, but he leads and I follow, and I kiss him back with a desperation that feels just as dire as life or death. And considering the two of us have recently walked hand in hand with death himself, this feels more than accurate.

I bite into his mouth, our teeth clashing as his tongue snakes through my lips, curling around my own, mapping my mouth like he's memorising it. The tip of his tongue traces the roof of my mouth, every ridge and dip, sliding over my teeth, dipping into each molar, and grazing across the tops.

It feels like life and death, horror and romance. And when he kisses me, surging against my hips, pelvis lifting, thrusting his hard cock up against my arse, and flipping me onto my back, cradling my head, the wood of the wrap around porch snagging at the cotton of my shirt, I melt.

Wolf grinds himself against my bare cunt, the thin material of his joggers doing absolutely nothing to hide his erection. His mouth explores every inch of my face, his tongue caressing the bullet graze along the side of my head, before dragging down, mouthing at my cheekbone, the corner of my jaw.

On all fours above me, he spreads me out beneath him

like a picnic blanket with a mouthwatering buffet. His tongue searing hot as it scorches down the column of my throat, dipping into the hollow at its base, and then grates his teeth along my exposed collarbone, the oversized t-shirt I wear having slipped down. He bites into me so hard that pain explodes in my temples, his palms flat on the wood either side of me, only his hips dropping to collide with my own, gyrating unconsciously in a filthy display of need.

"*Wolf*," I gasp, my breath rushing out of me as I dig my nails into his scalp.

He lifts up, hissing at the sting, skin embedding itself under my nails as I let them bite into him harder, and then he's lifting back up onto his knees. His hands fisting at the neckline of my shirt and ripping it clean down the middle. My back lifts with the tug and tear before the warm summer night's air is pebbling my nipples, his tongue lapping over the left one and then the right.

Frantically, Wolf's hands claw at my hips, his thumbs pressing divots into my pelvis, and then he lifts them up into the air. Head dipping, his mouth suctions over my clit, his tongue flicking savagely over the pulsing bud clenched between his teeth. A rumble ripples its way up his chest as he clings onto me, my weight balancing on my shoulder blades, my chin dropped to my chest so I can watch him tear me apart with his teeth.

He sucks his way lower, his tongue plunging into my hole, in and out, in and out, his nose burrowing against my clit until my entire body is trembling and the flat of his tongue is lapping up the length of me. Teeth nibbling the hood of my clit, and then his mouth is over me, sucking, sucking, sucking.

I grit my teeth as I come. Heat washing over every inch of me as wave after wave of pleasure wraps itself around me like a corded noose made of passion and lust. Black spots sluice across my vision, these splodges of darkness blurring my sight as Wolf laps lazily at my cunt, making sure he gathers and consumes every drop of my release.

When he lowers my hips back to the floor, settling me down on the torn t-shirt, pushing my arms away from his hair and down to the wood beneath us, his fingers latched around my wrists, so my elbows are bracketing my head, he follows. Bracing himself on his forearms on either side of my head, my own arms between. The lower half of his face is shiny and slick, and he sinfully drags his tongue across his lips, first the top and then the bottom, savouring my flavour with a deep rooted groan.

Heart pounding, my breath heaving in and out of me, I stare up at him.

My protector, my saviour, my wolf.

No words pass between us, but I can feel his cock pressed firmly against my wet flesh, my legs spread wide to cradle Wolf's hips. I flatten my feet to the deck, squeezing his sides with my bent knees, and then I curl my legs around his hips, crossing my feet at the ankles and tugging him down so he's completely flush with me, letting his weight press me further into the deck.

There's resistance from him, but not enough for me to relent. He comes willingly, and I can tell he's only holding back some of his weight so as not to crush me. The press of thin, worn cotton against my naked flesh feels obscene, but the press of his thick, swollen shaft beneath has my hips rotating unabashedly. My knees tighten around him, and he gives in.

Grinding himself against me, his gaze holding mine, his nostrils flare wide, his breath coming hard and fast between his teeth. It's like something else takes over, and neither one of us is completely ourselves. Lost in the throes of love and death, deep rooted want is the sharp reminder that we're both still here.

Wolf draws back, staring down between us as he circles his hips, pressing himself against me so hard that the friction of his clothes feels like fire. He stills suddenly, his breath a wash of heat rushing over my face.

His whiskey coloured eyes find mine, holding my gaze and then he dips down, his lips barely a caress over my own, as he whispers, "*Mine.*"

Wolf bites my lip, my chin, his chest smushed up against mine so hard I can feel his heart, can feel the erratic thudding of it as though it's beating inside the cavity of my own chest. His lips feather along my collarbone, his teeth grazing my shoulder.

"More," I breathe, my fingers coming to rest against the base of his throat, the top of his chest. The whisper just enough to still him completely, even his breath is held in his chest, "More, *Wolf*, please."

A whimper slips past my lips, breathless and needy as he growls, a deep grumble rolling its way up his throat as my bloodied nails scratch into his chest.

"Not all the way," he tells me. Shaking his head, like the action is more for himself than it is for me, "Not tonight."

"Okay, *okay*," I squirm beneath him, his hands rough but gentle as he grasps my face, kissing my lips fiercely, "just, please, *more*." I plead with my eyes, the pout of my lip as he lifts his head just enough to look down at me properly.

Without another word, he pushes up onto his palms, lifting one and threading it between us.

"Watch," he instructs, gritting his teeth, his neck corded with strained tendons.

Wolf wraps his hand around his cock over his joggers, squeezing. He slips the elastic waistband down lower, exposing more of the neat, dark trail of hair that stretches from his navel to his cock. His Adonis belt carved like cut marble between his hips, but he doesn't push them off, his cock still covered, the worn fabric almost moulded around his length in a way that makes my lip tremble seeing the size.

Wolf is a large man in every way, he's six-foot-six, as broad as a house, and has muscles more solid than diamonds, but I didn't think I'd have to worry about the size of his cock. I've never even thought about it until right now.

"Don't move," he whispers over my mouth, both of us still staring down, between the length of our bodies, "and just let me in."

He brushes the tip of his nose across mine, his top lip ghosting across my mouth, and then the tip of his dick is pressing to my opening, pushing in no more than an inch, the material of his joggers between us. The wetness of my cunt soaking the fabric covering his dick, and he groans, watching as he drags the tip back out, the light grey material now a deep, dark charcoal.

"*Fuck*, Little Moon," he breathes. "You are such a good girl," he grunts, dipping back inside me, stretching me, the material rough against the silken opening of my pussy. "So pretty and pink," he praises, lifting his eyes to mine, one hand planted beside my head, his other combing through the tresses of my hair, cupping the side of my head in his big hand. "Perfect little cunt, all wet, just for me, huh, baby girl?"

"Yes," I respond breathily, my eyes on his as he pushes just a little further inside me, "just for you," I gasp, the crown of my head grinding into the wooden floor, my spine curved and lifted in an arch from the deck. "Yes, Wolf."

He shudders, his hips dropping lower so he's further inside of me, his eyes heavy lidded, making me catch my breath at the slight burn. And then he's pulling out, tearing his hand from my face and shoving his waist-band down. Taking his cock in his hand and pumping it insanely hard, once, twice, and then he's groaning, this deep, guttural, animal sounding roar, the slide of his hand a firm corkscrew curl up his length.

Cum shoots from his tip, painting me in his creamy release, hot, sticky ropes of white land on my pelvis, my belly, the top of my thigh. Wolf stares down at it, his back heaving with his panting breaths, he pushes up onto his knees, his cock hanging heavy and thick despite it going soft, it's the biggest thing I've ever seen.

The tip of that was just inside me.

My cheeks flush, warmth pooling in my belly, my thighs clenching as I stare at it, still exposed over the elastic waistband of his joggers. Shyly, I flick my gaze up onto Wolf, but he's not looking at me, he's staring at his hands as they come up to my hips and then he's pushing his hands up my lower belly, rubbing his release into my skin, both hands landing in the streams of silky cum and massaging it into me. He watches his hands, and I watch his face, his eyes hard, a scowl settled in his brows like he's taking this task very seriously.

My lips are parted, and even as he pushes too hard over some of my bruises, I don't flinch, I don't ask him to stop, and I know he would, if he knew it was hurting me, he'd ease off. But those tender spots his strong, thick fingers work over, just make me tremble with his attention, like he's replacing the pain put there by someone else with a piece of him. It feels settling.

Heat between my legs warms my thighs, a quiver running through them as Wolf's hands palm my breasts, his callouses catching my tight nipples, making me gasp, arch my back, push into his palms. His eyes lift to mine then, his face hard, features set like stone.

"I'm never letting you go, Little Moon."

My chest rattles as my heart attacks my sternum in a quick, constant clap, thundering and battering my ribcage as his yellow-honey eyes latch onto mine.

There's violence in the way he says the words, this black, glittering thread that wants to tether our souls together.

And I allow it to.

This darkness, it creeps from him, oozing possessively from his pores, tiny, clawing whispers of smoke extending towards me like reaching fingers, and I let them in. I invite it inside of me, this piece of him, and let it make itself a home there. It feels heavy. Tears springing to my eyes as Wolf's hands still, their grip possessive. His own eyes burning into mine.

"You're mine, Luna. And no one is ever going to take you away from me."

CHAPTER XVIII

The sun is like lava, its rays licking over my exposed skin. My black hair is twisted in twin French plaits, a middle parting with one on either side of my head, they hang down my back, their tails kissing my lower spine. I have shorts on my long legs, only reaching the top of my thighs, my knees and lengths of my shins pushing into the cool earth, my weight depressing the tall, dry grass in the middle of the graveyard.

I hold a large white sheet of paper against one of the crumbling headstones, and then grab a crayon laying in the grass, a green one this time, the paper already peeled off of it. I rub the side of the crayon as hard as I can with taped fingers over the paper, watching as the words etched into the stone start to appear.

A tiny smile curls one side of my mouth, pulling at the wound in the side of my head. I was careful to braid over it when I combed my hair through this morning, managing to avoid injuring myself further, but it still hurts. Pulling the paper away from the stone, I place it atop the gathering pile I've already made, laying the green atop a pink one, and securing it with a small rock. Then I number the corner of the paper in purple pen, scribbling the same number down in a little notebook I procured from a room gathering dust inside the mortuary.

Purple, blue and white flowers dance in the warm breeze, the overlong grass swishing with this beautiful rushing sound I feel as though I've never heard before. My eyes close, achy fingers gripping the grass, I tilt my head back, face pointing towards the sky, I let the sun heat my eyelids, my cheeks burning, but it feels good. The air, the sun, the beads of sweat gathering in my hairline, at the nape of my neck, all of it feels foreign, good, sacred almost, in a way I fear this will all be snatched away from me.

As a dark cloud descends in my mind, I feel the

coolness of a shadow pebbling my skin, and when I look up, my eyes opening, squinting towards the sun, I see a large dark cloud has swept across it, smothering its rays, seemingly appearing from nowhere. Goose-bumps smattering up my arms, I frown, a trickle of sweat bleeding down the valley between my breasts.

"I'm like a bad omen when you're out here," Wolf grunts broodily from behind me, his deep voice gruff.

It sends a shiver through my entire body, as though my bones should quiver with disgust, but all that rocks through my veins like an unsteady heartbeat is pure, thrilling, lust. I may not remember much about my life, apart from the fact that bananas make me gag and the smell of cigars is ingrained so deeply inside of me it's as though I can smell them on my skin even after shower-ing, despite there not actually being any here. But I feel like I would remember if I'd ever felt like *this* before.

Darkly, obsessively, infatuated.

Wolf's shadow falls across me as he approaches, he's so tall it's like being eclipsed by the sun. His upper body bare, sweat glistening on every darkly tanned, olive inch of his skin. The scar over his heart is lumpy and red, but healing, and he's going to the hospital today to have it checked.

He has silver-grey basketball shorts on, the shiny, loose fabric swishing around the tops of his knees. He wears them extremely low on his hips, that dark trail of coarse hair thickening the further it tracks down from his navel. I want to thread my fingernails through it, scrape them across his skin. Claw until the skin is lifted and pink, then red and split, blooming with blood and little beads of weeping.

Craning my head back, twisting over my shoulder, I peer up at him as he finishes approaching, a small, plastic, orange container clasped in one hand, a frosty bottle of water in the other. His knees creak when he crouches down beside me, his elbows resting on them as he squats. Weight on his toes, heels lifted from the ground, the long grass tickling the sparse, dark hair on his legs.

"You have to eat," he says roughly, planting the open lidded box beside my crayons, a sliced apple and cubes of cheese inside of it, along with a handful of blackberries that he let me pick this morning. "And drink," the water plops down beside it, landing on its side. His hand comes to cup my cheek, the rough pad of his thumb brushing across my bottom lip. "You're going to get burnt sitting out here during the hottest part of the day." The back of his other hand comes to my bare shoulder, my body trembling as his knuckles scrape across my skin. "You need more cream on," he scowls, grunting as he grazes his hand down my bicep, curling his fingers around my elbow.

"I'm fine. I like it," I tell him, my lips wanting to smile, but they don't. "It feels good," I shiver as I say it, Wolf letting the circle of his fingers slide down to my wrist, lifting my hand to his mouth, he brushes his lips across the tips of my fingers.

"Yeah?" he whispers, gently nipping the tip of my index finger, since last night out on the porch, he hasn't been able to stop touching me. "You're going to be alright here with me gone." I stare up at him, blinking as he sucks the entire length of my finger into his mouth, curling his tongue around it before grating along it with his teeth, popping it free. "Haisley will take care of you."

Haisley.

That's Thorne's fiancée. Thorne, the oldest brother of the six Blackwell brothers. Wolf told me I've met him before, at the hospital, but I don't remember. I've never met Haisley, and she's coming to stay with me whilst Wolf's older brother takes him to his check-up appointment. I don't really want to stay here with a stranger, but I also don't want to be alone.

"I want to come with you," I whisper, my eyes heavy lidded as Wolf kisses every one of my finger tips.

It would be sweet if he didn't bite them after,

replacing the kiss with a feral clench of his teeth that leaves little blue bruise marks in each. It hurts, but I like it, so I don't say anything. He smirks at me then, like he knows what I'm thinking as my eyes drag up from our hands unto his.

"I know you do," he looks like he's going to say more, but whatever it is, he keeps it to himself. "But I wouldn't leave you in danger." His eyes are so bright out here in the daylight, the dark cloud overhead finally shifting enough for me to feel the sun's heat once again, they look like liquid gold. "Ever again."

He explained to me what happened, the things he knows from the moment he last saw me in the hospital hallway to when he found me in the river. I swallow hard at the thought.

What happened to me in those thirty or so hours when we were apart?

"Wol-"

"Shhh," he interrupts, pressing his fingers to my mouth now, "don't say anything." Wolf smells like lilies, teakwood, rich and warm with a subtle floral sweetness. "They're coming up the driveway now," he tells me, Wolf says the drive from the road to the house is miles long, it'll take them a while to arrive.

I nod, blinking hard, trying to swallow past the dry feeling lodging itself in my throat. I'm not sure if I have friends or family, but I feel uneasy, the pit of my stomach roiling with acidy sickness at the thought of interacting with anyone but Wolf.

"It won't be for long," he reminds me again, but I can already feel the frown wanting to settle in my features.

"You said a few hours."

"I did," he nods, smoothing his thumb beneath my eye, dragging it upwards to trace the healing scrape along the side of my head.

"That feels like a really long time," I whisper, an ache in my voice that bleeds need, but he doesn't scold me for it, or for the way my fingers find his forearms, my hands circling around his muscles like cuffs.

"It'll go quick," he promises, "I'll bring something nice home for dinner, yeah?"

My knees dig into the cold earth as I squirm, squeezing his arms tighter, "With them?"

Wolf's black brows draw together, creasing his fore-head, "They're good, Luna. Nice, protective, *safe*. You liked my brothers when you met them before. You'll like them again," he says with full confidence. "I will never endanger you. Haisley is going to be my sister. I've spent a lot of time with her, she's a good girl, Luna. You'll see."

It's as though hackles ripple their way down my

spine, tearing up the back of my neck. I go stiff, like the rotted corpses six feet below me. Jealousy surging up and blooming in my chest. My fingers carve into his flesh, his skin filling the undersides of my nails, the bones aching with my tight grip, but I don't let go and he doesn't so much as flinch.

"There are so many differences between you two," Wolf says plainly, and I can feel the still tired muscles in my arms shaking. "The most important one," he brushes a single strand of hair away from my face, dipping his own closer, "is that *you* are *my* girl." And then he kisses me.

Wolf drops down onto his knees in the grass as I lift up on mine. Our teeth smashing together, my hands clawing at his arms, grating his skin. His big hand closes over the back of my neck, my hands releasing him to bite at his shoulders instead. He guides my head with that hand, his thumb and fingers squeezing tightly over the bones, his other hand clamped over my waist, fingertips flexing their hold over my ribs.

The hot heat of his sweat-slicked skin seeps into mine, the sun beating down on us, our chests flush together. I only have a thin, black, spaghetti-strap top on, no bra beneath, and it's almost like we're naked. Bared to each other, in more ways than one.

Sinking my teeth into his tongue, I bite down hard

as he tries to tear it free, his hands tightening and loosening, and then I release him, his blood on my mouth, my teeth, smeared across his lip.

Hands in my lap, I look up at him, his huge frame towering over me, his chest heaving hard. With my thumb, I reach up, smearing the blood from the corner of his mouth up towards his cheek.

The rumble of a car stills us both, this smooth vibration that seems to roll through the earth.

"They're here," Wolf says, but he doesn't look, neither do I, as the car continues past us towards the house. "Be a good girl for me, and I'll reward you later," he doesn't smile at me, but he isn't really a smiler, though he has, *for me*.

"I want to come with you," I whisper again as he pushes to stand, his huge body shadowing me like the dark cloud from before.

He reaches down for me, offering his hand and pulling me to stand, "Not today, Little Moon."

Wolf

CHAPTER XIX

"How we gunna do this without Archer?" Hunter asks from the backseat of one of Thorne's many cars.

This one happens to be a more basic, blacked out Range Rover, as though it won't draw us any attention, but I think Thorne's got a funny idea about things that *won't* bring us attention. We're three very large, broody, intimidating men, it's not about the vehicle.

Turning around in the front passenger seat, I peer at him, slumped against the window, the glass slicked with condensation, the air conditioning filling the car like ice. "You're going to work that charm you've got, little brother," I grin at him and he scowls right back.

"I don't got any charm, you dickhead," he shoots back.

"We know," I snort, "but you'll intimidate, be a prick, and then I'll swoop in, soothe them with smiles and soft brushes of my fingers and Thorne will analyse the words they spill to see if they're hiding anything." A chuckle pops up my throat as I turn back to face forwards, "Just another day, Hunt."

Hunter blows out a breath, dropping his temple back to the glass, "Whatever."

When we reach the hospital, Thorne pulls into the first space he sees. The three of us get out of the car and make our way straight through the busy halls, up in the lift, and then we're spilling out like overdressed mob members into the ward I was kept in while I was here.

I see her straight away, bleached-blonde hair, up-turned nose, fake laugh. *Felicity*. She's a bitchy gossip, and she said shit about my girl that I didn't like, however, she also doesn't know how to keep her goddamn mouth shut. That's what I'm relying on today.

Hunter stalks towards her down an empty corridor when I point her out. His long legs carrying him right up to her, one of his big hands drops to the wall beside her head where she leans back against it and he immediately has her attention. Her eyelashes flutter, her head tilts, and I wonder if Hunter's actually switched on the charm, or the woman just likes moody, psychopathic, arseholes.

Unable to hear what he's whispering in her ear, Thorne and I hang back, watching other staff members rush around, all of them so busy, no one has time to take note of us. It's unlikely, if questioned, any of these people could confirm they saw us here today.

"Think he's choking her out?" I ask, sweeping my gaze to my older brother, his black eyes coming to mine with a raised brow. "Joking," I shrug, *sort of*.

"If he is…" Thorne trails off, a heaviness cloaking his eyes. "Go check on him," he sighs, nudging my arm.

Rolling my eyes, I push off the wall, dropping my crossed arms to my sides, and then Hunter's barrelling around the corner, a deep set scowl tightening his features.

"That girl has some serious issues," he grunts. "Also, we're dumb motherfuckers," he spits, like the statement is both an insult he accepts and one he equally loathes. "We need to go to the security room." That's all he says as he stalks ahead of us, as though he already knows where he's going.

We follow at his back, slinking through the busy hallways like ghosts, everyone too preoccupied with their own shit to pay us any attention. After a flight of stairs up, Hunter finds the door he's looking for, and without preamble, he cracks the round knob counterclockwise at the same time he shoves his shoulder into it, busting it open with a lot less effort than it should take for a secure room.

Screens are set up and it's obvious this system is old, but Hunter drops into the seat like he thinks he's Raine and starts clicking through menus and tapping in dates.

Then he brings up multiple feeds of the day I was discharged. Inside of the elevator, the hallways, my room, the front entrance, reception desk, all angles of the car park.

"That girl, who is disgusting by the way," he snarls, curling his upper lip as he tosses me a glare over his shoulder, "said Luna has a guardian but no one's ever seen them. Doesn't know if they're man or woman. Doesn't know if there's more than one. Can't tell me if they're family or whatever. All she knows for certain is Luna walks to and from work every shift, of which she only works nights. Which makes me think the address can't be that far away if she's walking it. She also said that Luna never takes time off, never calls in sick, is always clean and tidy and put together like an '*ugly doll*', her words, not mine, man."

A literal growl rumbles in my chest, and it's like a baser instinct to protect my mate by ripping out the bitch's throat for daring to insult her.

"Anyway, says that the only time she's ever been off is when you were in here. And that she's never seen her be picked up in a car before, that no one had ever spoken to her guardian's *people* before either. She insinuated that Luna's family, or whatever they are, have money, and that that's why she didn't bother to work her four weeks notice when her guardian's assistant called in last week to say she's quit and won't be returning."

Hunter says all this as he clicks through monitors, playing and pausing images across the vast array of screens. He leans forward, snatching a pen from a red wire pen pot and scribbles down the make, model and number plate of a car on a stack of pink post it notes.

The car, I realise as I watch a slow motion picture of Luna ease herself into the back seat of a blacked-out Mercedes.

"All we had to do was trace this," Hunter says, deleting the footage of all cameras from tonight, before tossing the pen haphazardly onto the desk, following it up by peeling the sticky note off the top of the pad and flinging those carelessly back onto the desk too. "We're dumb fucks," he shakes his head, straight, black hair dripping into his eyes. "I didn't need to waste time talking to that bitch. Which, by the way, I think she really dislikes your girl, man, probably means Luna's a keeper." He grins at that, this slow stretch of a sardonic smile slithering across his mouth. "The unusual ones are where it's at." He throws out, shoving himself like a brute out of the squeaky, leather, roller chair. "So, shall we go?"

And just like that, we're back in the car and tracking the Mercedes that drove my girl to her death.

"This is Italian run," Thorne says sharply, a moue on the unimpressed slash of his mouth. "Luckily for us, Vito owns this place," he says simply, and then he's getting out of the car, shutting the door behind him and walking towards the entrance.

Hunter and I rush to follow, the car beeping once as both of our doors close simultaneously and Thorne clicks the lock button on the key fob without turning back.

Thorne steps up to the door of what looks to be a gentleman's club. The outer walls are red brick, the small windows are tinted with that reflective stuff, so everyone inside can see out, but nobody outside can see in. And the door is a bright, glaring, red steel that quite obviously is intended to intimidate.

To warn off.

We don't feel intimidation.

Not Blackwell men. And, clearly, not their women either. We're gathering quite a collection of strong women it seems.

Thorne knocks once, waits, knocks three times more in quick succession and then takes a good solid step back, and kicks the base of the door with his foot. He doesn't look particularly happy about that part, staring down at the toe of his shoe as if he can feel a scuff mark appearing before he can see it, but Thorne is a perfectionist in all ways, especially when it comes to his appearance.

The slider in the top portion of the door opens in a rush, dark eyes appear in the gap, followed by the slamming of the slider once more, before the door is opening outwards with a groan.

"Thorne," the bald headed man greets as he allows the three of us entrance, his large body packed with muscle ushering us down a short hall. "No trouble," he calls out behind us, his Italian accent thick.

My older brother clicks his tongue, leading the way deeper inside the building, "Non c'è problema, Matteo," he calls back without looking.

Smoke is a dense wall that we have to walk through as Thorne pushes inside what appears to be the main room of the establishment. There's a long bar along the far wall, stretching from one corner to the other. There are a couple of pool tables off to one side surrounded by men. Bets in the form of money and expensive pieces of jewellery and watches perched amongst it line the wide wooden edges of the tables as men jostle each other and yell.

Our eldest brother takes us right up to the bar, weaving us between rowdy men and a collection of topless women serving drinks and holding trays of drugs. Thorne takes a seat on one of the many vacant bar stools, Hunter and I doing the same on either side of him. It only takes a moment for a guy to come over, and without taking his order, plants a short tumbler of bourbon on the wooden top in front of Thorne.

"Thorne," the man greets, not pleasantly, but not entirely impolitely either. "What do you need?" he asks immediately, ignoring both Hunter and I, his dark eyes don't even quiver in their sockets to glance at us, it's as though we're not here at all.

Thorne reaches into his pocket, pulls out a small roll of notes and pushes them across the bar, the man takes them without looking, slipping the wad of cash straight into his trouser pocket.

"I would very much like to know who this vehicle belongs to." He slides the pink post it note across the bar next, and the man glances down briefly before flicking his eyes back up and over my shoulder.

"Carlo Costa," he says, flicking his chin whilst screwing up the pink slip of paper and tucking that too into his pocket. "He's a driver."

"For?"

"Vito," he says thickly, like that's a stupid arse question, but my brother is undeterred.

"Obviously," Thorne drawls.

"He ferries around a suit," the barman says, grabbing a cloth and absently wiping down the polished wood.

"Contractor?" Thorne queries.

"Solicitor," he rests his hands on the bar, palms flat, fingers splayed. "One of Vito's personal legal team."

"And this Carlo, he drives the man when?" Hunter asks, but the man keeps his eyes on Thorne, and my brother, he just lifts one dark brow and the barman sighs, rolling his eyes.

"When Vito calls legal meetings."

Thorne nods, tapping the wood of the bar with two fingers, and then he slides off of the stool, throws down a crisp twenty and turns away. His obsidian eyes scan everyone in the room as we head back out of the doors we entered through. And I know when he sees Carlo Costa because he blinks, just once, shuttering those frightening black eyes, and then we're all back inside the car.

Waiting for Carlo Costa to make his grand exit.

Wolf

CHAPTER XX

Carlo Costa is a simple man, with a normal wife, a well paid job consisting of ferrying important men to and from discretely chosen venues. Which is probably why he doesn't expect someone like me, an unholy monster, to be in his back seat on a normal weekday evening.

I cut off his scream with a simple slap of my hand across his mouth, oh, and my other arm barred across his throat, but it stops him from making a fuss, something I'm not particularly in the mood for.

"Settle down," I grunt into his ear, applying pressure to his windpipe with my tensed forearm. "I just want to ask you a couple of questions, and I'll let you get on your way home to your wife, Suzie." He whimpers, his nostrils flaring wide as he sucks in panicked breaths, both of us watching each other in the rearview mirror, his eyes wide, mine almost drowsy looking, I've been sitting in this car quite a long time. "I'll let you go now, but only if you promise not to scream." He mumbles beneath my hand, attempting to nod his head, I think, but I squeeze his throat just a little harder once more before I release him completely.

And just as I predicted, he grasps the handle of the door, thrusting it open before it comes ricocheting back towards him, bouncing off of my younger brother.

"Jesus, fuck, you shithead," Hunter snarls, booting the door closed in temper on the guy's foot that he threw out of the gap in his haste to escape.

"Ahh!" Carlo cries out, snatching his foot back inside the car and gripping onto it tightly.

Me, I just lean back in the centre back seat, stretch my arms across the length of it and wait. Once he's finished snivelling, which to be fair to the guy isn't overly long, he sniffs hard, his breath catching, and then his eyes come back to mine in the rearview mirror.

"What do you want?" his voice trembles, and I smile at him, this manic sort of psychotic, snarling, grin.

"You drive for Vittorio Gambino," I state factually, cocking my head. "More specifically, you drive around one of his solicitors."

"Look, Vito would kill me if I told you anything, and I don't know anything! I don't ever get the drop off addresses for meetings until the hour of!" He panics, sweat running down his temples, his dark hair sticking up in all sorts of directions as he shoves his clammy hands through it.

"Mm, well, you see, Mr Costa, it must just be your lucky day, sir, because all I want is the address for the solicitor with the surname Beaumont."

"I- I see," he stutters, one of his hands moving towards his suit jacket.

I cluck my tongue sharply before reaching forward and slamming his face into the dashboard, "Hands where I can see 'em, shit for brains."

"Ahh!" he cries out again, "I was just going to retrieve a handkerchief!"

"Don't care, you're lucky I didn't fucking shoot you." Carlo quivers, still staring at me in the reflection of the mirror as he cups his bloody nose. "Both hands on the dash, Costa." His hands fly up, splaying over the dashboard. "Now," I start, but he interrupts me before I can finish.

"Yes, yes!" he squeaks pathetically. "I know the

address! Big money house up in Oakwood. Huge, pillared thing, peeling paint, rusty railings. I can give you the address!"

"I want his full name too," I tell him, reaching forward with a notepad and pen.

"Yes, o-of course!"

"And the woman who lives there, what of her?" I ask numbly, trying to remain detached.

"What?" he trembles, staring at me hard in the mirror.

"The young woman, you collected her from the hospital only a couple of weeks ago, surely your memory is not so poor that you are unable to remember her?"

"No, yes. No! I mean, I do recall!" he smacks his lips together anxiously, licking the dry skin. "She's his niece, but I don't drive her often. Ever! That was the only time!"

"Why?"

"Why don't I drive her?" he mumbles, frowning further.

"Why that night?"

"I don't know! I was dropping him home after a meeting and he requested I swing by the hospital to collect his niece on the way, that was it! I never even got a look at her!"

I hum, holding his gaze with a single lifted brow, "Now, Carlo, this little chat of ours…"

"I won't say anything to anyone! I never saw you!" he squeals, and although it's making my job easier, seeing as I truly believe this squealing man is going to keep his mouth shut, I'm almost a little disappointed at how easy this all was.

"And your foot," I start, "your nose?" I raise a brow, his head nodding already.

"Fell! Drank too much, lost at biliardo," he spits out, voice a quiver.

"Excellent," I smile, slowly reaching down into the pocket of my slacks for the small pad of post it notes and pen I brought along with me from the hospital. "You don't want to see me ever again, Carlo," I start to explain, "So, write that shit down, and anything else you can think to tell me, I want to hear it and I want to hear it now."

Large Sash windows line both the upstairs and the downstairs of the large, white, Victorian home. There's a straight, red brick pathway that leads up to it, weeds growing between the cracked cement. On the upper floor, three big windows sit on either side of a rusted, white railing enclosed balcony. On the ground floor, there are three matching windows framing the front door. The balcony above is held up by two column pillars that stand on either side of the front door.

"What d'you wanna do?" Hunter asks from the front seat this time, me in the back, Thorne behind the wheel, all of our eyes on the house that my Little Moon came from.

Clearly, a house of horrors.

I think of her now, at home without me, her pale skin turning pink in the sun, those ice-blue eyes wide, wholly focused on me. I'd lay her out in the dry grass between the crumbling headstones, the sun on my back, my shadow eclipsing her. The warm breeze tightening her nipples, I'd peel off her clothes, lick every inch of her, and then drive my cock into her so hard it kills us both. Right there in the cemetery she likes so much.

"I'd feel better if the curtains were open," I toss out, scratching fingers through my short stubble.

"That's weird isn't it?" Hunter comments, "the curtain thing? It's the middle of the afternoon."

Thorne remains silent, a million different things likely floating through his mind as he looks upon the house. Usually, I wouldn't ask, but I'm wondering if he's thinking the same thing as I am. Our mother would close drapes and blinds and shutters to hide her abuse from the world beyond the glass. Perhaps Hunter isn't as caught up in his mummy trauma quite the way we are.

Good.

Thorne killed her. He was only seventeen. We've never spoken about it, even to this day. The way he hunted her down to make sure she met her end. I loved her, and I hate myself for it, because Matilda Blackwell was a horror only Satan could have produced, and even then I wonder if she weren't just straight up infected with Lucifer himself.

It's something, I think, that will remain inside me forever, this twisted, warped love for a mother who did evil, vile things to her devoted children. Six boys who were obsessed with her, even though she terrorised us.

I think she was sick. Hunter pretends she didn't exist. Archer thinks she was a witch. Thorne won't talk about her. Arrow says she did it because she was dealing with her own trauma, but Rainey? Our drug-addled, youngest brother, he says she was possessed by *them*. The other half of the Blackwell family and their cult, using blood magic to curse her.

The Obsidian.

"I think it means the house is hiding nefarious things, little brother," Thorne finally says, catching my eye in the rearview mirror.

And I know, right then, that he was thinking about Matilda too.

CHAPTER XXI

Haisley has pretty red hair. Wild ringlets framing her face where they don't quite pull up into the thick, high ponytail she's sporting. Her eyes are green, these big emerald orbs split with oceanic blue, framed in thick strawberry blonde lashes. Her freckled skin is almost as light as mine, but you can tell she's seen the sun regularly for there are criss-cross tan lines across her upper back, the royal blue sundress she wears now showing off the marks.

With my crayons and papers, like I'm a child, I'm still sitting in the grass as the sun starts to lower. But when we were inside after the men left, something that's still making me nervous, the old stone building echoey and cold even in this heat, Haisley moved around the space like she lived here. She knows where everything is, she knows how to use all of the appliances, and how to find an old bookshelf full of gothic novels.

Watching her, so *free,* flitting around the space made my insides churn. I got *jealous.* Deep down, I know I don't need to be, she's marrying his brother, but Wolf is the only thing that I have, and he has so many people that care for him, and they all *know* him. The way Haisley has chatted about him today, almost gushing, has made me realise that I don't really know Wolf Blackwell at all.

Back against a headstone, the rough sandstone grazing my skin with every shift in my shoulders, I watch the wildflowers sway, the tall grass swish, and that's when she comes back.

The bunny.

A large white rabbit sits just a mere foot away, its pink nose working overtime to find the slivers of apple I placed out for it. There's something wrong with it. Its eyes are all squished closed, red, weepy and crusty, and its pretty white fur is balding in places, its skin beneath raw.

Still, I sit quietly, unmoving as it hops closer, studying the whiskers on either side of its face twitch insanely fast, it makes me think of the butterflies surrounding me earlier, their wings open, relaxed, and then suddenly like they were catching fire they took flight.

The bunny finds the first piece of apple by scent alone, the pale flesh of it browning in its pink skin where I've left it in the sun for too long, but the rabbit doesn't seem to mind as she gobbles it down. I nudge the next piece a little closer, the seven slivers of fruit like a little trail leading towards me.

Wolf's been gone for hours, and he said he'd only be a *few*, but I'm not so sure that's true. My skin ripples with goosebumps under the warm evening breeze, my skin chilly and too pink, burnt. I already know what Wolf will say about it when he gets home.

Home.

It's a funny thing to feel, the warmth of him in this cold, unusual place.

Only death existed here.

Until me.

The bunny is right beside my bare thigh now, nibbling on the last piece of the apple trail, the final piece is in between my fingers. I'm sure the rabbit has already scented me, but with dirt on my knees, and the smell of the grass and flowers smeared across my skin, maybe it makes me more palatable. Or, perhaps, she's just starving.

Unsure how to feel about that, I cautiously twist my wrist, offering the final slice of apple up. The white rabbit presses a little front paw against the side of my thigh as it gnaws on the fruit in my fingers, and then, very carefully, I lift my right hand, reach across my lap and stroke up the length of its twitching nose. It flinches at the contact but then carries on enjoying the apple.

"Oh."

The one word is breathy and feminine, but it feels cold as ice as the sound travels down my spine like splintering glass. Slowly, looking up, Haisley stands a few feet away, a scattering of crumbling graves between us. Her blue dress ruffles around her knees as the breeze picks up, and I think she's going to stand there, unsettled by the zombie-looking bunny.

But she doesn't.

Haisley comes closer, her short, curvaceous body folding neatly to her haunches at the end of my outstretched legs, my own feet bare, hers in pretty sandals with painted toes that she covers with the skirt of her dress. She watches the rabbit with a soft smile on her face that makes my own cheeks ache.

She's so pretty. The white length of a scar through the bowtie shape of her upper lip only adding to her beauty. Her cheeks are round and high, her lips thick, a natural, dark blush. The outer corners of her bright eyes turned up, like a feline, and she doesn't need anything to help her. She's natural, and she smiles like that, too, is natural.

"Poor thing, looks like it has myxomatosis," Haisley tuts softly, her eyes still on the rabbit, but mine are on her.

"What's that?" I ask her, still staring at her unblinking, it's a little hard to look away from her actually, because the woman is truly beautiful, young, happy, *free*.

"It's not curable, unfortunately, widespread through rabbits, they get swelling around the eyes, genitalia. Lethargy. A cruel end, really."

I stare down at the rabbit, still stroking its nose as its whiskers twitch. Its eyes red and weeping. My head pounds, a burning ache along one side of my skull, and I'm feeling that thread of irritation at not knowing anything. Maybe I had pet rabbits before, maybe that's why I've been coaxing this one closer for the last couple of days. Maybe I miss them. I should have gone in earlier for my nap, perhaps I wouldn't feel so *off*.

"It's such a nice day out," Haisley hums, more to

herself than me, she's been doing things like that all day.

Saying things that allow me to feel like I can reply if I want to, or to stay silent if I don't.

It's been very quiet here at Cardinal House today.

"I'm looking forward to the summer," she says whimsically, breathing out as she looks down at her hands, a large diamond that almost looks like a boulder on her tiny ring finger. "Thorne's taking me to Sicily. I love the beach, the sound of the waves, the scent of salt. It's my favourite thing."

There are boats on the water, a deep crystal blue with white foam. I've got a pinwheel in my hand, a rainbow of colours trilling in the hot breeze. The sun is burning the top of my head and I'm waving to someone I can't see clearly under the haze of the sun.

Blue eyes, familiar, but they are not my own.

"Luna?"

I blink, look at Haisley as she stares at me with wide eyes, her lip trembling.

"Yes?" I reply, feeling adrift, but Haisley looks like she's seen a ghost.

"I think the boys will be back soon," she says next,

changing the subject. Leaning back on her haunches, her eyes leaving me and scanning across the fields and trees and forest all around us, "It's just after eight." She pulls a phone from a pocket in her skirt, a smile lighting up her face, "Oh. Yes. They're almost home."

I can't stop the frown, but I don't think it actually shows on my face, it's just something I can feel deep inside, right beside the little black thread of Wolf. His darkness hollowing out its space inside of me even further, burrowing deeper. I want to stitch it there.

"I'm going to go and set the table," she beams, pushing to her feet, her smile bright and white. "Do yo-"

"Okay," I say quietly, cutting her off, holding her gaze like a stare in defiance until her smile drops away and she turns back towards the house.

I track her with my eyes as she goes, watching the dress drift around her, her huge, thick, curly ponytail swishing. My fingers curl over the poorly rabbit's neck just as Haisley hops up the front steps to the house, her head coming over her shoulder to glance back at me as she pauses in the open doorway. I don't smile at her, holding her eye, and when she disappears inside, I feel the crack vibrate up the length of my arm more than I hear it as I snap the sick bunny's neck.

Wolf

CHAPTER XXII

"And she was fine?" I ask Haisley for the fifth time since Thorne and I walked in the door less than twenty minutes ago.

Luna is still outside, sitting between tombstones and crumbling rock headstones. She saw the car pull in, but she's still out there. She likes the fresh air, the open space, she doesn't much enjoy staying inside this dark and dingy old house. Not that I blame her, it could do with a good clean and the windows need some serious help, they're awash with a layer of grime from the heavy snow and rain of winter. Still, I think she just prefers to feel the air on her skin.

Haisley has her back to me, reaching up to grab a stack of plates for the dinner we brought home from a cabinet above the microwave. I watch her clasp four of them in freckled fingers, a big glistening rock on her left ring finger, a thin, gold band securing it. She places the china down on the counter and then turns to me, resting back against the work surface, her eyes flicking hesitantly to Thorne as he leaves the kitchen before coming to mine.

"She was fine," she licks her lips, dragging my attention to the scar in her upper lip, it snags her sharp cupid's bow up a little higher on one side.

"But?" I cross my arms over my chest, leaning back against the opposite worktop, circular wooden dining table between us, six chairs tucked beneath it.

Haisley chews her bottom lip, slipping on a cropped black cardigan as Thorne re-enters the kitchen, passing the knitted item over to her with an outstretched arm. She flicks the end of her ponytail out from beneath the fabric and then looks back at me. Sighing, her shoulders drop and she rubs the side of her fist across her forehead.

"I think I might have upset her," she hedges, swallowing and tangling her fingers together in front of her.

"Upset her how?"

I feel it then, that dark, whispering, poison filling my arteries.

Obsession.

"I'm not really sure, I think- just because- I don't know... Maybe, she just wanted you, and I'm a stranger, just like everything else in her life right now. She probably just felt uncomfortable with me," she shrugs, frowning down at her feet.

Thorne curls his hand beneath her chin, fingers spanning over her slim throat, his body towering over her short frame. The way they look at each other, hold each other's gaze, it's this filthy, possessive, ownership. He owns her. She owns him. And they both love it.

"I'm going to get Lu-" I start, but I don't finish.

Luna pads softly into the kitchen, footsteps light across the stone tiles, blood smeared over her upper thigh, a limp white rabbit in her hand, the length of it swinging beside her shin, its back legs clasped in the delicate hold of her long fingers.

She swings the dead animal with casual movements, and drops it onto the laid table. Then she reaches up, long black hair in twin braids that hug the shape of her skull like thick ropes, and wipes the back of her hand across her mouth, blood staining her pale skin, she licks it from her lips without even blinking.

Haisley makes a strangled sort of sound in her

throat, but Thorne and I make no sound at all, watching her pause at the edge of the table, place her fingertips to the pale wood, the tips bending back sharply as she leans her weight forward on them.

"I'm not hungry," she announces quietly, her breaths slow and even, her attention on the rabbit.

Then, she turns, unhurried, and exits the wide archway opening of the kitchen. Her steps are slow as she turns down the hall, and I watch her leave for a moment, listening to the creaks and groans of the wood echoing back to us. And then I move.

She knows I'm there, following behind her, my footsteps not shy, my boots heavy as she floats through the shadows. She doesn't turn towards our makeshift bedroom. And she still doesn't look at me. I follow her silently through the darkened halls, stone walls, and ancient wood flooring until we reach the morgue.

Luna isn't shy as she depresses the door handle, opening it wide and taking the three steps down. She doesn't flick on the bright overhead light as she passes the switch, the room is empty now, the shattered coffin burnt to ashes in the furnace room, all that remains in here now is a trolley of clean instruments, and the fixed slab.

Not fully entering the room, I stand on the top step, watching her shadowed form sweep fingers across the side of the tiled slab in the centre of the room. She circles it, her fingers bumping over the little dips of grout between the tiles.

This is an original fixture, most tables like this are crafted of metal now. It's more hygienic, easier to clean, but I haven't the desire to change it. This one's been here as long as the house. Buildings live and breathe too. It felt wrong to rip it out.

Luna pauses at the drain end of the table staring up at me, my hands in my pockets, the black slacks too tight across my hips with both curled fists in my pockets, but I don't withdraw them. Her blue eyes set my skin on fire as she leisurely roves her gaze up from my black, laced boots to my crisp, white, collared shirt, the sleeves rolled up to my elbows, the top few buttons open revealing the tanned, olive skin of my chest.

"Did you put me here?" she asks me quietly, in the same way she always speaks, that soft, cracked, whisper.

"Put you here?" I ask, pushing thoughts of the dead rabbit out of my mind for now.

"On this table," she blinks hard, her face blank, "when I was dead."

The way she throws the word out, *dead*, I bristle at the casualness of it.

"Yes, I laid you there," I tell her, wondering where the fuck this is going, but I'm trying to let her walk through things, talk out thoughts, memories, coax her into finishing half sentences.

I want her memory back.

I'm going to bring you heads, severed, bloody, heads, Little Moon.

She glances down at the pristine table, her taped fingers gliding back and forth across the square tiles.

"Lift me up," she tells me, an instruction, one that has the hair on the back of my neck shifting to stand on end, but I don't hesitate.

Cold and sterile, I move fully into the room, stopping in front of her, I grasp her hips in my hands, lifting her up to sit her on the long edge of the slab. She shivers as her bare thighs touch the cold tiles, and then I release her, take a step back.

She kicks her dangling feet gently, her fingers curling loosely over the edge. Her pale eyes look white in the darkness of the room, like she's not in there anymore, drifting around the space in a non-corporeal form, as though her soul uses those blue glass orbs as doors to drift in and out of.

Her gaze comes to mine, a shiver rocking through my body like I've just been electrocuted. She looks at me like she's looking through me. Then she swings her legs up, slides her body down the length of the slab and lies there. All delicate and quiet, calm. Staring up at the ceiling, unblinking, she has her hands over either edge of the table, fingers curled gently over the lip of the slab. Then with a soft flutter of her inky lashes, she closes her eyes and she looks like a fucking corpse.

Something *wrong* rushes through me, a fire in my veins like lava rushing down the side of a volcano, racing towards the little sleeping village below. She looks like a fucking corpse and my cock kicks to life like it's the only place on my entire body that requires blood. Heart thrashing around inside my chest, I go to stalk forward, to tear her off of the fucking slab.

"Did you take off my clothes here or was I not wearing any?" she suddenly asks, her voice a ghostly whisper.

It stops me from completing my step towards her so suddenly that I have to grab onto the metal counter at my back to stop myself from stumbling forwards.

"What?" I reply sharply, my head snapping up so it's straight on my shoulders.

"My clothes," she says, staring up at the ceiling. "Did you take them off of me or was I already without them when you found me?"

I swallow down bile as I start to taste that acrid flavour on the back of my tongue, at the same time my cock weeps in the tight confines of my slacks.

"I cut them off of you." The inside of my mouth is like sand as I say it.

"How?"

"What?" I repeat, staring at her blankly, seemingly so comfortable and relaxed on a table I regularly dismember bodies on.

"My clothes," she says whimsically, like she's smiling on the inside. "How did you cut them off of me?"

"Scissors."

I can't give her much more than blank answers, I'm equally terrified and morbidly excited to see where the fuck this is going. And I shouldn't be, should I. Like, this is beyond fucked up, and yet...

"Get them," Luna instructs, and my dick pounds against the inside of the zipper it's imprisoned by.

Without hesitating, I turn towards the shiny metal table of tools, and retrieve the black handled scissors.

"Now what?" I find myself asking, a shiver tearing up my spine as I hover at her side, my shadow, even in the dark, darker than the rest of the room, looms over her like a cold blanket of death.

"Cut my clothes off, Wolf."

Detachment.

That's what she sounds like, that's what it feels like,

as I step closer until I'm flush with the edge of the table.

Still, I reach over her, the scissors sliding down the valley between her breasts, cutting easily through the elastic material of her spaghetti-strap, vest top until it's falling open in two pieces.

My eyes move to hers, but her own are shut, heavy fans of black lashes like butterflies settled upon her cheekbones. She hums, not focussing on anything but the feel of the blades as I slide them down the dip of her belly, and start cutting through the shorts sitting low on her hips.

When I reach the hem of the last leg, I place the scissors back down on the table and then I gently roll her onto her side. She lets me move her like she really is a corpse, it's both thrilling and disturbing as I tug the clothing out from beneath her. Getting another good look at the fading bruises, yellows and sickly pale greens.

Once she's bare, she shivers, her skin pebbling with goosebumps, her dark nipples pricking into sharp points. My mouth waters with the desire to suck them into my mouth, to bite down so hard around each of them that my teeth marks scar into her perfect skin.

"Then what did you do?" she asks, her voice trembling.

"Luna-"

"*Then* what did you do, Wolf?" She cuts me off with a sharpness I've not heard in her before.

"I cried."

My lungs deflate as I admit it, my hands trembling with a mixture of rage and hatred and so much fucking lust, it feels like it's going to explode out of me at any second.

I think of my mother, the way she would mock me for being soft. When she lopped my ponytail off and then taunted me with the rubber band of chopped hair, I cried, and she would scold me for it, mock me.

"Oh," Luna says breathily.

"I fucking cried, Luna, that's what I did," my voice is like the crack of a whip, dark, violent. "Then I cleaned you up, and I washed your battered body and I fucking cried every moment while doing it, before I laid you in that coffin. Then I sobbed all fucking over again."

Luna's eyes pop open, her lips parted as she watches me grasp my hair in my hands, losing the elastic tie and yanking at it so hard it makes my eyes sting.

This is like reliving my own fucking trauma, and I feel selfish for even thinking about my own feelings in this moment, but I just... today has been a long fucking day.

"Did you find me attractive?"

"What?" I feel like I'm coming unstuck, I'm a good man to her, but I feel unhinged, here, in this moment, I feel like a monster.

"When I was dead, did you look at me? Did you think I was pretty?" all of her words were cold, but these ones, these questions, *fuck*.

My breathing is ragged, loud, rasping heaves of breath, my heart battering against my sternum, the only thing containing the wild, erratic organ, because I can't lie, "Yes."

"Did you want to fuck me?"

An eruption of stars explode in my vision filling the dark room like a clear night sky. Ears muffled, the pounding of my blood shooting through my veins the only thing I can hear, can focus on as I think of her, only days ago, lying here, upon this slab, in this same position, naked and wet and bleeding.

Did you want to fuck me?

There are no morals with obsession, nothing can quell the desire, murder the lust, decapitate the hungry, pounding need to consume.

I am a monster, but I know I am, and I'm not ashamed, so I speak the only truth I know.

"Yes."

"Wolf," she says, a hitch in her voice.

At the same time I say, "Luna."

"Kiss me," she quietly demands, and I'm gone.

There's no real way to explain what it feels like to kiss a girl I once thought dead. Laid upon this morgue slab and readied to cremate. But the way her lips feel moving against mine with wild, hungry desperation, fills the hole in my soul like a black, poison laced, cure.

Quite literally, every ounce of hesitation, of worry, about what the fuck is happening here, dissolves like smoke whipped away in the wind. I throw myself up onto the slab, knees and hands bracketing her in against the tiles. My mouth descends on hers with the wild ferocity of an animal. She groans into the kiss, the sound rocking through her entire body.

Tongues tangling, violent, quick, collisions, I growl into her mouth, tasting her sweetness, consuming it.

My teeth clash with hers as we fumble together to get my slacks down. Her hands lift first, those long taped fingers struggling to pop open my button, but she tears down the zipper as I aid her, and then she's shoving her hand beneath the waistband of my boxers and dragging my cock out in a grip that's so tight it actually hurts.

I nip her lips as she tugs on my cock, but not like

she's trying to make me feel good, more like she's trying to fucking direct it. I'm not thinking straight as I let her. The soles of her feet come up, pushing down my slacks and pants, kicking at the fabric, and then she's lifting her hips high, tearing at the final few buttons of my shirt and shoving it off of my shoulders.

My hands planted either side of her head, her teeth in my tongue, my cock finds the heat of her cunt, her folds all slippery and wet, and I'm inside of her in one quick slam of my hips. The tip of my cock punches against her cervix, and I can't stop.

The noises that fall out of her throat only spur me on. The urge to devour her nice and slow for our first time comes in last place. The primal, frantic need to fuck her so hard we crack bones is the only thing in the forefront of my mind.

Her nails cut into my back, her fingers running down the planes of tight muscle like carving knives scoring my skin. Her scent fills my nose as I tear my mouth from hers and bury my face in her tits. Her usual smell of sweet peas and clean cotton is there, but she smells like sunshine and earth and there's the unmistakable copper taste of blood as I lick over her breasts. Sucking on both nipples, one and then the other as I piston my hips into her like I'm trying to drill my presence inside of her.

"Wolf," she pants, cutting her nails into my shoulders, the long lengths of her scratches burning with the sting of split skin in the cold air of the room.

My shirt flaps against my lower back as I fuck her, drawing my cock all the way out of her before slamming it back inside of her, and I know I can't last. The silken walls of her tight cunt squeeze so fucking deadly around my cock, it's hard for me to breathe.

Luna pants as I bury my face back in her tits, biting and sucking and marking her ice-white skin with savage little nips and ferocious, scarring bites.

Tearing myself out of her, knocking her legs from around my back, I dip my face down to her cunt, breathing her in like some sort of wild fucking animal. I breathe her in so hard, she's all I can sense. The room falls away and all I can hear is the moans and cries drifting like lyrical notes from her dry throat.

There's blood on my tongue as I lap up the length of her cunt, which almost gives me pause, but then my mouth is suctioning over her clit, teeth burying themselves into the flesh surrounding it. My tongue lashes around and around inside the circle of my teeth, sucking on her flavour like she's cake batter on my fingers. Forbidden and so fucking rewarding.

Her knees draw up, her thighs clamping down on either side of my head, she lifts her hips high, my hand grabbing her hip and slamming her back down into the table as she starts to come.

"Don't stop," she breathes, delirious and blissful.

And I already know I'll do anything this woman fucking demands of me. I rear up onto my knees as she finishes coming, slamming my cock back inside of her to feel her muscles clamp down around me, push me out and suck me inside. My thumb rubs torturously over her swollen clit as she thrashes beneath me.

"Don't stop," she breathes again, a chant, a dark summoning of my soul that licks at the base of my spine and triggers my own release.

I dip down, my mouth finding hers as she detonates around my cock, soaking me with a groan that rattles its way up her vocal cords like a demonic prayer.

"Wolf," she shudders as I fill her and fill her with ropes of hot cum, my hips clacking against hers as I push in deep one final time.

"Luna," I say softly, panting for breath, her nails still cutting into my shoulders.

She looks up at me in the dark, her face in shadow, but her glacier-blue eyes glisten like her soul's sighing with pleasure, and I feel it in my chest, that glittering black tether.

"I'm a monster, Luna. Your monster. Use me,

muzzle me, unleash me like a hound of hell and I'll tear out the throats of all of your demons."

Her eyes flicker between mine, her fingers digging deeper into my skin, "Wolf."

"Luna," I whisper, dipping down to take her mouth once more with mine. "I'll do anything for you," I confess, drawing back just enough that I can see her face, even in the dark.

"I know," she breathes, and then she smiles.

This pure curl to her mouth that hits me in the heart like an arrow of love, and it feels like I have so many things to say now, but I don't, I don't say any of them. Instead, I bite my tongue and kiss her again, clawing her closer with a sigh of pure happiness.

CHAPTER XXIII

There's blood between my thighs.

Wolf carries me through the dark, placing me down on my feet once we get inside the bathroom. He pulls on the light, reaching over the tub to start the shower. But I'm just staring down at my legs, a weird mixture of disbelief and horror clawing through me. This nervous thread of panic tying me all up in knots.

"Luna, it's okay," Wolf tells me in that quiet, softness used just for me.

"No it's not," I whisper, voice cracked, my breath catching in my throat.

"It's fine, really, Luna, it's my fault, we didn't know."

I'm not looking at him, gaze fixed on my blood smeared thighs, but I imagine Wolf is shoving his hand through his hair, and I should look up, I should tell him it's okay. It's not his fault.

Logically, nothing is wrong here at all.

I wanted him. He wanted me.

It was perfect, *for us.*

But all that's happening to me is a sharp seizing sensation in my heart like locusts have hatched inside my chest cavity and are swarming wildly around my heart like a crop field they're going to devour.

"Luna."

"I need to clean the mess," I mumble, shaky hands reaching out towards the sink.

My fingers fumbling over the taps, I swallow past the lump in my throat. I'm not even sure what this means, but I think about it, my virginity, and pure terror washes over me. I scrub my hands under the scalding water, lathering soap in my palms and slapping them against my thighs, clawing at the soapy, red skin.

"No, no, no, *no.*" A cry wrenches up my throat, dry and scratchy. "I shouldn't have done that." My fingers bend back with a sharp pain, the tape holding them together drenched, washing away the adhesive.

Wolf snatches up my hands as I cry out, pinning both of my wrists in one of his big hands, and raising them high, away from my legs.

I'm breathing hard, my eyes wide, bulging in their sockets and I have the most vivid imagery of them popping free, hanging down my cheeks.

"Luna," Wolf grunts sharply, his free hand grasping my chin. "Baby girl, look at me." He tilts my chin, my neck craning back, "You're safe. I've got you."

My teeth chatter, skin rippling with a tremor, "Something's wrong."

"Okay," he replies calmly, just like that, listening, unquestioning, not making me feel crazy.

"I don't know why," my teeth chatter so hard they clack in my mouth.

"It's okay," he soothes, cupping my cheek, pulling me into his muscular body, moulding my softness into his hard ridges. "It's okay."

"Wolf," tears streak down my cheeks, "I'm sorry."

"No, no, no, Little Moon, you don't have anything to be sorry for," he tells me, "nothing, okay?"

"I don't think I was supposed to do that," I confess in a small voice.

I feel him inhale sharply, his grip on my wrists releasing to haul me into his arms. He sits on the lip of the bath, cradling me to his chest, his palm curling over my head, protecting me.

My armour against the world.

"I know things right now are hard for you," wolf says calmly, his deep timbre gruff and low, softening, as it always does, *for me*. "But I'm not ever going to let anything bad happen to you. There will be no punishments, no scolding, no cross words. You could murder every bunny on the planet," he snorts at that, as though he finds it amusing, "and I will still-" he inhales sharply, his chest expanding beneath my cheek.

I blink, feeling him hold his breath, his arms a tight barring around me. The rush of the shower pounding against the base of the bath echoes in the quiet like hail on a tin roof, the spray dusting us, him more than me because his big body shields me from it.

"You will still what?" I whisper, my fingers pressing firmly to his chest, my eyes on the lumpy, red scar.

I cover it with my hand, my palm directly over the thrashing of his beating heart. Something that stopped, multiple times.

Because I bring death.

There's blood and bone and that putrid, sticky-sweet aroma filling my nose. It is sunken into the walls, staining the white ceilings yellow. The drapes are always closed, the fire always lit, but I am forever cold inside this house.

A spectre drifting through guarded halls, always watching and invariably watched.

"Luna?"

"There's a house with big windows that never open and doors that are forever locked. A garden I can't play in and guards always on watch." The words stream out of me like birdsong at dawn. My eyes lift to Wolf's perfect yellow-caramel orbs, "I think-" I glance back down, staring at my pale fingers flush with Wolf's suntanned olive skin. "I think I know where my house is."

Wolf drives us slowly down the dark roads, it's the first time I've left Cardinal House and the further away from it we get, the worse my tummy feels.

He thinks it's good for me to see if anything jogs my memory by seeing it, a house, he confessed, he had also driven by earlier today. I didn't ask why, but he told me anyway.

To protect you, Little Moon.

That was enough for me.

There are tall street lamps dotted along both sides of the road we come to a stop on, and Wolf parks the car a little way down from the house, in a spot that isn't under any light.

We sit quietly for some time, just us in the gloom. It's late now, early morning hours, but I'm not even a little bit tired.

"Do you recognise anything, Little Moon?" Wolf breaks the silence with his deep gravel, low tones, my right hand in his left, our fingers laced together.

Without words, I lift my left hand slowly, pointing at the large white house of horrors a little way up on the opposite side of the street. I don't know what happened to me inside that house, but somehow, deep inside, I know it wasn't good. Evidently, someone or some*thing* inside that large mansion killed me. It could have been something else. A stranger attacking me when I went out for a walk, perhaps. But deep down in the pit of my stomach, I know it was this house.

"Do you remember anything else?" he asks me a few more silent minutes later.

"No," I reply quietly.

"Luna?"

"Yes, Wolf?"

"The rabbit," he starts, his head turning towards me, his eyes burning into the side of my face, I keep my own gaze on the house. "Did you kill it to frighten Haisley?" he asks me so simply, emotionless, I almost feel like smiling.

Blinking, without turning my head in his direction, I glance at him from the corner of my eye, "No."

"Did she do something to upset you?" he asks next, my focus back on the house, the curtains drawn, no light spilling out from inside.

"No," I say, but I frown, and this time it shows.

"Are you sure?"

I think of the frothing water and the rainbow pinwheel and the blue eyes.

"I killed the rabbit because it was sick." The words drift out of me almost silently, my frown pulling at the healing skin of my head, making me want to wince.

"Luna-"

"There's a man," I gasp an inhale, squeezing Wolf's hand as a man exits the house.

He steps out onto the front porch, dressed in all black, and I have an urge, like a compulsion, to drop my gaze, to look away. Instead, I can hardly even blink. My throat gets tight, my mouth dry, tongue thick and

K.L. TAYLOR-LANE

heavy in my mouth. It feels as though I've licked sand-paper and shaved off all of my tastebuds.

"Do you know him?" Wolf is quieter now, watching the man like a predator readying to pounce.

No. That's what comes to mind first, but my gaze drifts to the spark of a lighter, his fingers pinching a cigarette between his lips, and even though we're far enough away that I can't see any details, my skin crawls as though it can feel his phantom hands holding my naked body down.

"Yes." I answer, taking in a nice slow breath.

"Did he hurt you, baby girl?" It's a loaded question.

I can hear the violence in the strain of his voice.

Can feel it thrumming through the interior of the shadowed car we sit in.

Taste it on my tongue, blood, as we sit here in the quiet.

A ghoul and her monster.

'The only monster here is me, Luna. And I'm yours.'

"Yes," I breathe, heat building between my thighs, my heart racing in my chest.

Anticipation.

He told me to use him.

'Use me, muzzle me, unleash me like a hound of hell and I'll tear out the throats of all of your demons.'

Wolf was right.

He is a monster.

My monster.

But… so am I.

"I want his head," I breathe, my entire body trembling, hands shaking, chest quivering.

Wolf's hand tightens in mine, strong fingers flexing until his fingertips dig painfully into my broken knuckles and I want to cry out at the pain. But I am silent, we are still, and then he brings my hand to his mouth, laving his hot tongue over the shattered bone like he knows he hurt me.

"Anything for my Little Moon," he breathes across my wet skin, placing my hand gently in my lap.

Then he gets out of the car.

An unholy terror released into the night.

Wolf

CHAPTER XXIV

I t's easy enough.

Slipping into the shadows, a copse of trees on either side of the house, like separators for property lines. The houses down this street are huge. The mini mansions of Oakwood line the quiet road like chunks of old money. People feel safe here, it's quiet, undisturbed, nobody overlooks anyone else's gardens, all of the building secluded in their own ways.

That's why it's fairly easy.

On his third circle of the house, my hand slaps over his mouth, his second cigarette falling to the dewy grass as I drag him kicking and flailing back into the over-grown bushes.

I don't waste any time with interrogation. Instead, I kick the man's legs out from under him, slam him into the hard packed earth and drive a knife into his chest. My hand remains over his mouth until his final breath rushes over the back of my hand, and his eyes roll back, the glare of the moon turning the whites of his eyes an eerie blue.

'Bring me his head.'

My cock is so fucking solid in my slacks right now, I don't know how the fuck I managed to climb my way out of the car. I wanted to lick her from head to toe, bite every inch of her skin, and then fuck her until neither one of us could walk.

But this first.

Like a courting gift, I must bring my queen a head. If I had time, I'd find a box, a big, over the top, velvet thing with bows and glitter, to present it in. As it stands, I don't have that luxury.

Sawing through a neck, especially when it's as thick as this one, takes monumental effort. It's not like slicing through a piece of meat, there are tendons and bone, sinew, tissue, veins, arteries. That's not easy dicing shit. Especially when I don't know how much time I have before someone comes out looking.

Sweat runs down my temples, my neck, coating my chest and sticking my shirt to my back, but I saw and saw, and I think of Thorne. Watching him do this in the back of a car. I thought he was crazy, like, sectional. Beheading a threat to his girl and then sticking it on a spike in front of a safe house owned by one of the most important families in the Irish mafia.

But, I get it now.

When I finally, *finally* hack through the final bones with tools I always keep in the car. The spinal column severed, nerves and tissues hanging free, I card my fingers through the light hair and heft it up under my arm.

My back is fucking killing me, my knees aching from being in a crouch so long, the hard packed earth beneath my boots having done my joints no favours, I casually make my way back to the car. I'm not taking the body with me to discard it. I'm not actually bothered if the man who owns this house, *Nolan Nicholas Beaumont,* finds one of his men missing, and a headless corpse in his shrubs.

I'm making a statement.

And he won't know what the fuck sort of monster is coming for him. Only that one is. And he can't prepare for the unknown, not one like me.

She's watching me, my blood thirsty little ghoul. I can feel her glacier-blue eyes burning my skin with every step that I take across the perfectly tarmacked road. It sets a fire in my belly, heat burning bright in my chest, like the sun's rays scorching me from the inside out.

Rounding the front of the car, I open the passenger door, crouching low in the space, the open door my shield, I offer her up the head. I hold it up high, gripping the hair tight between my fingers.

"Little Moon," I purr, the sound a horrifying mix of lust, love, and poison.

Luna's blue eyes are white in the dark, wide and burning on mine. Tentatively, she reaches out, and I think she's going for the head, but then her hand brushes past it. Blood catching on the back of her hand as she does, and then her fingers are touching me. Pinching my chin in violent fingers, she leans in. And then in a total contrast to the way she squeezes my jaw, she kisses the corner of my mouth. This light, feathery, airy, little kiss that sets my insides into full blaze, my heart pounding so hard in my chest I'm sure she can hear it.

"It's beautiful," she whispers, her breath ghosting over my mouth, dizzying me with the scent of sweet peas and clean cotton and a little hit of me, dark teak-wood and lilies. "Thank you, Wolf."

We're back on the road in less than a minute, my bloodied hands tight on the leather of the wheel, a severed head rolling around in the floor well between my girl's feet. And all I can think about is the way her thighs squeezed around my waist as my cock plunged into her. The way she tasted on my tongue, her wetness, blood, mixed with the scent of me.

My cock thickens even further and I'm certain it's going to burst through my zipper, and the button is going to shatter the windscreen as it pops free. What I'm not expecting is Luna to reach across the gear stick between us and cup the angry bulge in my slacks.

"Wolf," she says, that perfect, breathy, cracked, little whisper. "I want you now."

The tyres skid to a stop on the side of the road, gravel kicking up and attacking the paint like tiny bullets. Luna's already moving before the car's even out of gear, her fingers ejecting the clip of her seatbelt and mine, and then she's crawling into my lap. Fingers tearing at my blood drenched shirt, her nails scoring my skin, making me hiss as fire streaks down my flesh.

"Wolf," she whimpers, clawing at the zipper of my slacks.

I tear the skirt of her little, black, summer dress up

around her hips, stuffing the bunched, cotton fabric between her teeth, and thrust up into the hot, wet, heat of her dripping, little cunt. Silken walls strangle me, her wetness leaking out between us and coating my balls.

"Fuck, Luna," I breathe, biting into her neck, squeezing her ribs in the clasp of my hands. "Fuck, Little Moon, you feel incredible." I thrust up into her at the same time I drag her down hard onto my lap, then I'm guiding her back and forth, harder and faster. "That's it, baby, so fucking wet for me."

She whimpers around the fabric in her mouth, saliva dripping down her chin as she clenches her teeth around the black cotton. I lap my tongue in a hot, thick stripe up the front of her throat, before driving my teeth into her pulse point. She arches back as far as she can, thrusting her covered tits into my face. I bite her harder, feeling the hard points of her nipples through her dress rubbing against my chest. My tongue traces around the inside of my teeth, licking and sucking and tasting blood. Then I tear my teeth from her marked flesh, suck down to her bare shoulder, the skin tight and pink from the sun. I tear the front of her dress down with my teeth, baring her tits to me, no bra, no knickers.

"Fuck, Luna."

Using my punishing hold on her waist, I yank her

CARDINAL HOUSE

back and forth across my lap, her walls sucking me deeper by the second. Her cheeks are flushed pink, her eyes half-lidded, teeth gritted in a snarl around the fabric of her dress, holding it inside her mouth because I fucking put it there.

I suck on her nipples, flicking my tongue across them as I slide her back and forth over my lap, my dick weeping, spilling pre-cum into her. I don't think about it, fucking her raw, but only *I* have ever been inside her and it makes me feral.

I fist the fabric, yanking it from her teeth which give a clack, and I swallow the cry she yowls out, her teeth snapping tight on my tongue as I kiss her like I'm infecting her with me. Poisoning her with darkness and feeding it, letting it grow, tether our souls together. Tangle them so irrefutably that no one will ever be able to tell one of us apart without the other.

"Wolf," she pants into my mouth, moving with me as I grind bruises into her thighs, leave fingerprint markings along the dips of her ribs.

I nip her lips, suck on her tongue, drop one of my hands down between us, and pinch her clit like I'm trying to imprint my fingerprints into the swollen flesh for the rest of our lives.

"Wolf!" Luna jumps in my hold, her pussy clamping down around me as I thrust up, our pelvises knocking together, and rub brutal little circles over her.

"That's it, come for me, baby girl, show me how good you feel," I growl against her lips, sinking my teeth into her lip as she groans.

Her entire body locking up, her fingernails drawing blood from my shoulders, she comes around my cock and I can't bear not to watch her. I draw back, her head dropping back on her shoulders, eyes screwed tight, lips parted, she cries out, long and deep.

"Look at me, Little Moon."

A command of the highest order.

Her ice-blue eyes snap open, wide and surprised on mine as I keep pressure on her clit, and thrust up into her harder as she tenses, her muscles pushing against me, trying to force me out, and I'm coming too.

Ropes of cum shoot into her, painting the entrance of her cervix with my release, and it just doesn't stop, filling her and filling her. With frantic little twitches of her hips, she grinds down onto my lap and sinks her teeth into the side of my neck as I keep filling her up.

"Luna," I breathe out in a harsh rush of air.

Slowly, detaching the blunt points of her teeth from my neck, my pulse pounding so hard I can feel it in my toes, she uncurls her fingers from my shoulders, and stares at me.

I lick my lips, tasting her skin, my eyes on her as I loosen my hold on her waist, move my hand up from between us to cradle her cheek.

"Luna, baby, I love you."

There's this adorable little divot between her furrowed black brows as she looks at me, her hands coming to either side of my neck, resting there as she strokes the bitemark she put in my throat.

"It's okay if you don't feel it," I tell her, meaning it. Sweeping a stray lock of her hair off of her brow, I glide my thumb across her bottom lip, "I love you, and I'll take care of you for as long as you want me to."

Even if it kills me.

She jerks her chin up at that, her eyes the most expressive I've ever seen them, "It's not that," she says quietly, stroking my throat and sending goosebumps across my flesh. "It just doesn't feel right for us."

Us.

Her eyes flicker between mine, and she leans in to press a kiss against my mouth.

"We're more than love, Wolf," she says it as easily as breathing, her lips imprinting the words into my own. "What are the words you say to someone that you want to be buried with, same coffin, same headstone, same consecrated earth?"

"I don't know," I whisper, our mouths still touching. "That how you feel about me, baby?"

"Yes."

That's it, that's all she has to say. And I'm kissing her mouth and she's grinding herself back down on my rapidly hardening cock, and fucking me into the leather seats with nothing but pants and moans and love between us.

Cardinal House

Wolf

CHAPTER XXV

I don't know why the thought of Luna in my bedroom is such a big deal. It feels almost like a holy experience, walking her, hand in hand, through the dark, cool halls of Cardinal House into the newer wing of the single level-building.

The gloom embraces us, the shadows guiding us with cold hands and haunting fingers, like a cloak of darkness enveloping its monsters and welcoming them home.

My bedroom door is at the end of the furthest hall, leaving the heart of the house and moving into the bowels. The heavy mahogany door swings open with an eerie creak when I push down on the brass handle, and slip us inside.

The curtains are open, as they always are, because I rise with the sun, waking up with its rays on my skin, its warmth, when you live a life haunting the living before bringing them their death, you'll take any sort of light you can get.

The walls are painted a deep royal blue, a bright splash of aqua in the almost black colour that seamlessly melts into the dark mahogany flooring. A large, decoratively carved, sleigh bed sits in the centre, dressed in navy and rich gold. Washed out vintage rugs cover the floor surrounding it, and there are floating, industrial style bedside lamps attached to the wall on either side of the bed. Doors leading to a walk-in wardrobe and the en suite are opposite the bed. No tables, no dressers, just a mantle over the fireplace topped with cream pillar candles that smell like jasmine.

The only reason I chose this space was for the view. Perhaps that's why I'm so nervous about showing her my room, I've never let anyone in here before, not even my brothers have seen this. It is unshared with anyone, until now.

Luna leads me in as I shut the door at our backs,

her soft, padding footsteps heading straight towards the huge arched window.

That's the view.

Headstones and trees, grassy hills and wildflowers as far as the eye can see. It makes me feel like I'm outside even when I'm inside, and I need that.

Space.

Fresh air.

Freedom.

'I'm not free.'

"It's beautiful," Luna whispers, drawing my attention back to her.

Her fingers squeeze in mine, and I feel a little burst of excitement expand in my chest.

"You like it?"

Slowly, she turns to me, both of us standing side by side, hand in hand, like we've been doing this for centuries. I feel as though my soul knows her more than any other. Familiar and warm and full. Like a total eclipse, the moon obscuring the sun, that's how she's come into my life.

Obsession.

It's so much more than a need.

It's blood and bone, secretly shared smiles and love.

'We're more than love, Wolf.'

"Yes," she breathes, "I like to see outside."

I lift our joined hands up and curl my arm around her shoulders, her forearm coming across her chest to keep our fingers laced as we stare out at the view.

"I like to see outside too." I tell her, thinking of my mother.

The closed drapes and the shorn scalps, the cleansings and the midnight punishments. I want to tell her I understand her pain, even if I don't know what it is, even if she doesn't remember. I think sometimes we can have pain inside of us that doesn't feel like it has a source. It makes us dismiss the misery as inconsequential, but those dark holes can grow and stretch and swell, and before we know it, we're consumed by it, and there's no way of clawing our way out.

That was me.

Right up until I got shot.

When I died.

When some really incredible people massaged my heart and got it beating once more.

It was all an awakening.

So I could have this.

My brother shot me and killed me, but all his bullet really did as it slashed through my heart was bring me to life.

"Luna," I say, sweat slicking the back of my neck.

Obsession.

It swells and it grows and it consumes.

I don't think it's a curse anymore.

Unbelievably, I think, for me, it's a blessing.

"I'm never going to be able to let you go, Little Moon."

A sick confession.

Something horrid and rotting and possessive.

I have no regrets.

There's a part of me that worries, when her memories come back, she'll have had this whole other life, and there won't be space in it for me.

And even then, I know, as she tips her face up to mine, her ice-blue eyes stark white in the dark, I will never let her go. Even if she ends up somewhere else, with someone else, I will protect her from the shadows.

Lurk and stalk and creep.

I am a monster.

But I am forever hers.

Thorne is already on the porch when the sun rouses me from sleep.

His black on black slacks and shirt, shined dress

shoes, polished belt buckle. His appearance perfect in every way.

Mostly, I am his opposite. My chin-length, straight, black hair is scraped back with my fingers, tied in a bun at the crown of my head. There's a spliff tucked behind my ear, my chest is bare, and I wear loose gym shorts on my legs, feet bare.

Normally, I'd be going for a run now. Follow it up with weights in the small room I use as a gym, even if one of my brother's had stayed the night before like Thorne, but I don't want to stray too far this morning.

Having Luna in my bed for the first time last night was like a fucking dream. I almost feel weightless this morning. Floating on a cloud.

"We are having an engagement party," Thorne announces as I slump into the old rocking chair beside the wicker armchair in which he sits. "On the seventeenth." Looking up from his phone, he peers over the top of the thick framed, black, reading glasses he wears on his nose, flicking his gaze down the raised red claw marks etched into my skin. "I want everyone there."

"Okay."

"It is going to be at Lucia's. Haisley likes it there," he explains, even though he needn't bother, I know my future sister-in-law likes eating at that Italian. "Bring Luna."

"Thorne," I caution.

Not because I don't want to take Luna out.

Last night was a big risk. One I'm going to have to explain momentarily to my brother, because he's the boss, but taking her out to a restaurant owned by Vito Gambino, the Italian Don himself. After assaulting one of his drivers right outside his own bar, feels like pushing it a little. Especially considering we could bump into literally anyone that knows Luna, and we won't know it.

Neither will she.

"I know the risks, the entire family will be there. There are far more of us than there is one Nolan Nicholas Beaumont." My elder brother scoffs as he says it, returning his gaze back to his phone, just like our father does.

Taking the joint from behind my ear, I slip it between my lips and light it with the lighter always left out here beside the ashtray.

"I left a body in the bushes outside of his house last night," I say on an exhale, smoke billowing out of my nostrils.

My gaze on the orange-pink sky, I scratch at the lumpy, red scar over my heart and think of Luna's teeth sinking into it in the middle of the night. She swung her legs across my hips and sunk herself down onto my cock before even waking me up, I nutted in three minutes flat.

Not that I'm complaining.

Thorne sighs heavily, removing his glasses from his face and twiddling the arm of them between his finger and thumb, his elbow resting on the arm of the wicker chair.

"Why must you do these things at a time like this," he says, looking out at the hills, not as a question, and definitely not to me. I think my brother finds leading this family just as exhausting as our dad does. "You are a disposals expert, Wolf, why on earth would you *leave* the body there?"

I shrug, the joint hanging on my bottom lip as I lean my head back against the wood of the chair, rocking it back and forth with a creak, "It's only the shoulders down."

Thorne tuts sharply, but he doesn't sound the least bit surprised, we're all killers in this family, some of us are just flashier about it than others.

"And the head?" he asks, another sigh of exhaustion that makes me want to laugh.

"Threw it in the furnace when we got home last night."

"Wonderful," he chimes sarcastically, but because he's nothing if not well spoken, he clears his throat and purses his lips, his black eyes coming to mine. "We are dealing with enough messes right now without this, Wolf."

"I know."

"Then why?" he huffs, stilling the frantic twirling of his glasses, pinching them between his fingers instead.

"Luna wanted his head."

"Luna was there?" he asks sharply, "I assumed you had both retired for the night."

Now I've got his attention, "Nope."

"Explain." One word, and he's about to pull his hair out, it makes me smile around the butt of the joint.

I tell him what happened, a brief version of the events, but he still frowns at me when I finish the story.

"It'll be interesting, won't it?" I say then, pinching out the spliff and flicking the roach into the ashtray.

"What will be interesting?"

"Seeing if it gets reported," I shrug. "The man is a solicitor for a mafia leader, has a niece nobody knows about and has never heard of or seen. He hasn't reported her as missing, which means he either doesn't care, *or*, what's more likely is, he thinks she's dead after he administered the killing blow and got his goons to toss her into the river to wash up as a Jane Doe."

"Yes, we know all of this. You also know he will have that body cleaned up and gotten rid of before he can blink. All you have really done is make him question why someone killed a man on his property, one of *his* men I take it, retrieve the head like a trophy, and do nothing else. All this has achieved, is making him suspicious of everyone and everything around him, and be extra cautious *if* and when he leaves the house." He stares at me, and I look his way as I feel his eyes on me. "All this has done is put Luna in possible danger."

CHAPTER XXVI

Black satin slips down my body like water. Thin spaghetti-straps hold the skin tight silk up on my shoulders, the back scoops low, dipping all the way to the base of my exposed spine. The neckline is low too, a V shape that covers only my breasts, then hugs the rest of my dips and curves all the way down to the floor. My black hair is down in loose waves, and the front sections are pulled back, fastening at the back of my skull with a large, white, silk bow with long tails that hang down my spine.

"I can't wear those shoes," I say quietly, staring at Wolf, over my shoulder in the reflection of the mirror.

"They're too high," I tell him, referring to the shoes that Haisley sent over for me.

We had breakfast the morning before she left, and I think I liked her a little more than the day before. Seeing her with Thorne made me more comfortable too. She looks at him like sunflowers look at the sun.

"They *are* too high," he agrees from his seated position on the end of the bed where he ties the final knot in his shoelace.

His huge, muscular body is dressed in a white, long sleeved, button-up shirt. Pressed black slacks, polished dress shoes, black leather with black laces. A very large gold watch on his wrist, and black hoops through the piercings in the cartilage of his ears. His styled stubble is neat, black hair down, just the way I like it, a centre parting, and grease pulled through the lengths, so it tucks neatly behind his ears.

He looks perfect.

"That's why I also bought you these," he smiles, climbing from the bed, and hooking a pair of pointy toe, flat, black, silk shoes from a box on the floor I hadn't seen before.

"Oh."

"Lift your foot," he instructs, his warm hands sliding down the outside of my legs as he drops elegantly into a crouch at my back.

Pressing my fingers against the wall beside the antique mirror to steady myself, I lift my foot. Wolf's large hand sweeps along my skin, his thumb pressing into the arch of my foot as he places my toes inside the shoe, buckling the small strap that threads around the back of my ankle and placing it down. He does the same to my right foot, the small train of my dress hitched up around my knees, the excess hooked up over his shoulder.

Wolf runs his large, calloused hands up my smooth legs, under the black silk, his thumbs tracing the crease between my cheeks and thighs, he squeezes my hips, hitching the fabric up higher and higher as his thick fingers ascend.

"Wolf," I breathe out, bowing forward as he gently parts my thighs, dropping down onto his knees, and pushing his tongue up and into my cunt.

"Mm," he hums, not commenting on my lack of underwear once again, he never scolds me, never mentions it, never makes me feel embarrassed. "Always so wet for me, Little Moon," he rumbles against my wet flesh, sending me lurching forward as he grips my hips tight and licks a hot, wet stripe up the length of me, making me shudder. "We don't have much time before we need to leave," he chuckles, dipping his tongue into my hole and suctioning his mouth over me. "But I think

I'm going to take you to dinner with a little piece of me dripping down your thighs, baby girl. How's that sound, Luna?" he rumbles. "You want that?" he breathes, licking and sucking at me, one of his fingers meeting the swollen nub of my clit.

"Yes," I tell him desperately, my eyes bulging as I stare at him in the mirror, revealing the sight of his giant hand cupping my pussy.

"I can't hear you," he mumbles over me, his lips a delicious torture. "Tell me louder, baby girl."

"Yes!" I squeal loudly, lifting up onto my toes.

"That's better, Luna," he praises, my fingers bending backwards as I lean into the wall, his calloused finger rubbing firmly over my clit as he fucks me with his tongue.

When he sucks my wet flesh between his teeth and bites down, he slaps the heel of his hand over my swollen clit and sends me careening over the edge.

He's inside of me before the stars clear from my vision, fucking up into me only once, twice, and then he's shooting his cum inside of me, painting my clenching walls as I squeeze his cock so hard he grunts against my throat. Sinking his teeth into the slope of my shoulder, and sucking hard on my skin.

"I love you, Wolf," I tell him, staring into his eyes through the reflection of the mirror, his mouth still attached to my shoulder, those warm, whiskey eyes lifted up onto mine.

He detaches his teeth, kisses the side of my head, and sucks on my earlobe, all whilst holding my gaze, unwavering and whispering truth in my ear, "I love you, Luna."

Unconsciously, I stop walking as we arrive at the restaurant.

Nerves flitter around inside my belly, and despite Wolf reassuring me everything will be fine, I feel uncomfortable. I'd rather be back at Cardinal House, sitting amongst the graves and watching the sun set.

Wolf's hand squeezes comfortingly in mine, both of us staring up at the small, romantic looking building, baskets of bright flowers hanging on either side of the door, a red and white striped awning over the entrance. It's lovely, but I don't want to go inside. But then Wolf's stepping in front of me, his back to the restaurant, towering over me so he's all that I can see.

"You're missing something here," he tells me quietly, tracing the fingers of his hand not holding mine across the hollow of my throat.

"What?" I frown up at him, but I'm blinking hard just once and I'm unsure if the frown even shows, but he only smiles at me.

"This," he says, reaching into his black, suit jacket, and pulling out a long, emerald green, velvet box.

"Wolf," I breathe, staring down at the diamonds as he pops it open one handedly.

"There's studs in there too," he says casually, releasing my hand and picking one of them out. "Put these in."

I take the small, diamond, stud earring braced in gold from his fingers and push it into my lobe, doing the same with the next. Then he turns me around slowly, my back to his front, and slips the necklace, a line of diamonds from one end of the gold chain to the other and secures it at my nape. It sits in the hollow of my throat, casting rainbows across the polished black paint of the car as the evening sun lowers and hits the clear rocks.

"Thank you," I whisper as he turns me back to face him, his big hands wrapped around my biceps.

"Almost as beautiful as you," he smiles, kissing the tip of my nose, and stepping back.

My cheeks heat and my heart swims, and I forget all about my anxiety as Wolf leads me into the restaurant.

A man dressed in a black suit greets us politely and leads us to Wolf's family. He weaves us through empty tables and chairs, no cutlery or napkins or menus laid out, making me stare out across the large space with confusion.

"Wolf," I start, but he's already smiling when I look up at him, his pretty honey eyes focussed forward. "It's closed isn't it?"

"Yes, Little Moon, it's closed," he chuckles, glancing down at me with a wink, leaning down to whisper into my ear. "You think I'd let you come to dinner with my cum running down your thighs with strangers around?"

"Yes," I state simply, and he's jerking his head away with a barked laugh and a soft shake of his head.

"Fuck, you're perfect for me," he beams down at me as we reach the table full of the Blackwells.

After being re-introduced to Wolf's father and brothers, except for his youngest brothers, Arrow and Raine, who are noticeably absent. Meeting his sister-in-law, Grace, along with her and Hunter's three children, Atlas, River and Roscoe. Thorne and Haisley's engagement dinner goes well.

The table is surprisingly calm.

The three young boys are well behaved. Even

Roscoe, who is sitting in a wooden highchair beside his father, is patient and smiley as he plays with a pink spoon and feeds himself his food. Atlas is quiet, one hand always in Grace's, and River, who is apparently also lovingly nicknamed Trouble, sits himself in his father's lap and shreds the colouring sheets the waiter laid out for him instead of colouring them in, he stabs them with a metal fork too like he's trying to murder the paper. Not that anyone looks concerned by it, so I decide not to worry either.

Archer sits beside Stryder, who sits opposite me, but despite his polite smile, he doesn't seem to really want to be here. He has hushed conversation with his father, picks at his food, and downs pints of beer between courses without taking a full breath between gulps.

Haisley sits on one side of me, Thorne at the head of the table beside her. Her conversation is light and quiet, polite, kind. I wish I hadn't upset her with the dead rabbit, even though it wasn't entirely my intent, and when I tell her so, Wolf's father, Stryder's forkful of food pauses midair, hovering halfway to his open mouth, as Haisley chuckles lightly with a shake of her head.

"I'm used to worse things being a member of this family," she tells me lovingly with a bright smile, "I'm not worried about sick bunnies having their necks snapped."

I offer her a small smile in return, thinking of the bones breaking, the way it felt like a rushing vibration up my arm, and then hurry to pop a bite of creamy pasta into my mouth to smother the inappropriate curl of my lips.

Wolf's hand is on my upper thigh, his fingers splayed possessively over the entirety of my upper leg, and I feel relaxed, falling into what feels like easy conversation with Stryder, as Wolf converses with Hunter.

I can't help but keep glancing at Grace though. Her pretty eyes are unusual, both of them different colours, but it's the icy-blue one, that I can't help peering up at every now and then. It's so much like my own, it makes me feel a little warm inside. Maybe I'll find a kindred spirit in her.

Her hand rests over the large bump of her belly, a pretty white dress sculpted to it. I think about the baby in there. A girl, she said with a warm smile, who will be born into this family. A doting mother and father, three older brothers, who, from the way Atlas, the oldest of their three boys, keeps stroking his mother's tummy, will be fiercely protective of her.

I'm not sure if I grew up with siblings, but the

organ in my chest feels tight with want for one. Suddenly, I feel incredibly lonely, realising that the world really is a very big place, and I am, in fact, a very small part of it.

There's a very strange feeling in my throat, a tightness that makes my skin itch and my heart flutter, and I'm pushing up from the table, clanging glasses together as they slosh with wine and water.

Blinking hard, I keep my head lowered, "I'm sorry," and I realise with horror, that I'm waiting for something in return for my rudeness.

A punishment.

Wolf stands with me, his hand coming to mine, "We'll be right back," he tells his family calmly, without making a fuss, pulling out my chair quietly, so I can move away from the table.

Wolf leads me down a short, cosy hallway, before pushing open a wooden door that leads into a bright bathroom. He lets me enter first, pushing a lock across the door at his back.

"Come here, baby girl."

Wolf opens his arms wide, thick muscles bunching under his smart, white shirt, and when I step into him, those arms closing around me, I take what feels like my first deep breath of the night.

"You're okay, Little Moon. I've got you, take your

time," he whispers, kissing the top of my head, his hands a strong, hot heat over my bare spine. "I've always got you, baby."

He lets me close my eyes, sinking into his hold, his warmth drawing me in deeper, his strong body opening up to me, embracing me, cloaking me, shielding me.

I take long, deep breaths, breathing him in, lilies and teakwood, a strong, rich, masculine, scent with a subtle floral fragrance to break it up.

I could fall asleep like this, his hold firm and tight without squeezing, my face over his heart, the solid beat of it drumming loud in my ear, soothing me into a tranquil calm.

My monster.

"I feel better now," I tell him quietly, after who knows how long, but he still doesn't rush me, holding me nice and tight, his back resting against the door, his chin on the top of my head.

"We can take as long as you want."

"I know," I say, pulling back a little, so he can lift his chin.

Wolf stares down at me, the point of my own chin resting against his sternum, his warm yellow gaze flickers over mine, checking my truth.

I hear him saying it inside my head before he speaks, but he says the words anyway, "Blackwells don't tell lies," he smirks down at me, this decadent curl to his plush lips.

"I'm not a Blackwell," I respond, in the same way I always do.

But then he says with a sharp smile, "Not yet."

He doesn't give me enough time to react, to feel shy, for my cheeks to flush pink, because he presses his mouth to mine, slipping his tongue between my lips and devouring me like he's never tasted anything so sweet. He leaves me gasping and breathless when he breaks off the kiss, my eyes still closed, and his arms still embracing me. Curling me up into his chest and keeping me safe.

In this moment, I don't think about my memories, my past, all of the things that keep flicking through my mind, making me feel unsteady with the world and my place in it. Because Wolf Blackwell is mine and I am his and nothing could ever possibly ruin that.

Luna

CHAPTER XXVII

Wolf waits outside the door while I use the facilities and wash my hands. I look up at my reflection in the mirror, shaking droplets from my fingers into the basin, and reach up to sweep a few stray black hairs away from my face.

I hear Wolf's laugh beyond the door, this deep, gravelly sound that sets my core alight, and has one corner of my mouth lifting with a secret smile. I pull open the door, his broad back to me, shielding me from whichever brother it is he's speaking to, but he turns as soon as he senses the door opening. Twisting towards me with a dark, but bright smile, he takes me into his arms, pressing a kiss to my head.

"Vito," Wolf starts, turning us back to a man who is definitely not one of his brothers, "this is my Luna."

Suddenly, everything seems to happen in both fast and slow motion all at once.

The man's smile drops, morphing into shock, then a sharp, violent frown. His icy-blue eyes flare wide, and before I can blink, he's pulling a gun and aiming it at Wolf's chest.

I think it's my cry that startles us all, prompting the sudden sound of footfalls to come flooding into the hall. I'm in front of Wolf, despite his grunt, the harsh grip of his hand on the back of my neck, but my arms wind behind me, banding around his back, my fingers locking together, and the barrel of the gun is pointing in my face.

"You have three seconds to explain to me what the fuck is going on, Wolf."

"What the fuck do you mean?!" Wolf explodes at my back.

"Luna," Vito says, an accent curling my name, extenuating it with an *oon* sound in its centre.

The man, *Vito*, grabs hold of me and violently shoves me behind him, holding me painfully flush with his spine as I turn my head to find Stryder and Thorne in the mouth of the hall.

I'm trembling, my eyes wide, locked on Wolf's brother and father, my still taped fingers fisting up beneath my chin. I can feel my tears soaking into the fabric of the stranger's shirt, staining it with streaks of mascara. My knees wobble in time with my bottom lip and my breathing is too fast, uneven, my eyes bulging.

Lemon and rose fills my nose as I try to take deeper, even breaths, to slow my racing heart and to kill my panic. But the men are shouting, and I can't make out anything at all, peering around Vito's body, to stare at my Wolf with a gun in his face.

"Wolf!" I cry out, "Wolf!" I scream it this time, an earth shattering sound that has my throat cracking and aching as I repeat it in the same panicked tone again and again. "Wolf!" I struggle against the man's grip over my back, his fingers digging divots into my spine. "Wolf!" I yank myself out of his hold, stumbling backwards straight into the wall.

The back of my head smacks into the wall, silencing my panic, and I slide down the textured wallpaper as I slump to the ground.

. . .

There's a body sprawled out on a trolley, blood a dark crimson blooming across his chest. There are shouts, orders, instructions, the cloak of death is curling around my shoulders, a cold cape of finality as I stare at the man I can't fully see. Doctors and nurses a closed circle around him. His brothers watch on from the hall and I'm leaving the room to speak to them. One of them shouts, another scowls, the other, he is cold and kind and calm, all of them covered in blood. I take them into a separate room, and when I go back to the man, death has moved on, and he is breathing once again.

There's salt in the air, the breeze is too strong to be called as such, it's a wind, but it's warm, blowing my hair across my face like little lashes whipping my cheeks. The boy is not much older than me, but we have the same eyes and the same black hair. He passes me a rainbow pinwheel, and then takes my hand in his, stretching it out until our elbows are straight and the wind is whipping it around and around with a trilling sound that makes me bubble with laughter.

A warm hand comes over my shoulder, long fingers curling over the top of my chest. I tilt my head back, a bright smile on my mouth that makes my cheeks ache. But it only grows as I lean further back, tilting my chin with a laugh bursting free of my lips as the young woman beams down at me. Long black hair flapping across her face, her blue eyes like mine, but not quite the same, she smiles, and my chest grows as warm as my skin under the sun's rays.

"Ti amo, dolce ragazza."

The corner is dark, cloaked in shadows where I hide. My hand smothering my nose and mouth to hide the noise of my panicked rasps of breath. The smell of my skin makes me gag, my throat tightening and constricting until I have to retch into the cup of my palm. Cigars scent my skin, coating me in the rough, sweet aroma of him.

I ran, but I shouldn't have.

He's going to make me regret it.

Unafraid.

I let him take what he wants from me. Only touching my behind, never anything else.

If I'm good, it doesn't hurt as much.

If I'm still, he doesn't curl his fingers inside me, ensuring that I bleed.

If I bleed, it's worse.

My lips are bitten dry, but my eyes are drier.

I don't cry anymore.

Not for him.

Not for me.

I think of the blue eyes I don't understand and close my own.

CHAPTER XXVIII

There's a blood-red cardinal perched on the headstone of a Mrs Victoria Henry Jonathan Morris, with the dates eighteen-eleven to eighteen-fifty-six etched into the crumbling sandstone. That's all there is. I don't know if she was a mother, a sister, a *niece*.

That's what I am.

Confirmed with blood for DNA testing.

Vittorio Gambino's niece.

My memories are coming back like a fast-forwarded movie reel. Some things are flooding, others trickling, but there's nothing of him. My *real* uncle.

After we ruined Thorne and Haisley's celebration last night, Wolf hasn't slept much, taking calls on and off all day from Vito, and Thorne and Stryder. I've just been out here, breathing in the fresh air I've been deprived of for the last twenty-three years.

I remember him too.

Uncle Nolan.

And I wish I didn't.

Goosebumps prickle my flesh as I feel Wolf approach.

My dark, violent monster creeping through the night. Absorbing all of the shadows around him, his presence growing heavier, deeper, larger.

His warm breath fans across the nape of my neck, before his arms come over my shoulders, crossing over my chest and pulling me in flush with his front. His heart drums against my spine, echoing into the cavity of my own chest, thrumming through my veins like adrenaline in my blood.

"Hello, you," he breathes in my ear, his tongue curling over the shell, and making me shiver. "You cold out here, baby girl?" he asks, his voice rumbling heavily as his thumbs smooth up and down the bare skin of my biceps.

I'm in only a t-shirt, one of his, slipping off my shoulder, with nothing on my feet, my hair loose down my back, the ends of the strands reaching the base of my spine.

"No."

"You want to come inside, Little Moon?" Wolf kisses the side of my throat, nuzzling his face into the crook of my neck, a long, deep inhale has his nostrils flaring against my skin. "You smell delicious," he growls, nipping my flesh and making me press back into him further.

"What do I smell like?" I whisper, one of the first things I've really spoken aloud to him today, other than my usual yeses and no's, he hasn't gotten much from me in the way of conversation.

"Hmm," he hums, and I can feel his lips pulling into a smile against my skin. He huffs a humorous breath into my neck, grazing his teeth gently over my pulse, "You smell like mine."

And now it's my turn to smile.

I gaze up at the moon, my hands coming up to curl over his forearms where he holds my chest. Laying my head back against his shoulder, his chin over mine, our cheeks pressed together. We both stare up, stars and planets and constellations twinkling and burning bright in the night.

"Wolf," I whisper, the rough brush of his stubble

comforting as he nuzzles my cheek, marking me like wolves, and perhaps monsters, do.

"Yes, Little Moon?"

"I want you to make love to me under the stars."

Wolf's arms uncross, his hands smoothing down my front, thick, calloused fingers curling beneath the hem of my t-shirt, and stripping me bare.

With the moon as our witness, the stars our audience, Wolf caresses my breasts in the cups of his hands, his kiss dragging along the slope of my neck, mouthing over my shoulder, down my back. He spins me around, one arm going beneath my thighs, he brushes my legs out from under me and lowers us both to the ground.

The dry grass is rough beneath my spine, the scent of the wildflowers stronger under the light of the moon, small crumbles of headstone rock digging into my spine. Wolf's eyes connect with mine, honeyed-whiskey orbs oozing obsessive, possessive love.

Wolf spreads me out beneath him, holding my gaze as he lowers himself down my body. Laving his tongue down the centre of my chest, circling my nipples, and biting the diamond hard points. His mouth sucks down my belly, biting and sucking and marking a trail across my skin until he finds the glistening flesh of my cunt.

Lips curl around my clit, sucking tenderly. A deep,

throaty, groan rumbling its way up his vocal cords and echoing in the aching hollowness of my cunt.

Head digging into the earth, the grass tickling my face, my back arching, Wolf curls his arms around my thighs, lifting my hips from the ground and bringing me up to his mouth.

"Wolf," I say softly, drawing his attention with a quiet moan.

"Luna?" he rumbles, breath blowing over my swollen, wet flesh, sending a fresh smattering of goose-bumps up in his wake.

I lick my lips, looking down my bared body at him, his lips shiny with my slick, his eyes reflecting the moon, "I want…" I trail off, nerves shooting distress signals to my brain.

"What do you want, Little Moon?" he whispers, "you know I will do anything for you," his voice a caress of sinful delight.

"I want you to fuck me from behind," I tremble as I say it, staring down at him with wide, shiny eyes. "Not-not *that*," I breathe as he slowly lowers my hips back down to the grass, crawling his way up and over my body, shielding me from the blanket of stars so he's my only view. "But I want- I trust you, to be behind me."

"Luna," he licks his lips, me on his mouth, and

flicks those pretty eyes between mine. He doesn't ask me if I'm sure, he doesn't frown, he doesn't tell me no, he simply says, "You tell me if you wanna stop, baby girl, and we'll stop." Then he's lifting up onto his knees, staring down at me as he wears the moon like a halo, his black hair loose and fluttering, falling from its place tucked behind his ears and making him look like a fallen angel. *Mine.* "Stand up for me."

He hefts me up halfway, helping me to my feet as he rises with me. Dipping his chin as his bare chest presses to mine, he leans down, holding my gaze, our souls clashing and tangling through the windows of our eyes, and then he kisses me, and it's like the world stops.

My head spins and the planet goes dark, and his hands are firm, warm comfort as he runs them over my skin. Goosebumps erupt and shivers roll through me, and I can feel him in my chest, his fingers plucking at the valves of my heart and threading that dark, monstrous stitching through the organ, tethering me to him.

Healing and saving and loving me.

His tongue laps over mine with long, languid passes, and soft little sucks before he nips at the tip, nibbling on my lip and he tastes me like I'm something new but old, strange yet familiar.

Love untwists and expands between us, growing and swelling until my nails are biting into his arms, his hands cupping my cheeks tighten and burn.

And then he fucks his tongue into my mouth, biting hard at my lips, our teeth knocking together as he draws back from my swollen pout, using his thumb to force open my jaw, his eyes flicker between mine, and then he spits into my mouth, licking over his saliva on my tongue, groaning deep, and I'm swallowing him down.

"Turn around for me, baby," he whispers over my bitten lips, licking over them one at a time, the top then the bottom. "Put your hands here," he instructs, his own coming over mine as I turn around, his chest to my spine, and he wraps our fingers over the top of a headstone. "You say stop, I stop," he breathes, but he doesn't hesitate then, he doesn't wait for me to answer, to nod, to reply, he just thrusts his cock into me from behind and clamps a hand around my neck as a scream drops from my throat. "That's it, Luna. You feel so good, such a good girl for me, fuck, *fuck*, that's it, like that." He praises and murmurs and groans, biting into my neck as he wraps his giant body over mine.

"Wolf," I groan, a thick crack to my voice as my head drops forward, his splayed fingers holding me up with the hold he has on my throat. His dick pistons into me, our hips clapping together, fingers of the other hand laced over stone, "Don't stop."

"I'll never stop, I'll give you everything you need, everything you want. I'll bring you every head of every man you demand, my deviant little ghoul." His teeth sink into my throat, and I pant for breath as he bites, fucking into me harder and harder, and without any warning I explode.

My pussy milks him as I forget that's he's behind me, existing only in the pull and push of pleasure. His teeth scrape down the back of my neck, my hair hanging forward of my shoulders, curtaining my face. Dull teeth score my skin and then in no time at all, my cunt squeezing him hard, he thrusts in deep, holding himself still, and groans into my shoulder as he sinks his teeth in further.

My release ebbs and flows as his cock twitches inside me, setting off another climax. This one a soft, warm wave of pleasure that falls over me, and has my mouth dropping open in surprise.

"That's it, Luna, come on my cock, you're squeezing me so good, Little Moon, so fucking good, baby girl."

Wolf nuzzles my neck, kissing my spine and then he's pulling me down, into the crispy grass, still inside of me, his front to my back, but he's cradling me in his lap, kissing my hair and petting my skin.

Reverence.

That's how he holds me.

"I love you, Luna," he breathes in my ear, his heart pounding in time with my own through my back.

"I love you, Wolf."

CHAPTER XXIX

V ito's home is grand.

Marble floors and walls stretch through every room, Every surface hung with expensive art, gold, crystal chandeliers on every ceiling, and designer furniture in every available space.

It's nothing like Cardinal House, with its old stone, creaky floors, and history. This is clinical and cold and unhomely.

My skin itches where I sit on an expensive couch in a room the size of an echoey ballroom. Ceilings as high as a skyscraper and the long wall in front of me, just beyond this cluster of chairs, is made of all glass, showing off the manicured gardens and lawns.

It's uncomfortable, looking at a man who looks so much like me, but also, not at all.

Vittorio 'Vito' Gambino has a strong jaw decorated with a neat black stubble, pursed lips and a strong nose. His eyes are bright, icy-sky blue dressed in decadent curls of thick black lashes. A head of thick, black hair, straight, just like mine, styled neatly to one side of his head.

He smells like rose and lemon and a little bit like what I imagine to be the sea, salty and clean.

Vito is calm as he sits before me, a glass and chrome coffee table between us topped with an array of teas and coffees, sweets and pastries.

It is only the three of us in the large room, Vito, Wolf and I, when we first arrived, the men standing around like sentry soldiers made me not want to enter, so Vito just… sent them away. He didn't worry about security for himself, he didn't do it to be disrespectful to Wolf, making him feel like he's not a threat, but to make me comfortable.

Nobody argued. Nobody baulked.

But there were a lot of eyes on me that I wish there weren't before the room cleared out.

My knee jumps and I wish it wouldn't, my foot

unable to stay flat on the floor. I've got on a black sundress, a pale blue cardigan over the top, and that huge white bow in the back of my hair, pulling back the wavy strands from my face.

But Wolf is here.

His thigh pressed up tight against mine, black jeans and a white t-shirt on his muscular body, his inky hair pulled back in a bun. His fingers are laced through mine, the back of my hand pressing against his knee, his holding me solid and firm.

The men talk because I can't. I find myself incapable of words in front of the man, who's not that much older than me, that says he's my uncle.

Real uncle.

"How can you be my uncle when you're so young?" It's whispered, the question, haunting lyrics from a girl that feels like she's trapped between worlds, balancing on the veil that separates life from death.

The men quiet, but I can't look at either one of them, my gaze locked on a waterfall beyond the glass. A stone sculpted couple draped over one another, their legs and arms and torsos tangled together so much, it's hard to see where one begins and the other ends.

That's how I feel with Wolf now.

One and the same.

Vito clears his throat; it feels somewhat nervous,

given that this is a man who had no qualms about shooting my Wolf in the middle of a celebration. He didn't, obviously, but I'm certain, even without knowing him, he would have done it.

He's in a similar line of work to the Blackwells, they all work in the shadows, creating and cleaning up messes that those in the light need not know about. It doesn't worry me; it wasn't a long or drawn-out conversation when Wolf explained to me what he and his family really did a couple of weeks ago. I'm sure most people would find it morally wrong, but I suppose I have a rather unique perspective of things that go bump in the night.

"Your mother," Vito starts, a smooth, calming accent, he rolls his 'R's and hisses his 'S's, like his tongue curls the letters to be a seductive charm. "She was my elder sister, fourteen years older than me, and I am six years older than you."

Unable to blink, to look, my eyes burn, dry and wide as I keep watching the water spit from a cluster of cherubs around the carved couple's feet.

"Lucia," he says, and my body just goes cold.

It doesn't mean anything to me. Not that I can remember, but I lived with my un- with *Nolan* since I was just six years old.

"She did not want to be a part of the family business, not with a little girl. She worked hard to get away from our father, to prove herself, to bring you up in a safe environment away from the mob."

He says this all with warmth, something proud in his tone, even though I know this can't be a happy story, I can tell, just from that, that he loved his sister.

"The day you disappeared; I was twelve. Sitting in a tree, listening in on the conversations my father was having in his office. Trying to get information so I could prove myself. A boy of twelve, his father the Don of the Italian mafia, I had a lot to do to prove myself, but there were many conversations he left me out of, so I would crawl up into the tree outside his office and listen in."

A blackbird lands on the edge of the fountain, fluffing its feathers in the spray and dipping down to get a drink.

"He got a call, dismissed his men and then breathed *her* name into the phone. Lucia didn't ever call, trying to start a new life, but he put her on speaker, and she was crying, saying that someone was after her, that she needed to come home, that she was scared." Vito sniffs, drawing my attention, and I blink for what feels like the first time.

"You were sleeping in the back of the car, Lucia was racing to get you both here, and then the line cut off. Our father screamed at his men, barking orders as they flooded back into the room and then they all drove off, my father included."

Vito's nostrils flare, his eyes dropping to the table between us, just for a moment, and then those calm blue eyes come back to mine, a sad smile on his mouth.

"The car had crashed atop a bridge and gone into the river, it was empty, the door was open on the side where your car seat was. It was assumed Lucia had gotten you out and then you were carried away together in the current. It took seventeen days to find my sister's body, washed up miles and miles away, but we never found yours."

Vito shrugs loosely, his eyes shining. There's a lump in my own throat and my eyelids are hot, but I don't say anything. I'm not sure what there is for me to say, so I just nod, I don't know what else to do.

"We believed you to be dead," he breathes out in a rush. "That's why I reacted so... *impulsively* the other night. I didn't mean to frighten you. Honestly, you look so much like your mother, I thought for a moment that you were her. A ghost perhaps coming to scold me for my transgressions." He smiles at that, this soft curl to his mouth. "I- I was not thinking rationally, and for that I am sorry, Luna, I did not ever mean to frighten you, let alone hurt you."

"It's okay," I whisper, meaning it. "I remember things now," I say quietly, looking out upon the gardens again. "But you don't know how I ended up with that man." It's not a question because of course he doesn't, why would he look for a six year old girl that flew from a car into the River Thames?

"I do not," he says, and I hear him shift against the sofa, his suit sweeping over the bright navy velvet. "But we'll find out."

I know they will. Vito and Wolf have been on the phone non stop for the last three days, but I don't want them to find out.

I want to find out.

To know what happened.

How I ended up with *Uncle* Nolan.

"May I go out there?" I ask politely, tilting my head towards the gardens at Vito's back, peering into the trees.

Wolf's fingers squeeze mine lightly, comfortingly, because he knows I need the fresh air, or I feel like I can't breathe.

"Certainly," Vito doesn't hesitate, pushing to stand and turning towards the long wall of glass. His fingers find, what looks to me like, an invisible handle and then the glass is folding and opening with a gentle push.

"Do you want me?" Wolf asks, taking my chin

between his warm, calloused fingers, and turning me to face him. His yellow-caramel eyes bright on mine, he reads my answer without words, "You call me if you want me, okay?"

"Yes, Wolf," I nod once, his lips pressing lightly to the corner of my mouth, before he releases my fingers from his, allowing me to stand.

"Don't wander too far."

"I won't," I smile, and it's the first real lie I ever tell.

Wolf

CHAPTER XXX

Luna stares at the fountain for the entirety of the story that Vito tells. I already know it. Vito told me, repeatedly, this same story at least a hundred times over the last few days. We've discussed his *employee* and come to a mutually agreed upon end for him, after I'd told him a brief version of the story that Luna told me when she started to remember.

I don't take my eyes off of her as Vito talks and she stares out at the gardens. I know even before she asks that she wants to go out there. For the air. To breathe. So I'm not surprised when she requests just that.

Luna slips past Vito without really looking at him, and he watches after her as she passes the fountain she's been staring at for the last hour, before bringing his eyes back to me.

The sun is going down. The sky a deep pink, wisps of fluffy peach-orange clouds drifting over the tops of the trees. Luna follows down a winding path into the nearest copse of trees and then sits. I can see the top of her head, the large white bow secured at the crown of her skull.

"I'm going to marry that girl, Vito," I voice before turning back to face him.

He doesn't react outwardly, but the subtle tensing of his fingertips over his thigh is telling. He wants to be the one in control here, to be swooping in and saving her, keeping her, making up for all the years they've been apart. I understand it. I would be the same. But that's not how this is going to go.

"You are?" He lifts a single brow slowly, his bight eyes on mine in challenge, and I could smirk, I could say something cocky, annoyingly *knowing*.

But that's not, at all, what that statement is about.

"Yes, I am."

His eyes tighten just slightly, his brow dropping back into an arch over his eye, and then he sniffs, cocking his head to one side, before reaching forward for an empty glass on the table.

"I won't pretend I don't want her moving back in here with me, with la famiglia, but I have-"

A large bang sounds overhead, cutting him off, his bright eyes instantly flicking to the ceiling with a small twist to his mouth. Slowly, his chin lowers in time with his gaze, and he's levelling a look on me that speaks of darkness and sin.

"-Something I'm dealing with right now," he finishes. Smirking slightly as he says it, the space above us falls silent after several thuds and thumps. "And it is not... *ideal* for her to stay here at the moment."

"Luna will stay where Luna wants to stay," I tell him, levelling him with a look as my eyes flick back to her.

The top of her head still in the same place, the tail of her white bow flicking like an irritated cat's tail in the wind.

"She's spent her life being controlled, not being allowed to go outside in the sun. The last thing she needs is to be cooped up in here like a princess in a locked tower. We've got a good life at Cardinal House, and you're welcome to visit any time, but I have no intention of uprooting her, unless that's what she wants."

I stare him down, meaning every word, but I know, without having to ask her, that she won't want to be away from me. We've fallen into routine over the last few weeks.

She brought me back to life.

I love her.

And she loves me.

And no one has ever loved me as wholly as she does.

'What are the words you say to someone that you want to be buried with, same coffin, same headstone, same consecrated earth?'

"I want to visit," he tells me, lifting a foot to cross his legs, resting an ankle across his opposite knee, resting the empty tumbler he took from the table against his thigh. "I want to attend the wedding."

"Of course," I nod, as though she's already said yes, like I've already asked. "Unless she doesn't want that," I cock my head slightly, watching as his fingers tighten once more, creasing the fabric of his slacks as he does. "She does whatever she wants, she gets whatever makes her happy," I tell him blankly.

He purses his lips instead of scowling like I'm sure he wants to, but then he nods, "Good."

Vito stares at me, and there are so many things that either one of us, both of us, could say.

Instead, Vito lifts his chin, glances over my shoulder, and then pushes to his feet. Moving to a wet bar in the far corner, he ducks down behind it, and then pops up, crystal decanter in hand. Amber nectar flows into the glass he offers me as he sits back down, and I take it with eager fingers, not needing encouragement.

"I've always liked you, Wolf," Vito tells me, flicking his tongue over his lower lip as he brings his glass back down to rest on his thigh. "I respect your family, the work you do. I enjoy discrete."

"Well, we're nothing if not discrete," I say with a flick of my brow, swirling the whiskey around in my glass, and biting down on my smirk as I think about the decapitated body left in the shrubbery outside of Nolan Beaumont's mansion.

"Yes, so if anything should befall my niece…" he leaves the statement hanging for a moment. "Well, you already know, I know how to aim."

It pounds, my heart, as a smile curls my mouth, showing all of my teeth. One predator staring down another. There's a moment where we hold each other's gaze, and I want to tear his throat out for even daring to insinuate that I would ever do anything to hurt my Luna. But, equally, this really just means that Luna has an extra layer of protection now. The entire muscle of the Italian mob. Niece to the Don.

But then her mother had all of that and still ended

up dead in a river. Her daughter stolen, and somehow winding up living with a paedophile rapist for over twenty years.

"I don't think this should be something advertised," I say next. "In order to keep her safe, from your enemies, she needs to remain unknown. Just mine. A Blackwell."

He doesn't like it, the way a green vein protrudes in his temple, pounding as rapidly as his pulse, it's obvious that he didn't expect me to say that. That perhaps he hadn't even thought of it, but it's the only thing that makes sense.

I won't ever let her be put in danger again.

"Fine," he eventually grinds out, "but I want her to meet my brothers, her other uncles when they come over from Sicily."

"If that's what she wants," I agree, and he hates it, but he doesn't argue.

Both of us reach forward across the low table, nodding in agreement as we clink our glasses together and take a sip. The alcohol burns on the way down, but we're both smiling when I shake my head with a gruff laugh.

"We've had many drinks in the past, Wolf, but I never thought we'd be having a discussion quite like this one." Vito sighs, blinking down at his hand cupped over his glass, "I could think of worse for my niece."

I think of the early days at Cardinal House. The nightmares, the screams, the bed wetting. She never once hid herself from me, she never cowered away. I was her comfort, even when she couldn't remember me, didn't know me, a stranger who closed her in a coffin, she felt safe.

With me.

My eyes come up then, to where she went to sit outside, the sun almost set now. I'm climbing to my feet, my glass thudding down on the table as I round the sofa Vito sits on.

The cool wind whips at my skin and my feet are pounding over the stone pathway as I follow it past where she was when I last looked.

"Luna!" I bellow, real, true panic in my voice. I hear it in myself, as my heart pounds and my lungs squeeze, fear. "Luna!" The trees are dense, the path ending as it reaches the thick woods, shadows dancing, foliage ruffling. "LUNA!"

It's useless, the shouting, she wouldn't venture far, she wouldn't go anywhere without me, not on her own. Not like-

She's been so quiet since the night of the engagement dinner. After she fell, bumped her head, came to with the frightening realisation that she was remembering things. I should have seen it. The plotting. The carefully curated questions about my plans, what I was going to do to her abuser.

I spin on my heel, smacking straight into Vito at my back. His eyes wide with panic, "What is it, where is she?" he rushes out, scanning the dark trees surrounding us.

And I don't know what to say, how to tell him that she's willingly gone back to the place of her terror, so instead, I just tell him what we need, "Get a car."

CHAPTER XXXI

Staring up at the house, you wouldn't know what horrors live inside.

That the man who lives here is smart and neat and tidy but is really a demon in disguise. A fancy suit with soft eyes and cruel smiles. A man I still sought comfort in, even after he was the one defiling me.

Goosebumps tear their way across my flesh, the sky is dark, the trees and bushes rustle around me in the cool wind as I stand on the red brick pathway. My black dress lifting high, my pale blue cardigan with the white buttons doing nothing to keep off the chill of the night. It might just be me though, that's feeling the cold, and it has nothing to do with the weather.

I'm not trying to hide myself from him, continuing up the path, striding steps that take me up the three front stairs to the door. Fingers curling around the brass knob, I push it open, the scent of cigars flooding out into the fresh air, tainting the night with its vile odour.

Sickness swirls inside my stomach, bile rushing up my throat and coating the back of my tongue, but I step through the opening like I'm entering a part of my life I didn't believe was real until right at this very moment.

The foyer is full of guards, every instinct inside of me is screaming at me not to look at them, which is why I lift my chin, staring each and every one of them in the face. Not one of them shies away, letting me see them and their blank stares. Men who have had their big hands on my nude body, holding me down and muffling my screams with their palms as they helped my uncle abuse me.

Pain shoots up my spine. A phantom bolt of agony driving up through my coccyx and ripping its way into my chest. I know it's not real, I know there's no blood dripping down my thighs, even though my brain makes me believe that there is. The feeling of crimson running down the backs of my legs, leaving little bloody footsteps in my wake.

It makes the loose elastic around my hips, small cotton knickers covering my private parts, feel as tight as a noose as I start up the stairs. No one tries to stop me, as though they knew I was coming. Sentry along the walls, stationed on every fourth step. Lining the long hallway on the upper floor that leads to our rooms.

Our.

Nothing in this house was ever mine.

Not even me.

I'm numb by the time I reach the furthest door. The wooden barriers opening for me as I approach. Everything exactly as it was the last time I was here.

The drive home is silent, but I'm rushing with anxiety. Adrenaline pings through me like splinted shards of glass, nicking at my veins as they ricochet through me.

The guard who came to collect me isn't new, I can only tell that by a feeling, the way he moves like the rest of them, four steps ahead or behind me at all times, no eye contact, no touching. Opening and closing doors for me, ushering me silently into the car, in fact, the words he spoke to me in the hospital entrance are the only ones he ever has. I don't look at him, my eyes lowered to my hands in my lap.

I think of Wolf Blackwell, only moments ago, telling me he could keep me safe.

Me telling him I know but leaving without him anyway.

He's a stranger.

One that treats me with kindness and respect, secret smiles and soft touches. His scent of lilies and teakwood, makes him smell exactly like he is, strong but delicate. Soft.

With me.

I should have let him take me away, keep me safe.

I think of his mouth brushing mine, his whispered words pressing to my mouth, and I wish that I had kissed him. I wish that I had let my fingers dance across his tanned skin, let his rough hands meet my flesh.

It's too late for wishes now.

Mine would never be granted anyway.

The car door opens once we stop, my footsteps taking me automatically up the path. It doesn't occur to me to run, this is such routine now, that I just do as I should. If I were watching someone else do this, I know I'd be screaming at them to turn around and try to escape.

Instead, I'm walking through the upper floor of the house, and entering our rooms made to look like a romantic space, but instead hold sadistic intent and are used to inflict pain and torment.

"Luna," Uncle Nolan greets with that slash of a sick smile across his mouth, "I've been waiting for you, sweet girl."

. . .

That's how he greets me now. From his relaxed slouch in his leather chair, positioned in front of the fire, flames roaring behind the grate. His green eyes come to mine, hard and terrifying, and I feel as though I am six years old all over again.

"What did you do to my mother?" I demand it, my voice as loud as I can get to project from my wobbly lip.

My body trembles, teeth clenching, but he doesn't even look surprised by the question. Doesn't look like he's seen a ghost. As though he knew all along that I wasn't dead.

Nolan doesn't bother standing. Instead, he just smirks, running that gaze up the length of me.

"You're stronger than I thought, sweet girl," his lips curl into an award winning smile. "Much stronger than poor, ungrateful, Lucia." He chuckles, flicking a hand towards his guards, dismissing them from the room. "She was so perfect, looked just like you, you could have been twins." He sighs whimsically, like he would have loved to have the two of us together. "She spooked too easy. I came on too strong. I'll admit, I wanted to wine and dine her. I sent her lavish gifts, sent you plenty of toys, too, trying to win her over. But she rejected it all, every advance, every offer, every door I tried, she slammed in my face. Told me I was scaring her, lied about having a husband in an attempt to frighten me off. But I wanted you," he tells me, flicking his green eyes onto mine. "I wasn't going to take no for an answer."

"So you killed her?" It's a whisper, the question, and I hate that it sounds so small, so weak, but I'm trembling with rage.

"For you," he breathes, like it means something more than him wanting to kidnap and abuse a child. "Everything I have ever done has been for you." Nolan pushes up from the chair and I hold myself still, even though it takes every ounce of strength in me, I don't move. "So, how do you think it felt when I saw you with *him*." He spits on the floor at my feet, his upper lip lifting from his teeth, snarling at me. "I watch every fucking camera in that hospital when you're there. You think I was going to let you be stolen from me?!"

Nolan's face transforms into a twisted mask of rage. My heart is hammering in my chest, my fingers limp at my sides, my knees feel wobbly, and my lungs are heavy with a scream, but I don't make a sound as he slinks up to stand in front of me.

His acrid breath on my face as he towers above me,

the taste of cigars on my tongue. His fingers find my face, cupping my cheek, before he draws back his arm and slaps me with the flat of his hand so hard it sends me to the ground.

"You ungrateful little whore!" he screams in my face, spittle painting my chin, my throat, his tall, lean body dropping into an easy crouch. "I couldn't have you thinking you could *flirt* with men outside of this house. I had to teach you a lesson!"

"What did you do to my mother?" I spit blood onto the wood, feeling it coat my teeth, pushing up to my elbows to stare at him.

He scoffs, rolling his eyes, like this is so insignificant, "I had my men run her off the bridge, grab you from the back seat and bring you here."

"Why?" I feel like there's not even a real answer here, there's something wrong with this man's wiring.

"Because she wouldn't give you to me," he says softly, staring into my eyes with lust.

That simple.

"You're evil," I breath out, my bloody lip trembling. "You're disgusting," I hiss louder, "and vile," the word quivers off of my tongue as I push up to sitting, getting close to his face, "and a rapist!" I scream, making my tonsils ache, my throat crack.

Nolan's eyes widen, the shock at my outburst dropping him back onto his arse. He hits the hardwood with a thud, his hands splaying out behind him to catch himself, but he doesn't get a chance to right himself before I'm throwing myself into him. Barrelling him over, my knee colliding with his crotch, sending his spine crashing into the floor. Scratching and clawing and hitting his head, his face, everywhere I can reach, I pummel.

His hands try to come for my wrists, my knees digging into his ribs as I straddle his belly. He bars his arms across his face, cupping his hands over his skull to protect his head. I lash out with my hand, fingers curled like a claw, and swipe down his face, carving my nails into his cheek, raking a bloody trail down his face.

I'm screaming and panting and hitting him with all of my strength, and he's not trying to throw me off, just trying to protect himself, until I hear *him*.

"Lunaaa!" Wolf roars from below.

My head snaps over my shoulder towards the closed doors, and then the back of my skull is colliding with the floor, stars shooting across my vision, black blurring at the edges. Nolan rolls, flipping us so I'm trapped beneath him, his knees bracketing me in, pinning me to the floor by straddling my waist.

"You little bitch!" he screams in my face as I continue to hit him, punch at his chest, his neck, rake my nails down every bit of exposed skin I can reach.

Blood drips from his cheek, splashing across my lips and I buck my hips, trying to get him up, to shift him enough I could try to roll too, but he's so much heavier than I am, so much bigger. But his men aren't in here now, it's just us.

Me versus him.

One monster against another.

Adrenaline lights through me like a surge of electricity, strengthening me.

"You think he's going to get through my men, you desperate little slut?" he snarls with a laugh, and it stills me, the question, like a wash of calm rolling over me and reassuring me.

I blink once, his hands cuffing my wrists over my head, pinning them to the floor, I look him straight in the eye, our lips almost touching, and without hesitation, I tell him what I know, "Yes."

Then I scream into his face, throwing my head forward with all of my might so it collides with his nose. He flinches, releasing my hands to cup his face, and then I buck up, sending us into a roll towards the fire.

Gritting my teeth, I punch him, curling my still taped fingers, my broken knuckles screaming, I hit him again and again. Attacking his bloody face, trying to cave his nose into his skull until it's nothing more than a flat bloody splat on his face.

"I hate you!" I scream at him, my vocal cords screeching, my teeth gnashing. "I hate you! You ruined me!"

Time seems to slow as my arms ache, fists going numb as I hit him again and again and again. Tears are streaking down my flush cheeks, and then the door is bursting open at my back.

"Luna!" Wolf roars, this deafening, bellowing thunder of his deep voice that I feel all the way down to my core.

I feel myself slump with relief, all of me shaking, quivering, trembling.

That's my mistake.

Nolan lurches up from the floor grabbing me by the throat and rising effortlessly to his feet. Pulling my back flush with his chest, the clamp of his hand squeezing my jaw so hard my teeth cut the insides of my cheeks.

Wolf is standing in the open double doors, dripping with blood. His honey-whiskey eyes half hidden by the wet strands of his raven hair. He looks huge, broad and tall and wet with crimson, like the mass murderer from a slasher film. His fiery eyes scan over me, checking me for injuries, and I feel it, the moment his gaze locks on my split lip, a ripple of rage rolling through him and making his shoulders tense even further.

"I might not have killed her properly the first time, but I can tell you one thing," Nolan snarls as cold metal meets my temple, "I won't miss a second."

Wolf

CHAPTER XXXII

Tyres screeching, I careen around the street corner like a rally car driver, drifting the vehicle right up onto the front lawn, stopping directly in front of the steps.

Vito gets out at the same time as I do, barking orders at his men who pull up in hordes at our backs. Hunter and Thorne are running across the front lawn, meeting me at the front door.

"Let my men clear you a path," Vito says on a sharp exhale. "don't waste your time on the foot soldiers, when there's a grander prize for you just past them."

It makes sense.

Hunter scowls, but he doesn't object, and Thorne nods as Vito's men rush past us, breaking through both the front and back doors at the same time and storming in.

Despite their guns having silencers, the bellows, barks and cries of men is not going to go unnoticed in a lazy, little street like this.

We won't have much time.

I give the men an entire sixty-seconds to clean house, counting it down too fast in my head, and then I'm barrelling inside, grabbing the first guy I see.

My fingers close around his neck, slamming him back into the wall as his hands claw at my wrists. I knock him into it again and again, until blood is splattering over the cream wallpaper and the crunch of bone fills my ears.

"LUNA!" I roar, wondering if she'll hear me, be able to respond, give me an indication of where she is, but there's nothing in response, too much noise surrounding me, making it impossible to hear.

I'm heading for the stairs, because despite not knowing where Luna is, it's as though I can feel her, sense her. Somewhere, deep inside this house my heart beats and I just need to find it.

My knuckles crunch and pound and pummel, I fire off shots and stab my way through bodies.

Until I reach the upstairs corridor.

It's long and dark and dingy, wall sconces lit few and far between. It's like an underground tunnel, only it's upstairs, heavy velvet drapes are pulled across every window, shutting out the world to create a new one.

A hell.

He's big, I'll give him that much, the guard that steps out in front of me and blocks the door at the very end of the hall.

The one I'm heading straight for.

To his credit, he looks like a mean motherfucker. Shorn dark hair, hard eyes, broad shoulders and thick arms. He's only a little shorter than me, a couple inches at most, but we're evenly matched weight wise, his frame holding hard packed planes of muscle just as solid as mine.

"You're not getting in that room," he informs me, like I've come here to make small talk, but all he's done is confirm that's where my girl is.

"You touched her?" I ask him instead, because I'm almost certain, from the shit Luna's told me, every one of these fucker's have held her down to be tortured.

He lifts a dark brow, shrugs, and then the fucker smirks.

He's aiming a gun at me, but we know now, bullets don't fucking kill me, they bring me back to life.

I run, smashing into him, and throwing the bar of my arm up and into his outstretched one, knocking the gun from his fist as an errant shot goes off, hitting the ceiling and sending a flurry of dust down onto us. He grunts as my shoulder connects with his sternum, bending him in half and knocking him stumbling back a couple paces.

But he doesn't go down.

The guy brings up his knee, smashing it into my groin and making me see stars as pain explodes in my pelvis.

We go down together.

Rolling across the hardwood, my spine smashes into the wall, my heart thundering in my chest as I try to catch my breath, but there's no time, the guy's fist finding my face and crashing into my cheekbone as my own fist comes up, connecting with his kidney, once, twice, three times, before he's tumbling away, trying to put space between us. But I can't allow that. There's not enough time for space.

I reach down into my boot, gripping the handle of my knife and throw myself forward. The two of us tumbling directly into the double doors he was so adamant about guarding, and stab my blade into his upper spine, directly between his shoulder blades.

His eyes go wide, the heel of my other hand jabbing him in the throat, and then his lips part as I tear out my knife, stab it back in, again and again in quick succession. Pushing it as deep as it'll go until my hand is slippery and wet with warmth, and a breath coughs up his throat, blood spraying my face as he splutters. I shove him away from me, rolling his body off of mine with a thud.

Throwing myself into standing, I bend down to retrieve the discarded gun, yanking out the magazine and counting the seven bullets. I'm only gunna need one. Shoving it into the back of my jeans, I turn, facing the doors, taking one solid breath, my shoulders heaving, I grab hold of the handles, shove them down and thrust open the doors into the room.

My entire body is heaving up and down with my breaths as her name bellows out of my throat. Blood is dripping down my face, my hair wet with blood, my white t-shirt stained red, but nothing could ever distract from the fact that the man before me, squeezing my beautiful Luna's pretty face, a nasty split in her lip, holding a gun to her temple, is going to die.

"I might not have killed her properly the first time,

but I can tell you one thing," Nolan snarls, "I won't miss a second."

Even though my every hackle is raised, every instinct demands that I shoot him now, end all of this, save her, take her into my arms and kiss her better, I laugh.

It's a wild, throaty, psychotic sound that tears its way up my tonsils, barking free of my tongue. I shake my head, my body juddery and full of energy, a wolf pacing before an attack.

"You could shoot her," I shrug, "or you could shoot me and keep her."

It's all I say, holding my arms out at my sides, watching as he checks my hands for a weapon. This man's not a fighter, he's an overconfident moron. I can work with that.

"She's already mine," he spits at me, flicking his gaze up from my drenched boots to my crimson painted t-shirt, claw marks bleeding down his cheeks, his eye, it makes me want to smile.

"Not anymore, you threw her away."

"I thought she was dead!" he screams at me, his entire body shaking. "Those morons!" he shouts. "Can't do anything right, they were supposed to get rid of her body so even you and your filthy crew of mutts couldn't get your bloody hands on her."

He's a good looking guy, dressed well, neat beard, styled hair, money, that's what that is, a disguise paid for with blood.

"You think I fuck corpses?" I snort casually, wanting to glance at Luna, because even like this, that sentence I use mockingly to taunt, makes me think of treating her exactly like that, before taking her virginity on the fucking morgue slab.

Blood rushes to my cock, even in a situation like this, and I lick my lips.

Fuck, I love you, Little Moon.

"I think you would," he spits, snarling his upper lip, "she had to know who she belonged to."

"So you killed her?" I ask, genuinely trying to understand the logic here. "Why not just lock her up?"

"She wasn't meant to die, but seeing her on your lap in that hospital," he huffs out a sharp breath. "Disgusting."

"So you just... what? Got carried away?" I cock my head, staring at him, his chest heaving, his eyes bulging, his finger *not* on the trigger.

"It's none of your fucking business." He spits then, really spits, bloody saliva onto the floor between us. "Get the fuck out of my house!" he bellows, letting out his rage, and aiming the gun at me.

"Now, Luna!"

That's when I look at her, pretty and perfect in her summer dress, cropped cardigan, and ballet flats. She blinks, reaching up and over her head, plucking the long sharp needle out from her big, white hair bow and holding my gaze, those big, ice-blue eyes boring into my soul, she stabs it into his neck. The sharpened tip making it slide through his throat like a hot knife through butter.

Nolan chokes, not even managing to fire his weapon at me as Luna yanks out the long pin before driving it right back in again, his hand dropping from her face. When she pulls it out a third time, his body slumping to his knees, blood spurts out in an arc, decorating the wall and spraying her in splatter.

We both run to each other at the same time as the heavy thud of his face colliding with the hardwood echoes around the room.

"Luna," I breathe.

At the same time, she gasps, "Wolf."

Our lips mash together, my hands cupping her face, her fists tangling in my t-shirt. Tongues licking, our kiss tasting of blood and victory, I haul her up into my arms, her long legs wrapping around my waist. It's desperate and raw and violent.

She bites my lip and I suck on her tongue, and we cover each other in blood.

There's horror and violence, life and death, but above all else, when her lips press to mine, these gentle, urgent kisses, there's love.

Wolf

EPILOGUE

She's always in the cemetery.

Surrounded by crumbling stones, etched with names and dates that she finds utterly fascinating. Looking them up, finding out about the lives they lived before they ended up buried here, researching and scribbling it all down in her journal. I find her talking to them some days. When the rain falls and the clouds are low and the wind whips, I still find her out here, nattering away about fuck knows what, but it makes her happy.

And when she's happy, she smiles.

And those smiles.

Yeah, those smiles are worth it.

"Luna, baby," I whisper, coming up behind her, folding my arms around her throat, nuzzling my face into her neck, sucking in deep lungfuls of her.

A large white bunny sits in her arms, its little pink nose scrunching, whiskers twitching as it scents me.

"Wolf," she replies quietly, her fingers knuckle deep in the animal's fluffy white fur, her fingertips rubbing its back. "Do I have to come in?"

I look down at her little growing bump, only four months, but my hands can't stop grabbing it, before flicking my gaze back up to hers, a smile on my mouth and a shake to my head.

"No, just missed you, Little Moon."

We both glance down as another rabbit, not unlike the one in her arms appears at her feet and she smiles again, huffing a soft laugh, "They get jealous," she says lightly, my arms breaking free of her as she bends down, releasing the one in her arms back into the grass to greet the newcomer with a scratch between the ears.

"You wanna sleep out here tonight?" I ask her, trying to smother the smirk on my face by biting my molars into my cheek, but she catches it, tapping the back of her hand against my shoulder as she straightens into standing.

"You already put the stuff out on the porch,

didn't you?" she chuckles, that smile getting wider again, and I swear my heart fucking swells with that look.

"Might have," I laugh as she turns into my chest, pressing her ear over my heart and threading her arms around my neck.

Hanging onto me as my hand comes to her lower spine, pressing the little bump of her belly into the ladder of my abs, my other hand finding the side of her head, holding her tight to my chest.

"I'm going to take you everywhere, Little Moon," I whisper against the top of her head, pressing a kiss to her hair.

"I love you, Wolf," Luna breathes, making the whole world stop for a moment to let the words really sink in, the way she says my name still making me shiver.

I squeeze her just a little bit tighter, thinking of everything we had to go through to get to this. The good part. But I don't linger in the past, only looking to the future.

I dip down, dragging her chin up, pressing my mouth to hers, "I love you, Luna," I tell her.

And then she kisses me, the two of us tangled together, standing in the place we'll one day be buried.

Same coffin.

Same headstone.
Same consecrated earth.

The End.

Afterword

Thank you so much for reading, I'm so happy you're here for the fourth Blackwell book!

This series is one of my favourites to write, I love creating the locations, the settings, they really set the mood.

I absolutely loved writing Wolf and Luna, they drew me back into the Blackwell world and I enjoyed every second of it.

I always knew a lot about Wolf, but I never had any idea who he'd end up with, so, thank you Raine for forcing my hand!

And Luna, she was a surprise that appeared once I put pen to paper, but her connection to Vito? That wasn't planned, like, at all.

But Vittorio Gambino is one of my favourite characters from Swallows and Psychos, and since I haven't visited that series in a little while, I had to inject a little of it over here.

Also, that's not the last of him we'll see…

Moving on to the next announcement.

Book five will be a reverse harem featuring Archer, Arrow and Raine Blackwell in Magpie Manor. This also wasn't planned, I always intended for them to each have their own books, but they apparently chose otherwise.

That means this series will be complete with the final book being about Stryder Blackwell in an untitled book six!

Acknowledgements

Mark, as always, you have my heart.

Addie, for talking through the plot of this over and over, and thinking of dear Vito, dunno what I'd ever do without you.

Kayla for being my rock, thank you for all of your help with this book, thank you for reading it before anyone else, and thank you for listening to my endless hours of voice notes. I'm so grateful to have you.

Raeleen, for letting me ignore all duties for the past four weeks so I could get this baby done. I am so lucky to have you.

Leah, for creating magic, again. The cover, the graphics, the excitement. I love how much you love this world, for making me excited when I'm stressed, and inspiring me with visuals when I send you a random teaser line.

Mum, for texting me and cheering me on in the final hours of this book. Thank you for everything that you do.

And finally, to you, the reader, thank you. I hope to see you here again soon.

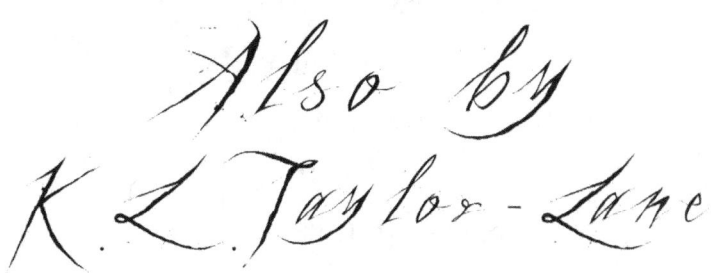

Also by K. L. Taylor-Lane

.

SWALLOWS AND PSYCHOS

<u>KYLA-ROSE SWALLOW</u>

A Dark Mafia Why Choose Romance

PURGATORY

PENANCE

PERSECUTION

.

SWALLOWS AND SAVAGES

<u>CHARLIE SWALLOW</u>

A Dark Mafia MMF Romance

RUIN

TBC

TBC

THE BLACKWELL BROTHERS

<u>HUNTER BLACKWELL</u>

A Dark Gothic Horror Stepsibling MF Romance

HERON MILL

HERON MILL TENEBRIS

<u>THORNE BLACKWELL</u>

A Dark Gothic Mafia MF Romance

ROOK POINT

<u>WOLF BLACKWELL</u>

A Dark Gothic MF Romance

CARDINAL HOUSE

<u>ARCHER, ARROW & RAINE BLACKWELL</u>

A Dark Gothic Why Choose Romance

MAGPIE MANOR

<u>STRYDER BLACKWELL</u>

A Dark Gothic MF Romance

TBA

·

THE ASHES BOYS

A Dark Bully Gang Why Choose Romance

TORMENT ME

BURY ME

TBC

RAVEN RIDGE HALLOW

BILLY BLACKWELL

A Dark Gothic Horror-Gore Cult MF Romance

HAUNT

LOVESICK

BRAM BLACKWELL

A Dark Gothic Horror-Gore Cult MF Romance

DEATHWISH

TOLLY BLACKWELL

A Dark Gothic Horror-Gore Cult Romance

HEARTLESS

GORE BLACKWELL

A Dark Gothic Horror-Gore Cult MF Romance

CRUCIFY

STANDALONES

NOXIOUS BOYS

A Dark College Bully Why Choose Romance

SICK LIKE ME

A Dark Gothic Romance

Coming 2024

DELIRIUM

A Dark Gothic Romance

Coming 2025

Find
K. L. Taylor - Lane

BOOKBUB - @KLTaylorLane

AMAZON - K. L. TAYLOR-LANE

INSTAGRAM - @kltaylorlane_author

TIKTOK - @kltaylorlane.author

PINTEREST - @KLTaylorLane

FACEBOOK - K. L. Taylor-Lane Author

GOODREADS - kltaylor-lane

FACEBOOK READER GROUP -

K's Southbrook Psychos - Reader Group for K.L. Taylor-Lane

Content Listing

Hurt/Comfort | Broody/Sunshine | Gun Use
Amnesia | Sexual Abuse (not by MMC/FMC)
Torture | Light bullying to FMC (not by the MMC)
Funeral Home | Graphic Gore | Shooting
Graphic Sex | Explicit Language | Drug Use
Nurse/Patient | Graphic Violence | Blood
Criminal Organisation | Murder | Spit Play
Dead Bodies | Morgue | Vengeance
Flashbacks/memories of child abuse/neglect
He falls first | Death | Mortuary | Death
Grieving | Hospital Environment
Anal Rape of FMC (not by MMC)
Animal death (animal is not a pet and is already dying)

*This list is not exhaustive - although every effort has
been made to include all potential triggers, there may
still be other content in these pages that may be found
triggering or upsetting to some*

www.ingramcontent.com/pod-product-compliance
Lightning Source LLC
Chambersburg PA
CBHW070835260626
47170CB00007B/2383